W9-DBM-892

THE LAST ANNUAL SLUGFEST

A Vejay Haskell Mystery

SUSAN DUNLAP

A DELL BOOK

Published by
Dell Publishing
a division of
Bantam Doubleday Dell Publishing Group, Inc.
1540 Broadway
New York, New York 10036

ISBN: 0-440-21558-7

Printed in the United States of America

Published simultaneously in Canada

September 1994

10 9 8 7 6 5 4 3 2

For Lillian Fujimoto
and Dave Hampton

CHAPTER

1

I slammed on the brakes of the PG&E truck. Barely a foot ahead, a mud slide covered the road. I had been pondering Edwina Henderson, the last Henderson of the town of Henderson, and her perplexing connection with tonight's Slugfest. I'd nearly driven into the mud slide.

"Damn!" Three more meters to read on this street, and one of them had to be blocked by mud! As I climbed down from the truck to check the mound, rain from the eucalyptus branches above splatted on my shoulders, and the fresh eucalyptus scent battled with the dank smell of mud. In March, at the end of the winter rains, mud slides were not uncommon in the Russian River area. It was not even surprising to find slides from last year still covering smaller roads. But this one was new; it crossed Kiev Road in a viscous drift and oozed down the hillside beyond. There was no way to drive over it or through it, and certainly no way to walk around it. Picking up my route book, I marked M-5—Road Blocked—where the read for the Yunellos' account should have gone. This Missed Meter, because of its acceptable reason, would be added to the office's count rather than to mine. But I would have to justify it to Mr. Bobbs when I got back—another nuisance.

The next account was a tiny red cottage whose owner had had visions of making a killing in real estate and had added a deck twice the size of the house to the rear; it looked as if the weight of the

deck would catapult the little dwelling down the hillside and into the river. But despite the winter rains, it
stood. And for me, the addition of the deck meant
that the meter, which had once been easily accessible
at the rear of the house, was now a full six feet under
the edge. Tucking my route book under my chin, I
crawled through the wet weeds to it.

The final account on Route H-4 (Henderson Office, Route 4) was the Victorian house of Edwina
Henderson herself. It had been built here on Kiev
Road near the top of the hill by her grandfather, the
town founder, Edwin Henderson. Unlike the cottages
that had sprung up around it, the pale blue-and-
white stick-style Victorian had been lovingly maintained. It occupied one of the few flat parcels of land
on the hillside.

I had read the meter here many times in the two
years I'd lived in Henderson, but Edwina Henderson
had never been home. There was no reason to assume she would be now, and even less to suspect that
she would tell me, her meter reader, why she had
pressured everyone from our local assemblyman to
the Chamber of Commerce to hold this year's Slugfest in Henderson. Still, I checked as I made my way
around the side of the house to the rear porch. The
meter was on the outside. Some meters were on en-
closed porches and customers gave us keys to get in.
This had been such a meter, but instead of entrusting
her key to strangers, even bonded strangers, Edwina
Henderson had had the meter moved. Jotting down
the read, I closed the route book and headed back
around the house.

A blue Volvo pulled into the driveway.

But Edwina Henderson wasn't inside. The driver
was a man I didn't know. There were faces I couldn't
put names to, but few that I didn't recognize at all
after two years of reading town meters. But this man,

who was probably close to forty, tall, with curly brown hair, a beard, and lapis blue eyes that shined through his rimless glasses, was certainly not one I would have overlooked. As he climbed out of the Volvo, I noted its parking sticker—SFSU—San Francisco State University. Was he a professor? In his brown herringbone jacket and black turtleneck, he looked the part.

Standing in the shelter of the house, I asked, "Have you come to see Edwina Henderson?"

"Right. She here?"

"I doubt it."

He raised his bushy eyebrows. "I have a four-thirty appointment with her. I'm already late. Are you sure she's not here?"

"Not positive. But it is Friday afternoon, and she does have a store to run. Maybe she planned on meeting you there."

"But this is the address on her correspondence."

I smiled. "She probably just forgot that, being from out of town, you wouldn't realize she'd be at the shop. In all likelihood, she's pacing around behind her special blends right now, irritated that you're late."

He shrugged. "Where is it?"

"On North Bank Road, the main street. It's the tobacco shop."

"Tobacco shop!" He laughed, and behind his glasses, his eyes relaxed. He had, I realized, quite a nice face. "You wouldn't think the lady of *this* house would be selling cigars."

"I suppose not. But Henderson Tobacconist's Shop is as old as this house. It was founded by her grandfather after he gave up logging for the comforts of the indoor life."

"He had the right idea. I had an awful time finding this place in the rain. I must have been up every winding dirt road on the hillside. Twice I had to back down. I almost went over the side the last time. If I had known about the shop being in the middle of town . . ." He turned toward the car, then stopped. "What do you do at night here?"

"Put on the headlights."

He laughed. "I mean, where's a good place to stay and what's here in the way of night life?"

"Genelle's Family Cabins, just west of town. And the bar."

"And?"

"If you want to drive into Santa Rosa there are movies and things you can find in any city. But here in Henderson the entertainment is the bar."

He sighed. "I was hoping for, well, something with a little more local color, something that would be sort of a memento of the area."

"An event you wouldn't find in the city? One you could tell your friends about?"

He nodded hesitantly.

"Well, if you want memorable, you should come to the Slugfest tonight."

"Slugfest! I was looking for colorful, not barbaric."

I laughed. "It's not what you think."

"It sounds like an event in a muddy field where the burliest drunks in town bash it out."

"It's not so violent, but it is probably just as disgusting. The Slugfest isn't a boxing match, it's an annual tribute to the California slug."

"What?"

The slimy California slug—the shell-less snail that slithers toward the tasty green of just-sprouted flowers, that decimates lettuce and spinach plants, and lops off every bud in an entire garden in one night's outing, leaving a trail oozing from the scene of one disaster to the next—moves most Californians to excess. Slugs range in size from those in the drier suburban areas that are no bigger than a finger, to the banana slug that makes its unwelcome home in damp spots like San Francisco and the Russian River area. Banana slugs grow up to twelve gelatinous inches long. Gardeners put out slug pellets, build moats of broken glass around their plants, and leave dishes of beer to lure the invaders to a sodden grave, but the slugs are undeterred. "At the Slugfest, there's a prize for the biggest slug," I said. "You have to be under twelve years old to enter one. It's the first of three events. The second is the slug race."

"A test of patience?"

"Very few photo finishes. The course is about two feet long, and the record is something like five minutes."

"And? You said there were three things."

I let a moment lapse. "The third event is the slug tasting."

He didn't speak; he just stared. I'd seen that expression before when people got their first inkling of the nature of that event. "It's a take-off on county fairs where people bring their favorite foods. The essential ingredient in all of these recipes is slugs."

When he still didn't speak, I could feel myself getting into the spirit of the Slugfest. "Slug Chili is a perennial favorite. Slug Dogs were quite a hit one year. And for dessert, there's Chocolate Sludge, and Banana Cream Pie—you know what kind of banana, of course."

"And someone eats them?"

"The judges have to. That's why they're judges."

"Where do they get these judges? The local asylums?"

I laughed. "The politicians find it hard to refuse. Every other year the Slugfest was run by *The Paper*, one of the area newspapers in Guerneville. *The Paper*

ran stories on whom they'd asked and what their
excuses were. The year Santa Rosa dumped its sewage into the Russian River the Santa Rosa city manager was a judge."

"That's real *mea culpa.*"

"He was a good sport. But this year the Slugfest
will be here in Henderson. Edwina Henderson is or-
ganizing it."

"*This* Edwina Henderson?" He glanced at the tidy
Victorian house, then back to me. Admittedly, it
didn't look like the dwelling of a Slugfest devotee.
"What kind of woman is she?"

Not knowing who this man was, I hesitated. Finally, I said, "She's the last of the founding Hendersons. She calls herself an 'historical environmental-
ist,' someone who wants to keep the area as it was.
Almost singlehandedly she got the county to pass an
ordinance making it a crime to deface the Nine Warriors—nine giant redwoods along the river. That
campaign was her great triumph. The trees are her
great love; I think they symbolize the natural history
of the area to her. She's also *the* authority on the
history of the town and the Pomo Indians, who lived
here before the white man. And she's fascinated with
Asia—the land, the cultures. If there's a slide-show
on China or a lecture on Bushido, she'll be there."

What I didn't say was that she was a wiry little
woman whom I had rarely seen without both a ciga-
rette and a cup of coffee. She was always rushing off
to a town council meeting, lobbying to restore the
Henderson railway depot, or circulating a petition to
save this or preserve that. No one could get an injunction or court order faster than Edwina Henderson. She knew the ropes and the judges. Her dedica-
tion to historical Henderson, to preserving the
Russian River, and to Pomo Indian history and rights
was nearly boundless. If you had a battle, tireless

Edwina Henderson was the woman you'd want in your corner. She'd give you her all, and the all of everyone she decided should be as committed as she was. But if you planned to relax back in that corner after the struggle, she'd drive you crazy in ten minutes. She was viewed, by the winter people in this resort area, with a fond but distant tolerance. Even members of the minority groups she supported and admired—Indians and Asians (groups with notably few members in our area)—found life on her pedestal trying.

I added, "She's the last person you'd picture at the Slugfest. I'd be willing to bet she never went near any of the ones in Guerneville. But for some reason, she had to have this year's Slugfest as a Henderson event, held in Henderson, with Henderson judges."

"Who are those lucky souls?"

"Well, there's Father Calloway of St. Agnes's."

"Showing mortification of the senses?"

I could tell I was dealing with a budding enthusiast here. "Then there's Angelina Rudd, the manager of the fish ranch out at the ocean, and Curry Cunningham, who runs Crestwood Logging. He's a member of the town council, the historical society, and an usher at St. Agnes's."

"Up-and-coming town leader?"

"The closest thing to a politician Edwina could get."

"And who else?" he demanded. It didn't seem to matter that he wouldn't know any of these local people.

"There's Edwina Henderson, herself, of course. And"—I couldn't restrain my grin—"the manager of the town PG and E office, Mr. Bobbs."

He glanced at my uniform. "Like having your boss eat his words, only better, huh?"

I nodded. At first glance, stoical Mr. Bobbs seemed

the antithesis of Edwina Henderson. In his tan suit, which was the color of the PG&E trucks, he rarely got up from his desk in the windowless cubicle that served as his office; he was as much a fixture there as the tan bookcase or tan chair. But his sedentary nature was not an indication of laziness. Far from it. He husbanded all his energy for his one passion: the management of the Henderson PG&E office. He was installed behind his desk before the first meter reader arrived at seven A.M. and still fixed in his chair when the last of us left. He could recall which meters had been tampered with in 1968 or what the read was for Fischer's Ice Cream Shop in June 1973. And he knew the Missed Meter Count of every office in Sonoma County, and doggedly struggled to limit his own—or failing that, to shift the guilt from the overall office count to the individual readers, as he would do with me today, when I got back to the office. A clear show of devotion to the company was his acquiescence to representing it at the Slugfest. The wonderfully ludicrous prospect of Mr. Bobbs downing a spoonful of Cream of Slug Soup could never be fully explained to a stranger.

"But why does Edwina Henderson want to have the Slugfest here? Does she have a bizarre sense of humor?" her visitor asked.

"No. It's odd. She doesn't have any sense of humor at all. But she wrenched the Slugfest from Guerneville, where it's always been. She has to have some reason. You can ask her when you see her, but I wouldn't count on getting an answer. You'll probably just have to come tonight to find out."

I gave him directions to Steelhead Lodge, where the Fest would be—clear directions. I was getting to like this man. I wanted him to be there. He would have to wait more than three hours to sate his curiosity, but Steelhead Lodge was on my route. I had saved that read for last. I figured if anyone had an idea why the Slugfest was going to be there it would be Bert Lucci, the manager. I knew what Bert Lucci thought of Edwina Henderson. If there was scandal or subterfuge involved, Bert Lucci would be delighted to tell me.

CHAPTER

2

Steelhead Lodge was one of those places realtors describe to prospects as "charming" and to each other as "dilapidated." Named for the river trout that was the focus of most of its guests, the lodge was a big wooden rectangle with a high, pointed roof. The roof sloped down over a veranda that ran the length of the building. Had it sported comfortable rockers, screens to keep out the mosquitoes, and a view of the river, the veranda might have been appealing. But it had none of those plusses. It was bare of furniture. Once, more than twenty years ago, Steelhead Lodge had been painted green, but now most of that paint had peeled off and what remained was coated with dust from the unpaved parking area. The long-ago-shingled roof leaned heavily on rough posts, and the thick railings between those posts looked like they had supported too many beer-sodden fishermen.

This, I thought, is where the first lady of Henderson has chosen to have her Fest! Perhaps she did have a sense of humor.

I had been inside the lodge a number of times when I read this route. The lodge was notorious among meter readers, especially female meter readers, because it was one of those old buildings built before anyone conceived of women having such jobs as meter reading. The meter was in the men's room! And in steelhead season, when every bunk in the lodge was filled with the Sonoma Fishermen's Asso-

ciation, or the Modoc Fly and Tackle Club, and a
goodly proportion of the club members were still suf-
fering from the previous night's drinking, making a
dash into that bathroom when it was empty was a
precision task.

Normally, at this time of year, the lodge would
have been full. The same groups came year after
year. The pine-paneled main room, with its sway-
backed sofas, rattan tables that sagged from the
weight of too many boots, and still-sticky spills on
the floor, would be strewn with forgotten clothes,
magazines, and aluminum cans that served as ash-
trays or spittoons. The smell of stale smoke filled the
room. This was not the type of place I could picture
Edwina Henderson choosing for anything, even the
Slugfest. I couldn't imagine her agreeing to be inside
here for two hours.

Another thing I couldn't imagine was Bert Lucci
working. But as I approached the front door, the
sounds of hammering inside were clear. Mr. Bobbs
might *appear* to be the antithesis of Edwina Henderson, but Bert Lucci *was*. Easygoing, he was always
willing to stop, talk, and laugh. It was as if the energy for two people had been split between Edwina
and Bert, and she had gotten it all. He was an aver-
aged-sized man, bald but for a few tufts of gray hair
poking out the sides. Habitually, he wore well-
stained overalls and a shirt, denim or plaid, that
matched the pants in accumulation of grime. He carried a hammer in his belt loop, but I had never before
seen him use it.

I pushed open the door and spotted Bert Lucci
perched halfway up a ladder fixing the paneling
along the back wall. Beneath him, the once beer-
stained, ash-scuffed floor glistened. And standing at
the foot of the ladder, clipboard in one hand, ciga-
rette in the other, was Edwina Henderson!

"Every panel on that side wall is loose," she said.
"You'll have to see to that, Bert. Move the sofas back
against the walls. The picnic tables can go by the
door. Set up the folding chairs, and the stage, of
course. And then there's my podium. Move, man.
We don't have time to stand and gawk."

"What about paint?" Bert asked. "You want the
place painted in the next two hours?" He glanced
back at Edwina and, seeing me, shook his head.

Edwina ignored his comment. "The kitchen, Bert.
Is that ready?"

"I had Helping Hands in here for three days scrub-
bing it out. It should be clean enough even for you."

Ignoring his sarcasm, Edwina nodded vigorously.
Her short, serviceably cut brown hair quivered from
the aftershock. She was a little, dark woman, with
pale eyes that bulged as if to spot the offending speck
of dirt more quickly. Her nose was narrow and
hooked. The observation that in profile she resembled a steelhead trout had not originated with me.
"And the folding chairs, Bert, you do have those,
don't you?"

"You had them delivered yourself. Mine weren't
good enough for you, remember?" he said. "Look,
don't you have something to do at the store? Aren't
you afraid Hooper's smoking a peace pipe in the
back and your customers are spitting on the sidewalk?"

His mention of the store reminded me of Edwina's
guest. "Edwina," I said, coming up to the pair,
"there is a man waiting for you at the store."

She spun toward me. "A man? Who haven't I
seen?" she asked herself, as if to short-cut waiting for
my reply.

"He's not local. Drives a blue Volvo."

"Maybe he's Chinese, Edwina, or an Apache,"
Bert said. "You better get down there."

Cutting him off before he could deliver a deeper dig at Edwina's well-known, unquestioning support for Indians and Asians, I said, "He's about six feet tall, and has curly brown hair and a beard." I was hoping Edwina would mention who he was, but my description didn't seem to enlighten her.

Still, she thrust her clipboard under her arm and said, "I'd best get down there. Can you manage now, Bert? I could have Curr drop Hooper off to help you."

"I've managed this lodge for thirty years. I think I'll make it through another three hours."

"Call me if anything isn't right." She was halfway to the door. "I can get back here." And then she was gone.

"Goddamned woman," he muttered as the front door banged. "Does she think nothing moves without the snap of her tongue? First she's got to have the lodge. Gives me three months' notice. I've got parties booked in here years ahead. Does that impress her? No, it doesn't." Still on the ladder, he leaned his arm on a rung. " 'Let them stay in a motel,' she says. 'They'll be in no condition to care where they sleep,' she says. What she doesn't say is 'Let me give you what they would have paid you, Bert.' No ma'am, I don't hear those words from her. You know her?" he demanded, looking directly at me for the first time.

"Not well."

"Save yourself the pleasure. Particularly if you're thinking of some kind of business arrangement. Once that woman's got a dime, it never leaves her hands."

"Why did you let her have the lodge?"

But Bert Lucci was too well launched in his monologue to be deflected. "So, once I agreed, then all of a sudden, it's not good enough. Now I ask you, is she planning to have the Queen of England here? Is she thinking of bringing her good family china and putting on a formal dinner? No. This is the *Slugfest* my lodge isn't good enough for. I had a janitorial service out here for three days. And you know who had to pay for that. They spent an entire day on the bathroom alone."

I pressed my lips together to forestall a laugh. I knew what shape the bathroom had been in. "She went to a lot of trouble to bring the Slugfest here," I said, trying to steer Bert Lucci back to my interest.

"Spent too much time in that cigar store. Last thing that woman needs is nicotine to speed her up. What she needs is a harness to keep her out of the way of normal people."

I laughed. "I heard you rather liked Edwina when you two were younger," I said.

"Like! A day with that woman is what convinced me to live here in the woods."

"If she's such a plague to you, why did you let her come here with the Slugfest?"

Bert Lucci stepped down from the ladder. "Curry Cunningham got me a group of logging crews from up north just for Saturday night. That'll make up some of the fees. But I'll tell you, if you know Edwina, you know Her Highness is not a woman you tell no."

"But why did she insist on having the Slugfest here to begin with?"

Bert Lucci's face softened. He eased the hammer back through the loop in his pants. "Don't make sense, I'll grant you that. Told her that myself, when I could get a word in between her orders. But you know she doesn't bother to explain herself." With a sigh, he said, "I can't stop and gab now. I've still got enough work for six days left. And if everything's not just right, you can bet I'll hear about it. Her

Highness wants it up to snuff when the television cameras get here."

"Television?" The Slugfest was a local event, more in the line of a church supper than a newsmaker. It hardly merited network coverage.

"So she says. She had me install two-twenty wiring for them. They'd better show. And it's already after five o'clock; I've got to get hammering."

After five! I raced for the men's room, pushing open the door without even a knock. It was empty, and spotless. It looked like it had been renovated rather than merely cleaned. I noted the read, and then ran for my truck.

When I got back to the PG&E office Mr. Bobbs would be waiting. It was just a question of what he would be more perturbed by—my late return and the Missed Meter, or his impending duty as a judge of the Slugfest.

CHAPTER

3

Mr. Bobbs was not seated in his cubicle waiting for me. He was out in the middle of the office, pacing. With his light brown hair and pale horn-rimmed glasses, his tan suit and shoes, he resembled a cloud of dust blowing toward me. Pointedly, he looked at his watch.

"I know it's after five-thirty," I said. "A number of roads were out. There are three new mud slides, not to mention the ones left from last year."

Before, he had looked distressed; now his eyes narrowed in suspicion. But I knew he was not worrying about the hazardous roads having endangered me; he was afraid of a Missed Meter.

I put the route book on the table before me. "There are no Changes," I said. "Changes" were notations we made when a meter had been removed or tampered with and required a repairman or an inspector. "But I do have an M-Five."

His pale eyes narrowed further. I was amazed he could still see. "Bad road?" he demanded. "Tell me about it."

He meant "justify it." "There was a mud slide across Kiev Road."

"Your truck has four-wheel drive."

"A tank couldn't get through that."

"Did you try?"

"If I had tried, the truck would still be there."

He eyed my boots for evidence of mud. With a

quick shake of the head, he said, "Clean. Didn't you attempt to circumvent the obstacle on foot?"

"Mr. Bobbs, Kiev Road is on the hillside. If I'd tried to walk around that mud, I'd have slid all the way down into the river. And," I added, knowing his weak spot, "I would have lost my route book."

He winced. I had lost a route book to an angry German shepherd three months ago. He'd been going for my leg when I proffered the book. Snapping his jaws around the tasty leather cover, he shook it till every page sailed out, half onto the muddy rain-covered hillside and the rest into the river. I'd spent days on the phone to the main office in San Francisco copying over all five hundred names, addresses, meter numbers, and reads. And while I had done that, my routes had gone unread. Late routes go on the office report—Mr. Bobb's report—as do unjustified Missed Meters. If I failed to read a meter because of a locked gate, or something blocking it, or because it was so obscurely placed that I just couldn't find it, then the miss went on my Missed Meter Count. It was my responsibility to contact the customer and deal with the problem. I was allowed only four and a half misses per thousand. But if I failed to record a meter because of an acceptable reason, like a bad road, then I was in the clear; it was the office's count it was noted on. And since the little offices in the rugged areas always had more Missed Meters than the city offices, where there were no felled redwoods blocking the roads or bulls huffing at outlying gates, Mr. Bobbs was always in the position of justifying his count. He fought us on every M-5. Presenting him with a Missed Meter was like telling Edwina Henderson to put up No Smoking signs.

He glared down at the offending route book. "We'll hold that read out." He looked back at his watch. "Too late to contact Public Works today.

First thing Monday. And you can drive by to see if that slide has shifted."

I was tempted to argue that my route for Monday was nowhere near Kiev Road, that I didn't have time to hassle Public Works about a slide I knew they wouldn't clear for months, and that Mr. Bobbs didn't need to hold this read out to badger me with next week (other offices didn't do that). But it was nearly six o'clock, and on Friday night, the night of the Slugfest, I had other things to do. "Perhaps," I said, "your sacrifice tonight will make up for this month's Misses."

Mr. Bobbs stared. One of the attributes he shared with Edwina Henderson was the absence of humor. To him, the idea that anything even this loosely connected with our utility company could be laughable was close to heresy.

Silently, I extricated the offending page and handed it to him. Route book in hand, I turned toward the storeroom, where I would drop it in the tan, dufflelike San Francisco bag that would carry it to the computer in the city.

"Miss Haskell!"

"Yes?"

"Your Missed Meter Count is already at four."

I nodded. As I put my truck key on the hook and signed out, I thought that no one but Mr. Bobbs would know by heart each reader's Missed Meter Count. I hoped that when he got his first bite of slug tonight, it would be raw.

It was eight-thirty when I pulled up outside Steelhead Lodge. The Slugfest was scheduled to start at eight, but the first event was the award for the biggest slug. Then there were the races, which went, as the master of ceremonies said each year, "at a snail's pace." Coming half an hour late, I expected to arrive just in time for the final heat.

The rain was lighter now, but the unpaved parking area had the consistency of chocolate pudding. Cars and pickups were parked every which way, and as I headed toward the veranda I could see the crowd huddled three and four deep around a Ping-Pong table. I glanced at them, looking for a tall, curly-haired man. But Edwina's visitor was nowhere in sight. In the middle of the onlookers, by the table, was Bert Lucci. "That's Sluggo in the lead," he was calling out, "with Escargot second, then trailing behind are Slimy, Spot, and it looks like Swifty is dead." All eyes were aimed at the table's three concentric circles. The slugs, I knew from last year's event, started in the middle and made their way to the outer rim. The contestants could be rented (with no possibility of return) for ten cents. And from the look of the crowd, every grammar-school child in Henderson was there, screaming encouragements that appeared to slide off the backs of their steeds. At the outer ring of the crowd, parents leaned back, oblivious to the decrepitude of the veranda railing, drinks in hand.

The Slugfest was symbolic of what the Russian River area had become: no longer strictly a secluded back country in the winter and a down-scale family resort of mildewed motels and poison-oak-covered campsites in summer. It was in transition, with its divergent groups: the old fishing families who had lived here for generations; the hippies from the sixties influx; the gays from the latest immigration; people who had summered here as children and come back "home"; civil servants from Santa Rosa and Sebastopol; and those who were fed up with the pressures of San Francisco life and marriages that had been no more personal than a business card, who longed for a place where they would be more

than a digit in the vacancy or unemployment rolls—
people like me.

The Slugfest was our spoof of "country-ness," of
the county fair bake-offs and black currant jelly tast-
ings. Its consummate tastelessness amused every seg-
ment of the river community. The more disgusting
the entrees, the better; the cornier the judges' comments, the more delicious we found them. Every year
The Paper in Guerneville devoted weeks to pre-Slug-
fest hype, selling Slugfest T-shirts, soliciting judges,
and quoting the excuses of those who couldn't stomach the molluscous repasts. They captured the
judges' gastric distress in print and on film; the post-
Slugfest issue of *The Paper* had a veritable bloat of
coverage.

The Slugfest was part church supper, part high
camp. Everyone understood that—everyone, it
seemed, but Edwina Henderson. She couldn't see the
tongue-in-cheek quality of it because, of course, she
had not a soupçon of humor. She must simply have
found the whole thing boorish, which made her desire to run it all the more puzzling.

"Going pretty well, don't you think?" Curry Cunningham was standing beside me. He was a smallish
man in his mid-thirties, with dark wavy hair thinning
across the top and cut river-chic long. With his up-
turned nose, thick eyebrows, and prominent jaw, he
could have stepped out of a St. Patrick's Day card,
had it not been for his slightly bulging eyes. Like
Edwina Henderson's, they looked as if they had been
stretched forward to see things first for so long that
now they found that vantage point normal. They
were the eyes of the man who, after only a year in
town, was already on the city council. Curry Cunningham ran Crestwood Logging, a small venture,
which, he was quick to tell you, was so ecologically

sound that it had been used as a showpiece by the State Forestry Department.

"I'm surprised to see Bert Lucci running this," I said.

"A natural choice. He's doing a great job." Curry smiled at me. "He's barely stopped talking in half an hour. And look at the kids. He's got them thinking the winner will take the race by a nose. I'm only sorry my own boy, Terry, can't be here."

"Is he sick?"

"No, no. Megumi, my wife, took him to Japan with her for the semester. She's Japanese. Her field is Eastern Buddhist Art. In that tradition they believe the most perfect work is the one that most faithfully reproduces an earlier great work. The continuity is through the work rather than through the artist, you see." He sounded as if he were repeating by rote what his artistic wife had explained to him. "So it's vital that she be where the great works are. She's been back to see the collections at all the museums on the East Coast. Still, it's a shame for Terry to miss the Slugfest. It's one thing he'll never see in Japan."

"There's always next year."

A woman with long dark hair caught at the back of her neck—Angelina Rudd—made her way in front of us, nodding curtly to Curry. I knew her by sight. She wasn't much older than me, maybe thirty-five, but already she managed the fish ranch at the mouth of the river and had a house near the top of the hill in Jenner by the Pacific. She was rarely home when I read her meter, and at the fish ranch it was the guard who unlocked the gate and accompanied me to the meter and back. So even if my face looked familiar to her, it probably fell into that uncomfortable category of those that couldn't be readily placed. And she was clearly too preoccupied to bother finding my niche at the moment. Looking past me, she took a long swallow from her glass.

"Don't ruin your appetite," Curry said to her, grinning. "We judges have to have fresh palates."

She scowled. "I hope Crestwood Industries appreciates this. If they hadn't insisted—if *you* hadn't told them about this—I wouldn't have set foot in here or have done anything to help that old witch out of a bind."

When she had moved on, Curry Cunningham shrugged uncomfortably. Both Crestwood Logging and the Russian River Fish Ranch were parts of Crestwood Industries. There had been speculation that Angelina, who had run the fish ranch since the property had been purchased a year and a half ago, would be given charge of all Crestwood's area industries. She'd even been called to the Crestwood headquarters in Baltimore to be interviewed. When Curry had arrived from there, six months later, with that job in the bag, Angelina hadn't hidden her irritation. Apparently, time hadn't diminished her bitterness.

"How come Bert is center stage here and not Edwina?" I asked, partly to fill the silence Angelina had left.

"Good sense on her part?" Curry replied.

"When she rushed out here this afternoon, she left him with enough work to keep him going till Wednesday. I'm surprised even she could get him to do anything else."

Curry grinned again. "Don't worry about Bert overdoing it. He called Hooper at the tobacco store. I dropped Hooper off here at five-thirty. So you can guess who's done the hauling and lifting since then."

I laughed. Clearly Bert had gotten to Hooper as soon as I had left, and well before Edwina had had a chance to get back to the tobacco store and intercept his call.

A scream went up by the table. "Sluggo," Bert announced, had triumphed. After a break, he added, the gourmet judging would begin.

I headed inside. At the left, a table was set up for a bar. Most of the crowd was either making their way to or from it. A few were settling on folding chairs by the stage. On the platform five chairs were positioned behind a long table. At each place was a soup spoon, the de rigueur utensil of the Fest. Cooks of the slug-filled entrees would hold their dishes in front of each judge while he dug in with his spoon. The dishes wouldn't be moved until he had taken his share.

I glanced to the right of the stage, at another long table where some of the entrees were already waiting. Hooper, Henderson's self-pronounced Pomo Indian leader (and probably the town's only full-blooded Pomo), seemed to be guarding them—not that I could imagine anything that could adulterate a slug dish. Next to the folding table was Edwina's podium. I wouldn't have been surprised to find Edwina up there already, assembling notes, preparing for whatever she planned to present to the television cameras. But her podium was empty.

I made my way through the crowd to the bar and bought a brandy and soda. Perhaps the receipts from the bar were the inducement Edwina had used to convince Bert Lucci to turn out the weekend's fishermen in favor of the Fest.

Inside the kitchen Leila Katz bent over a container of red sauce that smelled so enticingly spicy that I was almost sorry I wouldn't be offered any. Next to her stood Chris Fortimiglio—not the first person I would have expected to see here tonight. Chris, like his father and grandfather, was a fisherman. Now, with salmon season only three days away, I would have expected him to be at the dock in Bodega Bay, checking his lines or drinking with the fleet, listening for a hint of where the coho might be biting.

The Fortimiglios had been good friends to me when I moved up here from San Francisco two years ago. Chris's mother, Rosa, had fed me often, and I'd spent many an evening in their living room, listening to the Fortimiglios and their numerous relatives and friends (who comprised almost all the winter population of Henderson) passing the word of who was doing what. Gossip was as integral to the Fortimiglio household as pasta—but there was no malice in that gossip. If someone in town had a problem, they wanted to be there to help. They had pulled my pickup truck out of the mud; they had brought me a kerosene lamp the first time the lights went out, knowing that I, a new arrival from the city, wouldn't be prepared to deal with a power outage. They had made me feel a part of the town. And when we had all been caught up in a murder and it had separated us, I felt the loss. Chris was still friendly, but awkward about it, as if he was betraying a trust he didn't quite believe in. As for Rosa, it was as if the sight of me brought it all back.

But if Curry Cunningham had left my questions unanswered, I didn't expect that worry with Chris Fortimiglio. I glanced down at his tray. It held five small pastry shells, each filled with a suspiciously lumpy mixture in red sauce, topped with cheese, and sprinkled heavily with black olive bits. He was adjusting their positions on the tray. "What are they?" I asked.

"Slug Pizzas. They're good."

"Did you make them?" I asked in disbelief.

"Well . . ."

"Rosa?" Rosa's culinary renown was unequaled in Henderson.

Chris looked away. He was one of those blond

Italians—tall, already tanned from working on his boat. "Well . . ."

"How come she's not here then?"

"You remember my nephew Donny, Vejay. Well, he bought some tobacco at Edwina's store last fall, and he got sick. You know how bad his asthma is. We had to take him to the emergency room. Afterward, Mama told Edwina, and well . . . Mama's forgiven Edwina, but Edwina's still on her high horse. I was kind of surprised that she didn't find some reason to throw out my entry."

"I'm surprised you made an entry."

Chris hesitated, then grinned. "It was Donny's idea. His nose drops were pretty expensive. We could really use that fifty dollars. And you know, with Mama's cooking, we're hard to beat."

Behind us, Leila Katz spooned her spicy sauce into long-stemmed crystal dishes. The kitchen had a festive atmosphere, more relaxed than I would have imagined anyplace with Edwina Henderson in charge. I glanced around. "Where is Edwina, Chris?"

"Isn't she outside?"

"I haven't seen her. Her podium is empty."

Chris put down the tray. "She hasn't been in here. I don't know where she is. Have you seen her, Leila?"

Leila Katz was another person I wouldn't have expected to see here. She was Edwina's niece, though no one would have guessed by looking at her. Her short black hair hung in unruly curls, and her nose and cheeks were as soft and wide as Edwina's were sharp. Only in shortness did she resemble her aunt. She ran the Women's Space, a bookstore and general gathering place for women, straight and gay. It was no secret that lesbian rights was not one of Edwina's causes. As the creator of the town museum (a room connected to the tobacco store), Edwina was nothing if not traditional. The last I had heard, she and Leila weren't even speaking. "I thought she'd be here all day," Leila said. "Bert was afraid she'd commandeer one of his bunks at night."

"It's almost nine o'clock," I said. "She should have been here an hour ago. You don't think something's happened to her, do you?"

"Like she had a few too many to fortify her for her meal here?" Leila suggested.

All three of us stood silent, putting off the inevitable question. Finally, it was Chris who said, "Maybe someone ought to call her house and check."

There was another silence. Leila, the obvious candidate, was waiting for one of us to offer. Chris shifted his weight.

In the main room I could hear Bert Lucci beckoning judges to the platform. The shuffle of feet suggested a concerted effort by the audience to get one last drink before sitting down.

Bert Lucci stuck his head into the kitchen. "Almost ready?"

"Are you going to start without Edwina?" I asked.

"No. She's in her place. Looks a little green, but that's not unusual for a judge, or for Edwina at any time."

As one, Chris and Leila sighed.

I hurried out, and after a quick survey of the audience to spot Edwina's curly-haired visitor—he wasn't here—plopped down in the one remaining seat in the first row, right in front of Edwina. Bert Lucci had been right about her looking green. Unlike the Edwina of this afternoon, who could barely stand still long enough to give orders, now she slumped in her chair, noticing neither the audience nor the procession of platters from the kitchen. Maybe Leila had been right about her aperitifs. In the sticky heat of the crowded room, a number of drinkers were beginning to look sleepy.

The other judges seated themselves. Bert Lucci stood behind them demanding the audience's attention.

"Why doesn't he use the podium?" I asked Leila, who had come in and squatted beside me.

"Edwina told him to stay off. For herself only."

"How come?"

"Who knows with Edwina? Bert said he wasn't about to ask."

". . . Bobbs of our own Henderson PG and E office," Bert announced. Mr. Bobbs looked every bit as green as Edwina. He tried to force a smile. I couldn't remember ever seeing him smile, and this evening he didn't break that record. The crowd applauded first his introduction, and, more heartily, his vain attempt to look cheerful.

Curry Cunningham was next. At his name, he stood and bowed, holding his stomach. It was clearly a crowd pleaser.

Angelina Rudd did smile. "If my fish can eat worms, I can eat slugs . . . I hope." She was greeted by laughter. It seemed to surprise and please her. She hardly looked like the same moody woman who had snapped at Curry Cunningham.

The fourth judge was Father Calloway, the white-haired priest from St. Agnes's. His was the parish of the fishing families. Many of his flock were in the audience, and they applauded him with enthusiasm. Father Calloway shook his head. "I've taken vows of chastity and obedience, not tastelessness. I don't know why I'm here."

"Reward in heaven," someone called from the back.

"And, taking the last seat, the traditional Slugfest host's seat," Bert Lucci said from behind Edwina

Henderson, "is the lady who brought this auspicious affair to Henderson. And after the judging, if she can still speak, she tells me she'll have an announcement of importance to make."

I poked Leila. "Aha!"

The crowd applauded, but Edwina barely looked up.

I hadn't paid attention to the light, but now I noticed the hot bright lights necessary for filming. Glancing back into the room, I spotted a hand-held television camera, but I couldn't see the logo on it. Still, getting attention from any television station, no matter how small, was quite an accomplishment, one Edwina didn't seem to be taking advantage of.

But Bert Lucci certainly was. Thrust into the limelight, he blossomed as an emcee. "Let's hear it for the Grand Promenade," he called out.

Curry Cunningham got up and stood back. "Ladies first." He motioned Angelina and Edwina forward. Taking Father Calloway by the arm, he said, "Clergy second."

"Fools rush in, eh?" the priest retorted as he headed toward the display table.

Mr. Bobbs was still in his chair. Mimicking a head waiter, Curry pulled the chair back, assisted him up, and gave the chair a shove back in place.

On the food table, each dish sat on its tray by the front edge, ready for its creator to pick up the tray and carry it the few steps to the left and offer it to the seated judges.

"Take a good look, judges," Bert said. "Breathe in the aroma of garlic, and tomato sauce, and sautéd mollusk. Look for the best, the most slug-filled portions." He clapped his hands slowly, starting the audience off on the rhythmic accompaniment to the halting pace of the judges as he led them around the front of the table, stopping them in front of each dish, so that each judge stood before a dish, then moved a step and paused by the next dish. The funereal pace of this enforced march was popular with the audience, which added foot stomping to the clapping. Clearly, it was not with Mr. Bobbs. Bert had to grab his arm to keep him from sailing past the last two dishes and back to his seat. And even when he did make it there, he nearly knocked over his chair in his haste to get in it.

When the rest of the judges were back in their seats, and the audience quiet, Bert picked up the first tray, of what appeared to be shrimp cocktails in long-stemmed crystal, and held it out for the audience to see. "Looks pretty tasty, doesn't it? And that's just from a distance. If you were up here where these judges just were, or where I am now, you'd be able to see those scrumptious little feelers on each head. Leila Katz"—he beckoned her onto the stage—"tells me she boiled the slugs, cleaned them, and put them in her special spicy slug sauce. Leila, here, you can serve the judges, so you can enjoy every one of their eager expressions. They've had time to look forward to this dish now."

To the background of laughter, Leila Katz took the tray and held it before each of the five, as they took a cocktail.

"One bite," Bert Lucci directed. "Just enough to pass judgment. All together now. Get those tasty little fellows on your spoons, judges. Wait. No cutting! You can handle a whole one, right, folks?"

The audience applauded.

The three middle judges held their filled spoons up. Curry Cunningham glanced at his and rolled his eyes. Father Calloway took a deep breath. But Angelina Rudd now looked no more apprehensive than if it was indeed a shrimp awaiting her. I recalled she was a fisherman's daughter. She had probably eaten plenty more questionable things than this when playing around the docks. Edwina Henderson raised her spoon and held it steady, eyeing it with the expression from *American Gothic*. But it was Mr. Bobbs who garnered everyone's attention. His hand shook as he lifted the laden spoon. Swallowing hard, he stared at it as if face-to-face with an infinity of Missed Meters.

"All right, judges," Bert Lucci announced. "Down the hatch!"

Four spoons entered four mouths set in four faces filled with stoicism or disgust. The fifth spoon—Mr. Bobbs's—remained unmoved.

"Pretty tasty, eh, folks?"

Mr. Bobbs lifted the spoon up in front of his mouth.

"Oh, look here, one of our judges is savoring the moment. Well, we've got time, Mr. Bobbs. You probably just wanted everyone's attention, right?"

Mr. Bobbs stared at the spoon. His nostrils drew back from the smell.

"Ah, yes, the aroma of fine food, right, Mr. Bobbs?" Bert Lucci sounded more like an emcee and less like a handyman with each comment. Mr. Bobbs didn't move.

"Let's give him some encouragement, folks."

The audience began to clap rhythmically.

"Down the hatch!" someone called out in time with the clapping. The rest of the audience picked up the chant. I could make out the voices of two meter readers, loud and gleeful. "Down the hatch! Down the hatch!"

Mr. Bobbs opened his mouth.

"Down the hatch!"

He swallowed hard, shut his eyes, and shoved the spoon in his mouth.

The room shook with applause and stamping of feet.

Mr. Bobbs's eyes opened wide. Then he gagged. He clutched his throat, stumbled off the platform, and staggered into the bathroom.

CHAPTER

4

There was a moment's silence after Mr. Bobbs's dash for the bathroom, then a few unsure ripples of laughter came from the audience.

"Well, there's one opinion of Slug Cocktail," Bert Lucci announced. He paused for the audience's response as if he'd been honing his timing for years. When it was quiet again, he said to Curry Cunningham, "Top that judgment!" Handing him the microphone, he muttered, "I'll be back," and headed for the bathroom.

It was the custom for each judge to comment on each dish. This was what the audience really came to hear.

Curry Cunningham looked down at the remains of his Slug Cocktail. His brow wrinkled, and I could almost see him trying to assess what the proper tone should be. "I'd have to say," he said slowly, "that Slug Cocktail is a very moving dish."

His choice was correct. Bursts of laughter greeted him, and it was as if he had assured everyone that Mr. Bobbs need not be taken seriously. He passed the microphone to Angelina Rudd.

"Now I know how the salmon feel when they take the bait," she said.

"Have seconds," someone called.

Father Calloway took the microphone. He held it before him a moment, then said in a low, almost intimate voice, "You know those restaurants that offer free hors d'oeuvres . . ." The audience howled.

Edwina Henderson accepted the microphone. I realized I had almost forgotten she was there. "It's not likely to be in the *Henderson City Cookbook*," she said. Her words were so clipped, her delivery so schoolmarmish, that it was several moments before the audience reacted.

Chris had taken Leila's place. He nudged me. "Vejay, Bert's over there by the bathroom. He's motioning to you."

I looked up. Bert nodded at me. I raised an eyebrow. He beckoned me with a finger.

"What does he want with me, Chris?"

"Maybe you're Mr. Bobbs's nearest and dearest."

Chris was joking, but the thought struck me that perhaps Mr. Bobbs was sicker than we'd imagined. Still, I was hardly a friend of his. I was merely one of his employees, an unfavored one at that. But I couldn't refuse Bert's summons. I got up and made my way around the back of the stage to the bathroom door.

Bert was standing outside it. "He's in there."

I nodded.

"Look, I see men throw up every single weekend. That bathroom don't look right if there's no one hung over the sink. I haul them up, clean them up, steer them out, and drop them in bed. It's like those spoon cookies my mother used to make."

And that, I thought, was a comment worthy of the Slugfest microphone.

"But this guy . . . I don't know what to do. I don't want to leave him. But I can't stay. I've got to get back there."

Curry Cunningham called, "Come on, Bert. You can take Bobbs's place."

Bert nodded in his direction. To me he said, "You work for PG and E," as if that explained everything.

And before I could object, he headed back to the stage.

I stood outside the door, absently listening to the rhythm of Bert's comments as he introduced Frittata with Slime Sauce. I knew this bathroom—it was the men's room with the electricity meter. Whenever I had come here, I'd tapped on the door, waited, tapped again, and waited again. And even with that, I had surprised one or two surly Steelhead guests.

But there was no getting around the fact that I had to go in now. I tapped. "Mr. Bobbs."

No answer.

From the main room came a wave of laughter.

"Mr. Bobbs, it's Vejay Haskell. What can I do to help?"

Still no answer.

"Mr. Bobbs, I'm going to come in now."

I strained, hoping to hear even the faintest protest. But there was silence in there. I hoped he wasn't too far gone to speak. I put my hand against the door and pushed it in an inch and waited. Still no objection.

Taking a breath, I opened the bathroom door and walked in. I had expected to see and smell vomit. I wouldn't have been surprised to find Mr. Bobbs sprawled on the floor or collapsed against the wall. But the only smell was of ammonia, and Mr. Bobbs was standing upright in front of the mirror, his tan suit unmarred. He hadn't been sick. He didn't look any worse than he had before his bite of slug.

From outside came another wave of laughter.

Mr. Bobbs turned toward me. "Miss Haskell?" he said, as if I had just entered his cubicle in the PG&E office rather than the Steelhead Lodge bathroom. He wore the same expression he had this afternoon when he suggested I should have marched through the mudslide.

"Are you all right?" Even as I asked it, it sounded like a dumb question.

"I am."

"You don't have to go back out there. The judging is going on without you."

He nodded, as if I'd just handed him another Missed Meter page.

I waited.

He said nothing.

Enthusiastic applause came from outside.

"There's a back door," I said. "If you make a quick left outside, no one will see you leave."

He nodded again, but otherwise didn't move.

I swallowed, then, against my better judgment, asked, "Do you want me to drive you home?"

Now he stared directly at me. "I do not, Miss Haskell." He straightened his jacket and walked out.

I leaned back against the sink in relief. For once Mr. Bobbs and I had had a meeting of the minds. The idea of driving for twenty minutes or more with a humiliated Mr. Bobbs, a Mr. Bobbs who might even throw up in my truck, was appalling. And he, of course, would have been more horrified than I.

"Thanks a lot, Bert," I muttered under my breath. Irritably, I stalked out and made my way through the back of the crowd, where people had created a bleacher section from a picnic bench and table. Those on the table leaned back against the outside wall. I elbowed in front of the bench, just avoiding a slap as one enthusiast burst into applause. I stepped around a baby stroller and its sleeping occupant, and over a pile of jackets. When I got to my seat, it was taken. A pregnant woman I recognized from my H-1 route sat clutching two coats and a paper beer cup. She looked up at me guiltily.

I smiled and shook my head, indicating a forgiveness I certainly didn't feel. I had assumed that Chris's

involvement in my departure obligated him to at
least save my seat. Where had he been when I could
have used him?

Chris, I quickly realized, was on the stage, holding
out a tray of individual Slug Pizzas. Bert Lucci had
taken Mr. Bobbs's seat. He, Curry Cunningham, and
Angelina Rudd held their filled pastry shells in front
of them. Father Calloway reached for the closer of
the remaining two, and without looking up at Chris,
Edwina Henderson took the last.

"And here we are, folks, our last entry," Bert said,
from his seat. "A good way to end, with a Fortimiglio dish. You can bet this'll be more than you could
have hoped for, right, Chris?"

"Umm." Chris looked embarrassed.

"Chris is following the family tradition, right?"
Bert insisted.

"Umm." Chris reminded me of that nephew illic-
itly smoking Edwina's tobacco. Even though he was
well into his twenties, Chris wasn't skilled at deception.

"Fellow judges," Bert said, "one big bite now.
These pizzas are small. You can stuff them all in in
one bite."

Curry Cunningham rolled his eyes. I wondered
how many times those eyes had rolled in my absence.
Apparently I had missed the two middle entrees. Tomorrow the Slugfest would be the main topic of conversation in town, and there would be a lot of "Did
you see that?"'s I'd have no response for. Damn Mr.
Bobbs.

"Okay, judges, all together now."

They raised their pizzas and stuffed them in. The
audience held its breath, but it didn't take long to
realize that what we had here was an anticlimax.
Rosa's cooking had overcome the event. Even Curry
Cunningham couldn't disguise his enjoyment.

"So, judges, what's your verdict? You've had Slug Cocktail, not a universal favorite. Then there was Frittata with Slime Sauce, Slug Stroganoff, and now Slug Pizza. Give us your verdicts, judges." Bert poked the microphone at Curry Cunningham.

"Pizza."

"Pizza," Angelina seconded.

Father Calloway agreed, and though it was clear that Edwina Henderson begrudged the decision, she gave it her nod.

"And now a round of applause for our judges," Bert said. "We'll let them repair to the bar for a post-prandial cordial. You have any Slug liqueur back there?"

Amidst the laughter, the judges made their way off stage. Bert beckoned to Chris. I glanced around to see if Donny Fortimiglio, the architect of this scheme, was present to enjoy the victory. But I couldn't spot him. I also didn't see Edwina's visitor. So much for my careful directions to him. Apparently he'd decided that neither local color, nor me, was worth the effort of finding another building off the main street here.

"So, Chris, are you giving up fishing and going into chef-ing?" Bert asked, as he held out the check.

"No. I just have this one recipe. I don't think it will support a franchise."

"Well, here you go." Bert held the check high for everyone to see. "Maybe you can take your family out to dinner, unless you have some uneaten Slug Pizza at home."

Another round of applause followed. Then the people who had been sitting in the folding chairs stood up, and the ones who had been standing moved back to the bar. As I made my way there, I passed Father Calloway, drinking a brandy and saying to a parishioner, "You'll remember my sacrifices when it's hard to get up for Mass this Sunday, won't you, my boy?"

Bert Lucci came up next to me. "What happened with Bobbs? He's not still in there, is he?"

"No, I told him about the back door."

"And he left?"

"Like it was five o'clock and he was through for the day."

"A memorable performance." It was Mike, one of my fellow meter readers. "I wonder what we should do to commemorate it?"

"A slug on his desk Monday morning?" Sherman, one of the trouble men who dealt with electrical emergencies, offered.

Beverly, a meter reader-clerk, held up a camera. "I've got a shot of him just when he swallowed. We could present it to him."

"Whatever we do," Mike said, "I should be the one to do it." Ignoring the groans of his listeners, he went on. "You know where my wife is? Down in Puerto Vallarta turning brown. I'm here in the rain and cold turning purple. Her folks sold timber rights to a plot of land on North Bank Road. They used the money for the trip. They had an airline ticket for me, too. But I couldn't get time off. You-know-who wouldn't approve leave without pay."

"But Mike, it's worth it to have seen his face tonight. Come on, would you have missed this?" Sherman demanded. And that led to another rehash of Mr. Bobbs and his much-appreciated humiliation.

The crowd milled. A few people wandered to the table behind the stage that held the remains of the entrees. But it was clear the party was over, and in a surprisingly short time, people began leaving. Even the meter readers tired of recounting their own perspectives of Mr. Bobbs's debacle. In the cold of March, forty hours a week of climbing up and down the hillside to get near enough to read rain-splattered meters was exhausting. Soon, rehashing Mr. Bobbs's disgrace was not as appealing as bed.

The main room was virtually empty when a scream came from the kitchen.

I ran in.

Angelina Rudd was propped against the stove. Her mouth hung open. She was staring down at the floor, where Edwina Henderson lay.

CHAPTER

5

The sour stench of vomit hit me as I looked at Edwina's body. I braced myself against the doorjamb. There were three puddles of vomit on the floor near her. Edwina looked as if she had supported herself just as Angelina was doing now, leaning on the stove. And when her strength failed, she had slid down onto the floor. Her body was slick with sweat; drops still hung from the sides of her face; her hair stuck to her forehead. I couldn't see any signs of breathing.

I turned away and swallowed hard, willing myself not to be sick. When I looked back, Leila Katz was already on the phone to the fire department. They would send an ambulance and medics.

"Hey, what's going on in here?" Bert Lucci called cheerfully as he rounded the doorway from the main room. He stopped and gasped. His tanned face paled. "Edwina? What . . . ?"

We all looked at Angelina.

"I just walked in," she said. "She was there, like she is now. I don't know what happened."

Bert seemed to crumble down over the small body. It was a moment before I realized he was doing artificial respiration.

The siren sounded outside. The firehouse was only half a mile away. Bert pushed down on Edwina's ribs. The siren shrilled. Outside the main room, brakes screeched, metal doors banged, footsteps slapped up the veranda stairs and across the floor.

"Stand back," one of the medics instructed. We all stumbled back against the kitchen counters. One of the medics replaced Bert Lucci, kneeling over Edwina. Bert back-pedaled into me.

"Sorry," he mumbled absently.

As the medics hovered around Edwina's body and then lifted her onto a stretcher, it was like watching a movie. And like a viewer in the audience, I found a certain relief in shifting my attention from Edwina Henderson to Bert Lucci. What a surprising man he was. I had only viewed him as a marginally competent caretaker of this decrepit building. I would never have imagined him capable of emceeing the Slugfest. It would never have occurred to me that he knew CPR, much less that he would be the one to take charge and try to resuscitate Edwina. And it wouldn't have occurred to me, particularly after this afternoon's discussion about Edwina, that he would be so stunned by her collapse.

By now, I wouldn't have been surprised to see Bert Lucci insist on riding to the hospital with Edwina. But it was Leila Katz who did that. She grabbed her purse and ran after the medics, catching up with them outside. Their voices were muted, but Leila's sharp insistence that she be allowed to ride along carried easily. There was a pause, then one of the medics said, "Lady, she won't miss you in the ambulance. She's dead."

The room where we stood was so silent it seemed like we had all stopped breathing. Then I heard Leila, outside, say to the medic, "I'll be in my car behind you."

Doors slammed. Engines started. The siren cut through the silence of the night. And then all of them were gone.

In the kitchen, we stood silently. The medics had taken samples of the vomit, but the smell of the resi-

due seemed stronger. I pressed my lips together hard.
I could feel sweat on my face. And, as I surveyed
them, all four—Curry, Angelina, Bert, and even
Chris—looked ashen. We'd all heard the medic's pronouncement.

It was Curry who said, "I didn't realize food
poisoning worked that fast."

"It doesn't." Bert's voice was barely audible. "I've
seen plenty of bad food. Guys come up here for the
weekend. They make themselves a sandwich, lots of
mayonnaise, Friday before they leave home. Saturday they forget about it. Then, late in the night, after
they've been drinking all day, they get hungry and
drag it out. Maybe it tastes a little funny, but they
don't notice. They're doing pretty well to be moving
both jaws together, much less tasting. But that sandwich is a day and a half old, and it's been out in the
sun, maybe over a hundred degree temperatures, for
hours. It's like a laboratory specimen. And still the
guy may not feel anything till well into the next
morning." Bert was sounding like his old self now.

"That long?" Angelina asked.

Bert shrugged. "Sometimes sooner. But it never
starts in less than an hour or two, and then the symp-
toms are gradual. No one's stiff on the floor in ten
minutes."

As one, we all looked down at the spot where Edwina had lain.

"Could we move out of the kitchen?" Curry
asked.

With relief, we hurried into the main room and
headed away from the stage to the far end of the
room by the piano, and settled on the old, lumpy
couches or the rattan chairs. Chris perched on the
picnic table.

"What about botulism?" I asked.

"Not unless the slugs were canned," Angelina

said. "Botulism is caused by the exotoxins from anaerobic growth." She glanced at Chris, then added, "Anaerobes live where there is no air or free oxygen. They get their oxygen from decomposing compounds."

I knew Angelina managed the fish ranch, but I had half-forgotten she was a biologist.

There was another silence, longer than the first, before Chris said, "Do you mean, then, that she was poisoned?" It wasn't clear who he was asking, and when no one responded, he said, "But poisoned with what? What kind of poison?"

"Chris, there are all sorts of poisons," Angelina said, "from arsenic and strychnine, the common ones we all think about, to ones so obscure that only someone who was researching them would know they exist. There are whole books that just list poisons and their effects. What Edwina swallowed, it could have been anything."

"But how . . ." Chris held his hands as if weighing the volume of the question.

"She didn't look good when she got here," Bert said.

"That's right. And she was late," Curry added. "Maybe it was something she ate before."

He looked so hopeful that I hesitated before saying, "I can't imagine you judges would eat anything before the Slugfest. Did you?"

"Well, no," Curry admitted.

"Angelina?"

"I made a point not to. I didn't want the slug meat mixing with anything else."

"But she was late," Chris insisted. "Maybe she was late because she didn't feel well."

"No, Chris," Bert said. "She may have had something on her mind, but it wasn't affecting her body. Maybe you didn't see her drive up here, but one of

the guys who did said she came around the bend like
a race car driver. That's the way she drives. I didn't
see that. But I did see her tearing in here. There was
nothing wrong with Edwina Henderson then."

"And that was right before she sat down at the
table?" I asked.

Bert nodded. "Then you folks came out of the
kitchen."

The rain, which had blended into the background
before, struck hard against the roof. A gust of wind
shook the windows.

"If she was all right before the judging, then the
poison had to be in something she ate or drank
here," I said.

"Didn't drink," Bert said. "I know, because I offered her a drink and she turned up her nose. I figured she wasn't about to drink *here*."

"But wasn't the food all together on that display
table beside the stage?" Angelina asked.

"It was there, and I had Hooper keeping an eye on
it. I didn't want any funny business," Bert said. "I
wasn't going to have Edwina telling me afterwards
that there was a hair in the Slug Cocktail or a blade
of grass on one of the pizzas. That's just the type of
thing she looks for, always an eye for a speck out of
place." He stopped abruptly.

"But if there was something in the food, how come
we're not all sick?" Curry asked.

"Maybe the poison was just in one part," Chris
suggested.

"But most of the dishes had sauces with everything
stirred in." Angelina rested an elbow cautiously on
one arm of the rattan chair. "What was there? We
should be able to remember," she said with a touch
of disgust.

Curry leaned forward. "There was that incredibly
bland Frittata. I mean, you couldn't even taste the

slugs, which was the best thing about it. And then that awful Stroganoff, where you sure could taste the slugs. God, that was like someone had pulled them off a flower pot and dropped them into a glass of cream. Believe me, if that poison had any taste, it would have been noticeable in either of those dishes."

"What about the Slug Cocktail, the first dish?" Chris asked. "It made Mr. Bobbs sick."

"White bread would have turned his stomach then. That had nothing to do with the dish," Bert said. "The guy was just scared. And anyway, the sauce was cooked in one pot and poured into each glass. So unless Leila Katz poisoned one slug, in one dish—"

"But how would she know Edwina would eat from that dish?" Curry asked.

"She served you," Chris said. "The dishes were on the tray, two on each end and one in the middle. She could have figured that by the time it got to Edwina, only the back one on the side of the tray nearest her would be left."

"That's true," I said. "People almost always take the dish that's nearest to them."

"But if Leila had wanted to poison Edwina, she would have had to poison all the slugs in the dish," Curry said. "She couldn't be sure which one Edwina would eat."

"And every portion of the slugs equally," Bert added. "Leila's been around long enough to know the judges don't eat any more than they have to."

"Poisoning all the slugs in Edwina's cocktail would be pretty dangerous," I said, looking around. "Are the Slug Cocktails still here?"

"Sure," Bert said. "Leila lit out of here with the ambulance crew. She wasn't about to stop for her dishes." He glanced behind him. "There. They're still on the table."

"Well, the only other thing that had individual dishes was yours, Chris," Curry said.

"And that"—Angelina paused and swallowed—"we had to eat whole. Bert, you made us down the entire thing."

No one had to say that the poison could have been added to only Edwina's pizza. No one had to comment that Chris, who was serving it, could have watched how the judges took the dishes from the earlier trays and positioned the poisoned pizza so it would be the only one left when he held out the tray to Edwina.

No one needed to say anything, because the door opened and Sheriff Wescott walked in.

CHAPTER

6

Sheriff Wescott stood in the doorway of Steelhead Lodge, hands on hips, surveying the room. He looked like a sheriff of the Old West, as if he'd ridden in from the range after routing Black Bart, rather than having driven here from his new metal-and-glass sheriff's department building on the outskirts of Guerneville. He was not yet middle-aged, but his skin looked weathered, his light brown hair held a wiry curl, as did his mustache. At times I had seen his blue eyes sparkle and soften all his features. But this was not one of those times. Tonight, the tan of his uniform seemed to mesh with the tan of his hair. He looked all Government Issue.

He glanced around, assessing the room and its occupants. Then his eyes rested on me. "I might have known," he muttered. "Miss Haskell, I'm surprised you get invited out anywhere."

I could see Curry Cunningham staring questioningly at him. But I knew what the sheriff meant. In the two years I had lived in Henderson, I had been involved in two murders. He had suspected me of one. When he'd come out to investigate the second killing and found me there, he had said, in the same tone he used now, "Does no one die in this town without your attention?"

"The body was found in the kitchen, is that right?" he asked.

"By the stove," Bert said.

He strode toward the kitchen. Hesitantly, Bert fol-

lowed. After all, it was his kitchen. The rest of us
shifted in our seats but didn't stand. A uniformed
deputy and a camera-laden man in rain gear walked
past us and into the kitchen. I suspected that they
would be photographing the scene and preserving
what was left of the vomit. I could do without seeing
that.

Suddenly, I felt overwhelmed, not so much by Edwina Henderson's death as by the manner of it. Edwina had been a nuisance much of her life. Despite
the enormity of her devotion and energy, her
achievements had been scant and of importance to
few but herself. She was like a Fourth of July spark-
ler sending her flashes of light out to die in the dark.
She needed to be told to relax; she needed an arm
around her shoulder. But she was too prickly for
anyone to come that close.

She did not deserve having to force down offensive
food and die in her own vomit.

I hesitated, then, taking a deep breath, pushed myself up and walked to the bar, hunted around for the
brandy bottle, and poured myself another drink.

It was at that point that the sheriff walked back
into the room. "I'll need to talk with each of you."
Eyeing my glass, he added, "Keep yourself in shape
to tell me what's happened, Miss Haskell. I'll start
with you, Mrs. Rudd." Turning to Bert Lucci, he
asked, "Is there a private room we can use?"

Bert looked around the room. It was clear from his
expression that privacy had never been a request at
Steelhead Lodge. "My office, I guess. It's not very
large, and I haven't straightened it up—"

"That's fine. That door there?" The sheriff indicated a door at the back of the room.

"That's it."

Nodding to Angelina Rudd, the sheriff ushered her
through the door. A deputy settled himself on a chair

across from the half circle the rest of us formed. Still holding my brandy, I settled back down in my seat and took a swallow.

No one spoke. It was like a doctor's waiting room, where you're afraid to ask the most impersonal question for fear it will lead to a disclosure you don't want to hear. So we sat, occasionally shifting in our seats. Bert coughed now and then. Once Curry got up and paced toward the table on the stage, until the deputy called out, "Please don't go near the evidence." Then Angelina emerged, and, without comment, left. The sheriff called in Curry.

Bert got up and made a show of counting the folding chairs, pointing his finger at each one and mumbling the number. Chris looked as nervous as he had on stage. I took another sizable swallow of my brandy, and, feeling the sacrifice, handed Chris the glass. He hesitated, almost spoke, then took it and emptied it.

I thought Chris would be next to be interviewed, or possibly me. Leaving Bert till last would have made sense. He had to be awake until the last of us left anyway. But it was he whom the sheriff called in.

And when Chris's turn came twenty minutes later, he looked as if he could have used another whole glass of brandy. As I waited, now alone with the deputy (Bert had gone into the kitchen where the sheriff's team had finished), I wondered why Chris Fortimiglio was so nervous. Was he thinking that the poison had to be in his pizzas? Was he wondering if the sheriff had heard of the flap over Donny Fortimiglio and the tobacco? Was he afraid that the sheriff would discover that Edwina had still been piqued with Rosa, and that Rosa had made the pizzas but purposely steered clear of the Slugfest? Even if the sheriff knew it all, it was hardly incriminating enough for murder.

But if anything, Chris looked even worse when he emerged. As he passed me he paused and gave me such an open, frightened look that I had the sensation of peering through his irises into the hollow of his fear. Then he was gone.

"Miss Haskell?" the sheriff called sharply from the office doorway.

Suddenly I realized that it was the second time he'd called my name. Maybe I wasn't in such hot shape either.

When I walked into the office, he was already sitting in Bert Lucci's ripped and discolored Naugahyde lounger. The wide window behind him dominated the tiny room, and I could picture Bert relaxed in his lounger in the late afternoon, staring out into the stands of laurel and eucalyptus. There was a desk under that window, but it was clear that Bert never did any sustained business at it. The desk was nearly hidden under newspapers, flyers, magazines, paper plates, and crumpled beer cans. There was no desk chair, and the lounger was hardly suited for sitting up and keeping accounts, even if Bert had excavated a place to work on those accounts. Sitting on the hard wooden chair opposite the sheriff, I shivered in the chill of the closed-off room.

"Tell me about the events of this evening, Miss Haskell," the sheriff said.

There had been a time last summer when he had invited me for a drink at the bar in town, half to warn me to stay out of his case and half, perhaps, for more personal reasons. Then he had called me Vejay. For those few minutes while we sat drinking our beers, we had talked like a man and a woman, choosing each word, trying to be agreeable, but still just teasing enough to keep things rolling along to a more intimate connection. The potential had been there. I had seen it in the nervous way he fingered his mustache; I'd heard it in my own voice. And then the murder—what he viewed as an accident, and I saw as a murder—took over. The attraction between us was transformed into antipathy. His few moments of openness had made him resent what he viewed as my betrayal all the more. And when the investigation was over, the intensity of our meetings settled back not into promise but rather a brittle distrust. I had seen him around town, on duty, since then. We had been cautious, polite. It had always been "Miss Haskell."

"Edwina Henderson was inside when I got here this afternoon," I said.

"What were *you* doing here this afternoon?"

"Reading the meter. I *am* a meter reader."

"A coincidence?"

"You could say that."

"So, it wasn't chance."

"Well, the lodge was on my route for today, but normally I read it in the morning, before Bert's guests have time to get too lively. That can save a lot of hassle. But today I left it till last because"—I almost said because I wanted to know whatever had possessed Edwina Henderson to use this place for her Slugfest. But I had learned to be circumspect with the sheriff. I didn't want to offer any information until I knew what he planned to do with it—"because," I said, "I wanted to see how the preparations for the Slugfest were coming."

"And Edwina Henderson was here?"

"She was standing at the bottom of the ladder Bert was on, giving him orders. She acted like she always did."

"Did anything else happen then?"

"No. It was just the three of us. Just a couple minutes. I had to get back to the office and explain my reads to Mr. Bobbs. I suppose you've already heard about him getting sick."

"Yes."

"Do you think his reaction is connected—with Edwina's death, I mean?"

"Until I know more, everything's connected."

"Do you have someone out interviewing him?"

The sheriff jerked forward. The backrest of the old lounger bounced, then sagged back. "Miss Haskell, I've seen to Mr. Bobbs, Father Calloway, and Hooper, too. I can manage this investigation without your help. Is that understood?" Without waiting for a reply (which wouldn't have been forthcoming), he said, "Now back to your movements. After you left here . . . ?"

"I drove back to the office, turned in my route book, went home, had dinner, and got here about eight-thirty. I talked to Chris and Leila in the kitchen before the Grand Promenade and the tasting started."

"What were they doing?"

"Leila was just standing. Chris was arranging his pizzas on the tray."

"What do you mean by 'arranging'?"

I knew what he was asking. Was Chris aligning the five pizzas with four in the corners and one in the middle? Did he realize that the one in the left rear would, in all likelihood, be the only one left when he offered the tray to Edwina? "He was just putting them on the tray."

It had taken me too long to answer. I could see him noting that. I could see him reassessing his next question. "Then what?" he demanded.

"Bert called us in. The judges circled the food table. Leila served her Slug Cocktails. Mr. Bobbs gagged and ran to the bathroom. Bert called me to deal with him. And by the time I got back, Chris was serving his dish. Then the judges ate it. They all, every one of them, including Edwina, said it was the best of the dishes. I was right in front of Edwina. She didn't look any different after she ate it."

He nodded curtly. I had explained too much.

"Then the judging was over," I added. "The judges left the stage."

"Where did they go?"

"Bert suggested they have a drink. I passed Father Calloway by the bar later. But the others . . . I don't remember if I saw them then or not. The next time I specifically recall seeing any of them was when Angelina screamed when she found Edwina's body." I hesitated, then went ahead and added, "Of course, Chris and Bert were on the stage with the prize money."

He nodded again, making notes in what must have been his own brand of shorthand.

I leaned forward. "Couldn't Edwina have been poisoned after she left the stage? Maybe she ate something by accident. She could have wandered into the kitchen and picked up anything."

"Any small item so soaked with poison that it would kill her in ten minutes?" The sarcasm was clear in his voice. "I would assume, Miss Haskell, that after being a judge at this affair, eating would have been the last thing on Edwina Henderson's mind."

Much as I wanted to, I couldn't disagree. And that brought suspicion right back to Chris's pizzas. "Anyone could have poured a few drops of poison onto any of the dishes," I said. "This place was a madhouse before the judging."

"But, Miss Haskell, you have just told me that at least Mr. Fortimiglio and Miss Katz were working on their dishes until the judging started. At that point, if I understand it correctly, the trays were placed at the front of a long table on the stage. So it would have been rather obvious if the killer had stalked up and doused one dish with poison, don't you think?"

"Unlikely, but not impossible. People were still getting seated, the television camera was— The television camera!"

"Before you instruct me, we're getting the film."

I sat back. It was late, and suddenly I realized how exhausted I was—too tired to spar with the sheriff, particularly when I was losing. "Is there anything else I can tell you?"

He put down his notepad and leaned an elbow on the arm of the lounger. "I don't have any further questions. But, can we be straight with one another for a change, Vejay?"

I lifted an eyebrow.

"I'm not pleased to find you here. I'm sure you realize that. I would like to think that you were just a member of the audience who happened to stay late. I would have preferred you not to have been in the kitchen next to the food. And mostly, I would like to think that you will not try to do my work for me. Murder is a very dangerous affair. Someone has given a lot of thought to this murder. That person has arranged things so that Edwina Henderson could be poisoned in front of over a hundred people and a television camera. This is no ordinary spite murder. The person we're—*I'm*—after is clever and ruthless. You *don't* want me to tell you what happened to Edwina Henderson between the time she ingested the poison, the time she threw up three times, and the moment she died. Corrosive poisoning is a very painful death. Am I making myself clear?"

My first reaction was to remark that his patronizing attitude was unappreciated. But that would have escalated things into just the type of sparring I wanted to avoid. I sighed. "I saw her there."

"The point I want you to understand is that anyone who did that wouldn't hesitate to kill again. So do me a favor and just stay away from this one, huh, Vejay?" His eyes opened wider; his face softened. I knew he was sincere—if overbearing about it.

"I'm headed right home."

"Good. Do you want one of the deputies to accompany you to your truck?"

I stood. "No. I don't think I'll be in danger walking across the yard. I didn't see anything. I spent half my time in the bathroom with Mr. Bobbs. I'm the least likely person to be a threat to the murderer."

"All right. Keep it that way, okay?"

I turned and walked out across the main room to the door, aware of those familiar mixed feelings, annoyance and attraction. I never met the man when I didn't feel a pull; I never had a conversation with him that didn't irritate me. Only the balance between attraction and anger varied. But tonight I was too tired to consider what the ratio was.

I pulled on my jacket as I stepped outside. It was raining harder now, and the parking lot was muddy from all the vehicles backing out and turning around. I was at my truck, reaching for my keys, when someone grabbed my arm.

Stifling a scream, I spun around. "Donny! Geez, you scared me."

Donny Fortimiglio bore not even a familial resemblance to his blond, boyishly handsome uncle Chris. Donny was a stocky kid with shoulder-length brown hair that bushed out in all directions. It was only when he spoke that his earnestness characterized him as a Fortimiglio. "Oh, I'm sorry," he said, releasing my arm. "I guess I just didn't think."

"That's okay. The sheriff was trying to frighten me in there." I indicated the lodge. "I guess he succeeded." I shifted my purse strap on my shoulder. "But what are you doing here, Donny? It's after midnight."

"Grandma was worried about you." "Grandma" was Rosa. "When Uncle Chris got home he told her what happened, and she was worried about the sheriff keeping you here so long. She said she and Uncle Chris would still be up and you should stop by on your way home."

"How long ago was that, Donny?"

He glanced around the dark parking lot as if searching for the answer. The rain bounced off his thick hair. "I don't know. Maybe half an hour, maybe more. Why?" A true Fortimiglio, he wasn't about to let a question go unanswered.

"I just figured she probably didn't realize how late it would be before I got out of here."

"Oh, no," Donny said quickly, "Grandma said

you should come no matter how late it is. She said if it was later you'd need to come even more."

"Tell her I appreciate that, but—"

"She said she'd put an apple pie in the oven so it would be cooling when you got there."

I leaned back against my truck. Again, I was aware of how exhausted I was. It had been a long day *before* Edwina Henderson died. And after we discovered her body, I had been running on adrenalin and brandy. Now both were used up. There was nothing I wanted to do as much as go home, settle into a warm tub long enough to let the heat soak into my body, and then crawl into bed. But this was clearly more than a casual kindness Rosa was offering. It was Rosa's offer of reconciliation. And after a year of estrangement from the family, I wasn't about to refuse.

"I'll follow you there," I said, and climbed into my pickup.

Donny had jumped into his own truck, made a U-turn, sending sprays of mud in a semicircle across the parking area, and raced out the rutted, unpaved exit road before my engine was warm. By the time I started down the road, there were no visible lights other than my headlights. I turned left onto North Bank Road, going east toward town.

There were no other vehicles on the road. The overhanging branches of redwoods and eucalyptus blocked out the sky and held back the rain just long enough for it to weigh down those branches, and crash like a breaking wave on the windshield. North Bank Road curved as it ran beside the Russian River here; it was impossible to see more than fifty yards ahead on the straightest stretch. And now with the rain and the darkness, it was like going through a fun house tunnel, never knowing what could spring up around the next curve.

The Fortimiglios' house was up a driveway off
North Bank Road, just west of town, across from
one of Edwina's Nine Warriors. It was a dark red
rectangle that looked like a box for a long, narrow
shoe. Built into the hillside, the lower level had origi-
nally been foundation. Later, one year when the fishing had been good, they had added a recreation
room and two bedrooms down there. But to the un-
informed eye, the lower level still looked like the
foundation.

A screened porch ran the length of the main floor.
I could remember many evenings during my first
summer in town when I had sat on the porch with a
plate of homemade ravioli on my lap and a glass of
burgundy beside me. The spicy aroma of Rosa's tomato sauce intermingled with the fresh scent of eucalyptus outside, and occasionally a cone from one of
the smaller redwoods bounced off the porch roof.
And Chris's parents, his sisters and brothers-in-law,
the various Fortimiglio grandchildren, and five or six
of the people Rosa had run into in town that day
would be clumped in small groups around the three
green wicker tables. Rosa would join one group long
enough to see that everyone had full plates, and to
hear what they were discussing, then she'd moved on
to the next group, pollinating each conversation with
the insights from the last, so that even if we hadn't
talked to everyone ourselves, we all had the sense of
being together.

And that winter, when it was too cold to sit on the
porch, some of the ill-matched chairs were dragged
inside. Chris would light a fire, and when that
proved inadequate, would turn on the electric heater
at the far end of the oblong living room. We would
all line up in the kitchen, accepting more spaghetti
than we could hope to eat and a second scoop of
Rosa's homemade sauce. We would take the plates

and the ever-present glasses of red wine into the living room and settle on the maple sofas or the padded rockers, or perch on one of those ottomans that no longer had chairs to match. And we would down every strand of spaghetti.

After the murder we'd all been involved in, Rosa's dinners had stopped. Rosa didn't blame me—she'd told me that one awkward moment standing in the Safeway parking lot. It wasn't my fault. I had been the last person seen at Frank's Place before its owner, Frank Goulet, was shot. The sheriff suspected me, and in my struggle to clear myself, I'd discovered things my friends, Rosa's friends, and Rosa herself didn't want publicized. I'd discovered the killer. I was sorry. Rosa didn't blame me, but she'd never forgiven me either. A lot of people hadn't. The insularity that had protected Henderson had been pierced; Henderson, as it had been for the winter people before then, didn't exist anymore. People didn't blame me, but they watched what they said. I never again had the feeling of belonging that Rosa had given me that first year.

As I pulled up in front of the house, I realized how much I'd missed being here for the last year.

"Vejay," Chris called to me from the kitchen door. "Up here."

I made my way around the west side of the house to the kitchen door. There was a front door that led in from the porch, but I had never seen anyone come in that way. Regardless of their business, the kitchen was always the first stop for any visitor.

Rosa was putting the pie on the table when I walked in. Seeing her here after so long, I realized that she was smaller than I had remembered. She was probably not much taller than five foot—a sturdy, buxom woman with short, thick, gray hair and the bright blue eyes that Chris had inherited.

She took a step, reaching out to me. Then she stopped, her arms momentarily stationary in an aborted hug before they dropped to her sides. "Vejay, it's good to see you. It wasn't right that the sheriff should keep you so late. I told Chris that. The sheriff knows you work hard and you have to be tired. Now you sit down and let me get you some coffee. Or would you rather have something else?" Her words, the same things she would have said a year ago, sounded forced.

"No. Coffee's fine. Nothing keeps me awake." I sat at the table.

Through the doorway I could see only one dim lamp on in the living room, and I could hear the low sound of the television.

Rosa put the coffee cups down and began cutting the pie. As if on cue, Donny hurried in from the living room, accepted a piece that looked like an entire meal, and disappeared back through the doorway.

I stared after him. I'd never seen this house so empty of people. And Rosa, I realized, had never looked so clearly her age. A year ago I'd sat in this kitchen and she'd jumped up to get me coffee, to get the cream, another trip for the pie, and yet another for the forks and then the napkins—all interspersed with questions and, as she took in my answers, a smile of approval, a smile of speculation, of thought; even her nod of sympathy had held the remnants of that smile so integral to her that it was never totally absent.

Now she still bustled, still smiled, but the smile no longer fit. It was like the Sunday dress worn by a cancer patient for a last trip out that reminds one not of the happy times when it has been worn but only that those times are gone forever.

Placing my slice of pie in front of me, Rosa said, "It's so hard to believe. Edwina. Well, you know,

Vejay, she was a woman you could gladly have throttled. But you wouldn't kill her."

"Someone did, though, Mama." Chris forked a piece of pie. "If there had been another dish or two, after ours, she would have died right up there on the stage."

"Chris," I said, "do you think the murderer put the poison in your dish because it was the last one?" As soon as I said it, I looked guiltily at Rosa. If Chris hadn't told her the poison was almost surely in their pizza . . . but, of course, he had. By now he would have told her everything he had seen anyone do or say since his arrival at the lodge.

"I don't know," he said, glancing at Rosa. Then he looked back at me. "Vejay, someone put poison in my dish. Why *my* dish? I . . ." He swallowed, then picked up his coffee cup, took a gulp, and almost choked on the hot liquid.

Rosa put down the fork she'd been holding halfway between pie and mouth. "You're a friend, Vejay. You know us. We've been in Henderson for a long time. From when Chris's grandfather was a boy. You know that not everything we've done we'd want the sheriff to know about. There've been hard times, you know that."

I nodded. For fishing families seasons are boom or bust, and in recent years the boom seasons had been scarce. And when there aren't enough salmon to go around, there are still payments to be made on the boat, the insurance, the gas; and for the bait and the ice that are needed to go out into the empty sea every day, hoping that the cohos or the chinooks have finally come back. And there are house payments, and clothes and food. Most years, the old fishing families like the Fortimiglios cut back or borrow, or scrape by hoping for next year. But in the bleak winters that follow, there is always the temptation of those empty vacation houses, with the televisions and stereos and VCRs, the cabins or chalets of the summer people who have gone back to their real homes in San Francisco or Sacramento. There is the knowledge that whatever their loss, insurance will reimburse them. I knew that there had been times when that temptation had been too great for members of the Fortimiglio family.

I'd read in *The Paper* that this year promised a good salmon season. It would start Monday. And Chris needed to be on the water when the sun rose.

"Vejay," Rosa continued, "the sheriff won't know that Chris couldn't have killed Edwina, that murder isn't in him. He'll think about those things in the past —not that Chris did them; Chris was never involved. Chris was out at sea. But the sheriff won't care about that. The sheriff will think of us as a family of thieves."

"Maybe he'll get a lead to the real killer, Mama." Chris had put down his fork, too.

"Maybe, Chris, but . . ." A year ago, when the sheriff had suspected me of murder, Rosa had never doubted that innocence was protection enough.

"But he'll start with you, Chris," I said for her. "And when he's satisfied beyond a doubt that you couldn't have done it, then he'll look for other suspects."

Chris nodded grudgingly.

Rosa didn't say anything. She didn't look at me. But the request she'd invited me to her house to hear, the request she couldn't bring herself to make, was clear. To anyone else I would have protested that my familiarity with murders came accidentally, and that I, of all people, was not the one to deal with the sheriff. Edwina hadn't been dead four hours and already the sheriff had warned me to stay out of the way. I said, "How can I help?"

Rosa looked up. She smiled, but her eyes still couldn't meet mine.

"Tell me what you know about Edwina," I said. "Maybe we can think of who would want to kill her."

"Chris and I did talk about that," she said, now relaxed enough to pick up the pie-laden fork. "There are no secrets about Edwina. She helped out in the tobacco store when she was in school, and afterwards she was there full-time. She had had two sisters, both younger. One went to college and moved away. She had a son. They, the three of them, she, her husband, and the boy, came here to visit the summer we made our trip East to see our relatives, the year after the fishing was so good. That sister died years ago. But I remember Edwina talking about her nephew's visit. I remember her saying the trip was a sixteenth-birthday present for the boy."

"Then this boy will inherit?" I asked.

"Oh, I don't think so," she said. "Surely Edwina would have left her money to Leila. Leila's the only child of Edwina's sister Margaret, God rest her soul. Edwina and Margaret were very close. It was the other sister who was the outsider."

I had forgotten about Leila Katz, Edwina's niece. She had driven to the hospital with Edwina's body. "I thought they weren't speaking."

Rosa shrugged. "More coffee?"

"Thanks."

She retrieved the pot from the stove and poured. Putting it back, she said, "Edwina had her fallings out, but they were never serious. If she had lived, things would have come together for her and Leila. Leila was her niece. Edwina wasn't about to let that go. Edwina was very set in her view of family. It was because she couldn't understand Leila's way of life that she wasn't speaking to her. But that would have worked itself out."

Chris laughed. "If Edwina had changed her will every time she had a falling out, she would have had to write it on erasable paper."

"So what there is to inherit, Leila will probably get," I said.

"Oh, Vejay, you don't believe that Leila would kill her own aunt just to inherit some land," Rosa said. It was like Rosa to think too well of anyone she knew to imagine them a murderer, even if that meant narrowing the alternatives to Chris. But in this case she was right: Leila was a friend of mine and I didn't think she had killed her aunt—at least I didn't want to think it. I said, "Tell me about Leila. What was she like growing up?"

Rosa lifted her coffee cup to her mouth and sipped thoughtfully. "Leila was always different from the other girls. She dressed different. She seemed distant, controlled, like someone from the city. You know what I mean, Vejay," Rosa said awkwardly.

I smiled. "I lived in the city long enough to know. You mean Leila wasn't as friendly, as open as kids here."

Rosa nodded, clearly relieved that I hadn't discovered an unintended affront in her comment. "Leila's mother, Margaret, was in a wheelchair. Her father died quite young, and in any case, he never lived here. He wasn't Catholic. Edwina never could accept that, that her sister could have married outside the Church. I suspect that's one reason why they didn't live here when he was alive. But when he died, Margaret and Leila came back and moved in with Edwina. Leila must have been eight or nine then. Edwina kept close tabs on her. She insisted Leila go to every class or discussion or potluck dinner that they had at St. Agnes's. I guess she was worried about

Leila's soul. But that was too much for a child. Even Father Calloway told Edwina that. And Edwina was so piqued at him that she went to Mass at St. Elizabeth's in Guerneville for the next month."

"And after Leila turned eighteen," Chris said, "she never set foot in St. Agnes's again."

"Hardly surprising," I said.

"But you know, Vejay," Rosa said, "I don't think Leila ever really forgave Edwina, not so much for pushing the Church, but for how she thought of Leila's father."

"Anti-Semitic?"

Rosa took another sip of coffee. "I don't think that's exactly it," she said slowly. "With Edwina, it probably wouldn't have been much better if Raymond Katz had been a Baptist. You see, Edwina just felt that there were certain things the Henderson family should do. Marrying within the Church was one of them."

But clearly it would have made some difference, and to the daughter who missed him, that "some difference" would have been gigantic.

"That wasn't the only thing," Chris said. "Edwina was always stalking down to the school. She cornered Mr. Granger, the band director, and didn't let him go until he agreed that Leila could play the trombone. And she badgered Miss Hitchcock until Leila got a special place in swim class. I don't even know if Leila wanted to do those things before Edwina got in gear, but she sure didn't afterwards. The other kids were pissed about her getting special treatment, and they made jokes about Edwina. And Leila, well, she was just caught in the middle."

"She never really had friends then, did she, Chris?" Rosa said.

"No. I did take her to a dance one summer— Mama sort of pushed me into it, but I didn't mind.

Or at least I didn't till I got to Edwina's house to pick her up. Edwina must have kept me in the living room for half an hour, pumping me. She just kept on and on, and there's not much about our family that's a secret. Leila was so embarrassed she didn't do anything but apologize until the dance was half over."

"You know, Vejay," Rosa said, "I'll bet it's things like that that made Leila turn to women. She kept to herself all the time. Her only real friend was Angelina, and she was her babysitter."

"But it wasn't like Leila was strange or anything," Chris said quickly. "It was more like she didn't want to expose anyone else to Edwina."

I took a drink of my own coffee. We were all friends of Leila's, all sympathetic to her adolescent sufferings, all trying to put the best face on our observations, and everything we said strengthened the case for her killing Edwina. But there had to be others with motives. I asked, "Who made the two middle Slugfest dishes, Chris, the ones that were served while I was in the bathroom with Mr. Bobbs?"

Chris laughed. Even Rosa smiled. "The first one," he said, "was the Camp Fire Girls. The second was from Esther Grimes."

"Who's she?"

"You know her, Vejay," Rosa said. "She's the woman who does for Father Calloway. You've seen her."

I had. She was devoted to the priest. Her only complaint was that he refused to have a full-time housekeeper, as she felt someone of his station should. Under her care, his house sparkled and his larder stayed full. I couldn't imagine her having so secular an interest as the Slugfest. "Did Father Calloway ask her to cook?"

Chris nodded. "Edwina told him she was low on dishes. So Father Calloway asked her to make one."

"I guess we can leave her and the Camp Fire Girls out of our considerations." I forked a bite of pie. Despite her concern for Edwina, and for Chris, Rosa had managed to make the best pie I'd had in months. "The only people who had access to the food were the cooks, the judges, Hooper, and of course, Bert Lucci."

"Oh, not Bert," Rosa said.

I'd forgotten Bert was a distant relation. "He did grumble about Edwina."

"Oh, that," Rosa said. "Bert's grumbled about Edwina for as long as he's known her. And she's complained about him. It just seemed sudden because they had to work together on the Slugfest. Most of the time they didn't run into each other, so they didn't have the opportunity to moan. But I know they liked that, complaining."

"Well, Bert did give her mouth-to-mouth. Maybe he wouldn't have been so anxious if he knew there was poison in her mouth," Chris said.

"What about Curry Cunningham?" I asked.

Rosa finished her pie. "The man who runs the logging company? I don't know much about him."

That was another sign of how things had changed for the Fortimiglios in the last year. Before that, any new winter person would have been invited to one of their dinners. They wouldn't have rested till they had made him feel part of the community, and till they knew everything about him. But Curry Cunningham had moved here just over a year ago, when the dinners stopped.

"He was transferred from one of Crestwood's other companies," Chris said. "You know about Crestwood, Vejay. It's run by that guy James Drayton, the one who's so right-wing. He's against almost everything—drinking, sex, even dancing. That was in

the papers last year, when he came here for the opening of Crestwood Logging."

"I thought at the time it was lucky he wasn't going
to be in the river area long," I said. Guerneville, Henderson, and the other towns around, with their sizable gay populations, would hardly have been comfortable for one with Drayton's narrow beliefs.

"But Curry's not like that," Chris said. "I did a
little work up at the logging site before Christmas.
He was hiring anyone who could lift fifty pounds
then. You know Curry's so careful about his safe-
guards that the government has brought guests there.
And that's saying a lot. There was a time a few years
back that some guy—Opperman, wasn't it, Mama?"

Rosa nodded.

"Opperman clearcut an entire hillside in one day.
He brought in maybe a hundred guys and just went
crazy."

"What happened to him?"

"Not much. Once the trees are down there's nothing you can do. The timber industry has a lot of
power in this state, much too much. They've got so
much clout that environmentalists aren't even allowed to photograph the cuts from the air! They
have to make an appointment to inspect! That's how
it is when you clearcut the hillside. But if you're a
fisherman, Vejay, the government can board your
boat any time, with no warning, and go through everything you've got."

I nodded. I'd lived here long enough to have heard
plenty about the unequal treatment of the two industries. "But what became of Opperman's land?"

"The land?" Chris said. "Oh, it's a tree farm. Opperman made a big thing about replanting. But all
the trees are the same height. It looks like a giant
cornfield."

"But you were saying Curry Cunningham isn't like that?" I prompted.

"Oh, right. Curry's been real good. What I was saying was that he was transferred from back East. His wife and son had to fly back there a couple times. Now they're in Japan. I think she's studying there."

"They sound like a very ambitious couple," I said. Rosa nodded.

"Angelina Rudd?" I asked. Before Rosa could protest, I said, "Tell me about her. She was a local girl, wasn't she?"

"She was in school with my oldest daughter. Her family, the Longhitanos, have been fishing here since longer than I can remember. Mario, her father, was swept overboard in a bad storm when she was just a girl." Rosa swallowed, as if the memory were still fresh.

"That happens," Chris said quickly. "It's the risk of fishing. You're careful, and even if you never take chances, a storm blows up suddenly, and you can't get back to port." He shrugged. "There's nothing you can do."

"What kind of girl was Angelina?"

"She worked hard," Rosa said. "She always had a job after school. The family needed the money. She'd take care of Leila Katz and her mother every day after school until Edwina got home. Then she'd walk home—it wasn't close by, either—and study. Later, when Leila was older and her mother had died, Angelina worked at Fischer's Ice Cream." Rosa lifted her coffee cup, then, realizing it was empty, put it back in the saucer. "I can remember my Katie saying how hard Angelina worked in school. She was one of those kids who have to struggle for everything. Good grades didn't come easy for her. Or good times, or boys. Katie was always a very social girl. She always had more boys over here than she knew what to do with. Once or twice she invited Angelina over, I think because she felt sorry for her—Katie was that type of girl. But Angelina never came."

"I guess she got what she wanted," Chris said. "There she is running the fish ranch. And Katie's just a teacher's helper at the school, with four kids at home."

"Chris!" Rosa exclaimed. "Katie's a fine mother."

"I know, Mama. But Angelina wouldn't have wanted that. Besides, she has a son and a husband now. And she has the fish ranch. She'll make a go of that if it kills her. She doesn't have any choice. She told everyone that fish ranching was the way of the future. She said she'd make fishing with the fleet obsolete. She said we'd better think about going back to school and getting ready for some other kind of work. Maybe she's right." Slowly, Chris grinned. "But, Vejay, if she's not, everyone who's ever had a salmon on the line is going to be laughing. She'll never hear the end of it."

I nodded. Rosa didn't look up. I knew her well enough to realize that she couldn't imagine the women she'd known as children, or Bert Lucci, or the man who was an usher at St. Agnes's, killing Edwina Henderson. She could no more see them poisoning her than she could picture Chris doing it. As for Chris, I suspected he was thinking the same thing I was—that none of them looked as suspicious as he did.

I stood up.

"Won't you have another piece of pie?" Rosa asked.

"No, thanks. I need to get home. I don't want to lose time in the morning."

Surprisingly, neither Chris nor Rosa asked what I was planning.

When I got home, my house was damp and cold. I ran the tub, turned on the electric blanket, and poured myself a glass of wine. I felt both exhausted and wired—not a good combination.

The rain had picked up, the wind was gusting, and the bathroom window rattled ominously. When I had bought this house two years ago, I knew it would need some repairs. I made a list, hired one of Chris's cousins to deal with the foundation problems that couldn't wait, hauled the firewood, and lowered myself precariously to the edges of the steep roof to clear the gutters, not daring to look at the fifty-foot drop to the ground down the hillside. I assumed that when everything I had planned was finished, the work would be done, and I would relax and enjoy my snug home. I didn't realize that when that list was taken care of, there would be a new list. And another list after that. With a forty-year-old house on a steep hillside, only constant hauling, hammering, and shoveling kept it standing. That window was one of the items that had been on this year's list since last summer. It rattled more vigorously with each storm. But I noticed it only when I was in the tub, right before I went to bed. And when I got up in the morning, and had time to deal with repairs, I would invariably forget it.

The rattling was worse than I could remember. I did the only sensible thing. I pulled the bathtub plug, dried off, and went to bed.

When I woke, it was cold and barely light. I snuggled down under the electric blanket. It was five minutes, ten minutes, perhaps even half an hour before I realized that I was still cold. I reached for the control, wondering why it hadn't occurred to me to turn the blanket up sooner. The control was dark.

"Damn!" I muttered. The electricity was off. Outside, it wasn't raining, but the sky was dark and the wind was still blowing the branches of the redwood near the house. They scraped against the window. I wondered if one of the higher redwood branches or a branch from one of the laurels in front of the house had blown down on the electric wires, or if the outage was not limited to my house. A tree could as easily have fallen on a power main. I pulled on my bathrobe and headed downstairs to the bathroom. A shower would warm me up. But I was only halfway down the stairs when I remembered that there would be no hot water. The thought of a warm cup of coffee flickered through my mind, but, of course, the electric stove wouldn't be working either. The problem with electricity outages here in the Russian River area was that, unlike most of California, we were not hooked up to the natural gas lines. When the electricity failed, not only was there no light, but no power for cooking, and no hot water. When the outages lasted three or four days, as they did at least once per winter, I spent my evenings huddled next to the fire, with greasy hair hanging down my neck, eating tuna fish on crackers, facing another day of reading meters for customers who stormed out of their dark, cold homes to demand answers I didn't have.

But now the problem could be handled easily. I dressed, and drove down to the café for breakfast.

Weekends are big sales times in Henderson, as in all resort areas. But March is not yet tourist time. And at nine o'clock on a cold, windy morning, there

were few people on North Bank Road, and fewer in
the café.

Marty, the weekend waiter, waved at me as I
walked in. I had been there so often that I was a
regular, and my eggs, kraut, and chorizo sausage
went onto the grill before I sat down. The vinegary
smell of sauerkraut floated across the room and I
noticed the woman at the next table—obviously not
a sauerkraut lover—wrinkling her nose. While I
waited, I picked up a copy of the local paper. I expected to find an account of Edwina's murder on the
front page, but there was no mention of it. The paper
must have gone to press before she'd swallowed the
poison. But there was the weekly burglary report,
and an account of the chamber of commerce's fight
to have the summer dams put in the river before Me-
morial Day, and the fishermen's opposition to anything that threatened to block the movement of the
steelhead and salmon.

"Here it is, another peculiar meal," Marty said as
he put my plate in front of me.

"I thought waiters were supposed to be enthusiastic about all their fare."

"I deal in truth." He grinned.

In spite of the pie I had had at midnight, I attacked
my eggs and kraut with vigor. The café was beginning to fill with grumpy tourists, still wrapped in
jackets against the cold wind outside.

It was just nine-thirty when I finished, the hour the
Women's Space Bookstore opened. I walked across
the street.

The Women's Space Bookstore was next to the
Henderson Tobacconist's. I had expected the Tobacconist's to be closed, with a black wreath on the door
or a notice of Edwina's death in the window of the
town museum, which occupied a room to the right of
the tobacco shop proper. But there was neither. Over

the roof hung the lowest branch of a giant redwood, one of the Nine Warriors. Occasionally, when I read her meter in warm weather, Edwina would be sitting underneath it, eating her lunch. Once, she hadn't been eating but was just staring up at the branches. It was the only time I ever saw her look peaceful.

I pushed open the door to the bookstore. It was empty but for Leila Katz, slumped in an overstuffed chair beside a floor-to-ceiling bookcase. Women's Space looked less like a commercial endeavor than a family library in a beach house. Bookshelves covered the walls, four thrusting out at right angles into the room. Armchairs were strewn around haphazardly, some clustered in groups of twos or threes, others tucked away in the niches made by the protruding bookcases. By the cash register was a sturdy wooden table, with thermoses of coffee and hot water, earthenware mugs, and, frequently, a platter of cookies or savories. The store was meant to be more than a place to buy books. Leila had made it clear that she wanted to have a gathering place for women.

When I read the commercial route in town, I stopped in here on my break—after reading Edwina's meter—had a cup of coffee, a cookie, and slumped in one of the chairs with a magazine. But now there was none of the coziness that normally characterized the store. Leila herself looked small and tired. With the dark circles under her eyes, she resembled a raccoon wearing a short, curly wig.

"How late were you up?" I asked.

"I don't know, Vejay," she said, not moving in the chair. "Edwina was already dead when I got to the hospital, of course. But that didn't mean there was an end. There was still plenty to do, papers to sign, autopsy to be arranged. I felt I couldn't abandon her. It was ridiculous. She was already dead. It wasn't like there was anything I could do for her. But I just couldn't leave her there alone under a sheet."

"You want some coffee?" I asked. "If there's none in the thermos, I can run across to the café."

"No. I made some. I've already had three cups this morning, and God knows how many during the night, but you can pour me another."

I poured a mug and handed it to her, then poured another for myself. Sitting down across from her, I said, "You must have been quite close to Edwina."

She considered that. "From the way I reacted last night, you'd think so. From the way we'd gotten on for the past few years, it was like we were Hatfields and McCoys."

"But you were her closest relative."

"I guess so." She sipped the coffee. "That was good and bad. Edwina took 'family' very seriously. To her we were the village royalty. When I married Jeff, Edwina congratulated him on becoming part of the family; she considered him a sort of woodsy prince consort. No, not even that appendage-like; to her he was a full-fledged prince. She never referred to him as a nephew by marriage; to her he was a nephew proper—until he committed the unforgivable sin and opted out of the family. After our divorce, he simply ceased to exist for Edwina." Leila took another sip of coffee. "Edwina had a very rigid concept of the way a Henderson lived. 'That's not how a Henderson behaves, Leil.' Edwina always called us in the family by our first syllables—another of her eccentricities. I was Leil, my mother Mar. But that phrase—'not how a Henderson behaves'—I'll always think of that when I remember Edwina. It was her condemnation of virtually everything I did. Edwina's proper Hendersons lived in very narrowly defined ways."

"How did that fit with her being such a supporter of Pomo rights, preservation, and ecology?"

Leila nodded stiffly, and in that movement I could see a resemblance to her aunt. "Hendersons do charity. You'd think there was a fortune in the family, and we didn't all have to work. What money there was, Edwina controlled, and she didn't part with it easily. She deigned to give me a loan for college, and after I paid it back, she wouldn't consider lending it again so I could open this store. If I hadn't had a decent job after college, there would have been no way I could have afforded to be unemployed for a year, much less rent this shop, even from Edwina."

"She owned this?"

"She owned the entire block—this, her tobacco shop, Fischer's Ice Cream—all the shops. You can see why her tightfistedness grated on the family. It wasn't even like she had anything to spend it on. Her big outlays were for painting her house every couple years, and occasionally redoing the facade of the weed shop. She certainly wasn't spending it on Steelhead Lodge. That place could have fallen down before she would have put a dime into repairs. She was the typical slumlord with the lodge, and she would have died before—" Leila stopped abruptly, flushing. "She wouldn't have wanted people to know that that ramshackle place was hers."

"She was pretty safe. No one would ever have guessed." I had a hard time suppressing a grin. The thought of Edwina Henderson owning that sagging, beer-sodden building was as ludicrous as her determination to hold the Slugfest in it.

I took a breath. Leila was a friend. She saved books she thought I would like. She told me about the best used clothing stores, and the secluded beaches. And at those times when the panacea of small-town living wore thin, and I had second thoughts about having left San Francisco and my career in public relations, Leila, who had had her own career in merchandising, was there to remind me why both of us had opted for the Russian River. And when, after the closeness of my first winter here, the winter people and Rosa had kept a wary distance, reminding me by the formality of their greetings that I had proven myself an outsider, Leila had set aside another volume of Virginia Woolf's diary, or suggested we see a play in Santa Rosa. She'd told me about her brief, disastrous attempt at marriage when she was still fighting her attraction to women. "It took a year of living with Jeff to make me see that I really was happier with a woman. I guess I had always known that. But before then I had wavered back and forth," she had said. And I had recounted my own divorce, and told her about my family who had moved so many times when I was growing up that now, as an adult, when I thought of a house we'd lived in I couldn't remember which town or even which state it was in. "That's why it was so nice to be a part of the winter people here," I had said, then quickly changed the subject.

"With Edwina having been murdered," I said, "it's going to put you in an awkward position—you being her heir."

"You think I'll inherit this?" She laughed, a hollow sound. "Edwina wouldn't leave this to me, Vejay, not if she could find someone else. I may have felt a burst of affection for her last night, but before that we hadn't spoken more than ten words in months."

I was relieved she brought the subject up. "How come?"

"You know how Edwina was. Either she was all gung-ho to have the state erect an historical marker and couldn't understand that everyone wasn't able, or interested, in driving to Sacramento to petition our assemblyman, or she was out checking the bark on the Nine Warriors to make sure no one had carved their initials there. Or she was busy getting an injunction. No one could get injunctions faster than Edwina. With me, if she wasn't badgering me about a Henderson's responsibility to the community, she was complaining about my shop."

I waited.

"She said I was encouraging a bad element—that was her term—to congregate in Henderson. She was afraid that lesbians would be attracted to my store and find it so appealing that they would buy up every piece of property in town."

"That'd be quite a commercial endorsement."

"That's what I told her. But you know Edwina had no sense of humor. And when she got an idea in her mind, there was no changing it. I tried reasoning with her, asking her what it was that she objected to about lesbians. It wasn't like she had married, or had patience with men in general—ask Bert Lucci, he'll tell you that. She certainly wasn't opposed to assertive women. There was no logic in her prejudice against us, but I guess that's what prejudice is. I tried for years to get her not so much to accept the fact that I am a lesbian, but to tolerate it. I never succeeded."

"It must have been difficult to tell her to begin with."

Leila leaned over and refilled her cup. "I don't know when I would have been able to face that, but I never had to." Seeing my puzzled look, she said, "I mean, I never had to decide on a time and place. Edwina has viewed me as a sexual miscreant since I was in high school. I had an affair then, with someone she found 'unsuitable for a Henderson woman.' It was the great scandal of the decade, entirely contained within the walls of Edwina's house. No one knew but the family. Edwina was terrified that word would get out and the first family of Henderson would be disgraced. After that, no matter what I did, it was all downhill. She'd written me off. She made my life so awful that summer that I used to finish what I had to do at home and then sneak off to Angelina's house. If it hadn't been for Angelina, I don't know how I would have survived."

"Why *sneak* off?"

"Well, Edwina can be unreasonable. Even then I knew that, and I didn't want to taint Angelina with my sin."

"Well, who was this scandalous lover? Anyone I know?"

Leila sipped her coffee. "I've never told anyone. It was enough that Edwina knew. Edwina controlled the family money—what there was of it. She made it real clear what she'd do to me, through my mother, if I let people know. She showed me by taking out her indignation on Bear, my lover. Edwina did what she could to make Bear's life hard. She did well. She had more influence than I would have thought possible. It was frightening to watch how she kept Bear from getting the right job or a promotion well-deserved. She kept her eye on Bear for five years after that. Every time an opportunity came up, she had just enough influence to put first choice out of reach. It was awful. I was terrified, and furious, and I couldn't do anything. If I'd said anything, it would have just made matters worse." She took a long drink of coffee. "You know, I'd almost put that out of my mind till now. It was a long time ago. But eventually Edwina let up and things got better for Bear—a good position, community respect. Now I wouldn't say anything about our affair for Bear's sake."

I nodded. I also noted how carefully Leila had

avoided mentioning the sex, or the real name of her
lover. I wondered if the affair had been as hushed up
as Leila thought. In a town the size of Henderson,
very little was truly private knowledge. Rosa would
know all about it. I also wondered if this affair could
have any connection to Edwina's death all these
years later. "So that's why you figured Edwina
wouldn't have left you her property?"

"That, and her fear that I would open a lesbian
bathhouse, a lesbian erotic theater, and a restaurant
where women do obscene things with food. Anyway,
what she always told me was that she would leave
her house and shop to the town as historical buildings. And whatever money she had would be an en-
dowment for them and her town museum. So I don't
suppose anyone will really inherit anything."

I put my empty cup on the table. "You must have
thought about why she was killed."

"I've spent nearly the whole night wondering
about just that." She finished her coffee. "I just don't
know. She could be an annoying woman—vindictive.
But lately she wasn't badgering anyone any more
than usual. And she wasn't enough of a nuisance to
murder, certainly not like that. If I'd been told Aunt
Edwina had been killed, I would have expected to
find her bludgeoned in front of someone's door, still
clutching her clipboard. But this . . ." She swallowed hard. "It was so awful to see her like that. If
you knew how appalled she would have been . . .
and the pain of the poison . . . I stopped the doctor
before he could tell me what it had been like for
her."

"Don't you have any idea who might possibly—"

The door opened. Three down-jacketed tourists—
clearly a mother and two daughters—walked in.
"Mind if we look around?" the mother asked.

"Enjoy," Leila replied without enthusiasm.

Eyeing a poster for a lesbian support group, the woman said, "We're not . . ."

"It's okay," Leila replied. "The store's for all women." Pointing to me, she added, "She's not, either."

The three moved quickly to the farthest shelf. I looked at Leila. "No idea?" I repeated.

She looked as if she was about to speak, then decided against it. "Not that way, no. I can't imagine anyone doing that."

"Is this poetry that my girls should be reading?" the woman called.

Leila pushed herself up. " 'Erotic' is on the shelf behind you. Garden-variety poetry is where you're looking now, though I can't promise you there won't be any mention of breasts or orgasms in it."

I stood up, exchanging glances with her. "What will you do now?"

"Survive. I've got to be here all day. There's a feature writer from the *Chronicle* coming at six. She's doing a piece on women's bookstores. It's the worst possible time for me to see her, but I can't afford to scoff at publicity like that. It could make the difference between going further into debt and actually climbing into the black. So, even if I have to take uppers all afternoon, I'll be here, ready to show her around the store, book by book."

"Why don't you get someone to cover for you now, so you can go home and take a nap? Maybe Angelina would . . ."

"Can't do. I've got a colleague from Ojai dropping in some time this afternoon—a woman I have to see —and a customer driving up from San Francisco to get a copy of *Bodies Nearly Touching* that she can't find down there. So I have to be here. Besides, Saturdays and Sundays are the days that pay the rent here. But after that, Vejay, I am going home and falling into bed, and I don't plan to open my eyes till nine-twenty tomorrow morning."

"I'll look in this afternoon and see how you're holding up." I was tempted to offer real help if she needed it, but I caught myself. I had already promised all my help to Chris.

CHAPTER

9

I made my way through the traffic on North Bank Road. The café door opened, and out of it walked a tall, curly-haired man with a beard. He wore jeans and an Aran sweater. Seeing me, he grinned. "You're the meter reader, aren't you?"

It was a moment before I recognized him as Edwina's guest from yesterday. I smiled. "Yes. I'm surprised you're still here."

"Did I give you the impression I was passing through?"

"Well, no. I just figured if you were staying, you'd come to the Slugfest."

The smile faded. "Oh, that. I'd planned to. When you were telling me about it, I fully intended to go. But then I . . . couldn't."

I pulled my wool cap down farther over my ears. This would have to be the day I had no hot water and hadn't washed my hair. It was like my mother had told me: "Never go out of the house without makeup. You never know who you'll meet." The idea of being seen in public with stringy hair was beneath consideration.

"Listen, I just had breakfast, or I'd ask you," he said. "It was gigantic, so I can't even ask you to lunch. But what about an early dinner? My name's Harry Bramwell, so you know who you didn't have breakfast with."

I almost said I didn't know where things would take me today, but caught myself. I could hardly refuse a man who accepted me in this condition, particularly one to whom I had given so much thought last night. "I'm Vejay Haskell. How about five o'clock?"

"Good. I'll be at your house then, if it's not too far back in the hills. I don't have a very good record finding places in this town. I even had trouble spotting the Tobacconist's right in the middle of town."

"Just stay on North Bank Road for three blocks. It's a yellow house, perched on the hillside. Fifty-two steps. You can't miss it. My name's on the mailbox."

"I'll see you then," he said, extending a hand. He gave my hand a squeeze, then turned and walked toward his Volvo.

I watched as he jumped down from the high curb and climbed into the car. As he pulled out and headed toward the ocean, I smiled, delighted at his unexpected reappearance. With Edwina's murder, I had almost forgotten him. Now I recalled the San Francisco State University sticker on his window. Was Harry Bramwell a professor, or was he just going back to school for a second degree, or a late first one? I recalled reading that the average age of students at San Francisco State was twenty-seven. Yesterday, in his jacket, he had had a professorial look, but today, the Aran sweater suggested a traveler. Perhaps a photographer, or a journalist, or . . . But I could find that out at dinner. Till then, my time was committed to Rosa and Edwina's murder.

I turned my gaze back across the street to the Women's Space Bookstore.

I had hoped when we talked that Leila would explain away my misgivings. But with Edwina dead, she stood to inherit money and commercial space. (I couldn't believe that someone as family oriented as Edwina would leave her ancestral fortune to a trust run by strangers, regardless of what she had told

Leila.) So, with Edwina's murder, Leila could both inherit and get revenge for her father, her childhood, and her lover. What more could anyone ask for motive? For discoveries that would help my friends, I was batting substantially less than zero.

It was with relief that I noticed Curry Cunningham coming out of Gresham's Hardware. *He* wasn't a friend. I knew him mostly from reading the meter at Crestwood Logging. Unlike Angelina Rudd, who had set up the fish ranch so that getting past the gate was a major operation, Curry Cunningham made a point of meeting everyone who came to the site. He knew what day his meter would be read (anyone could call the office to find out, but few did), and he made sure that there were no logs stacked in front of it, or trucks parked in my way. His house site was on my H-1 route. Once he had stopped me and offered a tour of the unbroken ground. He was so eager that I hated to refuse, and half an hour later, I had seen blueprints that were unintelligible to me and had watched him pace out what would be a huge living room, a dining room, a country kitchen, and a studio for his wife. He had pointed up proudly to the air, where the second floor would be. I had seen the architect's sketches, heard about the copper piping and the redwood shingles. And I suspected, as he pulled me here and there, that this tour, given for the joy of describing his dream, could as easily have been given to the postman or the garbage man.

Curry stood on the sidewalk in front of Gresham's display of wading boots. His thick eyebrows were raised in question, his prominent jaw jutted even farther forward than usual as he tapped his teeth together. He looked like a leprechaun who had misplaced his pot of gold.

"Hey, there," he called as I stepped toward him, "when are you going to put the lights back on at my house?" By that, he meant the house he was renting in the ever-expanding interval till his own house was built. As far as I knew, there had been no progress on that since my tour of the grounds.

"When you pay your bill," I replied. I had been dying to say that to someone since the last outage, but it was hardly the kind of witticism that would have gone over on my route. It didn't seem to be a big hit with Curry Cunningham either. I added, "The lights are off at my house, too. I'm just glad the problem is so localized. It's really bad when the power fails here too, on North Bank Road. Then you can't even get a cup of coffee."

"I don't know if *I* dare stop here for coffee today." He glanced around conspiratorially. "I'm surprised you haven't been attacked by everyone in town who wants a firsthand report, but then, you weren't a judge."

"Oh, you mean about the Slugfest."

He nodded. "I just came down here to see if Gresham's had dimmer switches. I figured as long as the power was off I might as well make use of the time—"

"Don't do that. It could go on any time."

He laughed, a little leprechaun laugh. "I'm not that careless." Grabbing my arm, he made a show of pulling me into the café.

I stared at him in mock affront.

"That was Alphonse DiLeo from the Knights of Columbus bearing down on me out there. If he'd bagged me he'd have made the fifth this morning. I'm just going to have to keep off the streets." He sat down at a small table, nodding at the opposite chair for me.

"Let me be the fifth, then. How do you think Edwina was murdered?"

"Everybody in town knows she was poisoned.

They all know that only those of us up by the stage had access to the food. I'll tell you . . ." He grappled for my name.

"Vejay."

"Vejay, it creates an awkward situation when you deal with the public."

"How so?" I asked, anxious to get his particular slant.

Curry Cunningham was eager to explain. "These are the people I ultimately have to justify my operation to. You were in public relations, you know how important that is."

"Uh-huh." I was amazed that he, who hadn't a clue to my name, had recalled that one obscure fact from my past. I must have mentioned it while pacing his still-imagined dining room or kitchen.

Marty approached with the menus. As he looked down at me, he broke into a grin. "Our eggs with sauerkraut and chorizo are especially fine this morning, ma'am."

"We'll just have coffee," Curry said. "That okay with you, Vejay?"

Another cup of coffee was not what I needed, but I couldn't be bothered disagreeing. I nodded, thinking how Curry Cunningham balanced on the edge of annoying presumption, just pulling himself back in time. When Marty had retreated, I said, "So you figure Crestwood Logging is going to have an image problem because of you?"

"Well, I wouldn't say that." He looked offended. "But the thing is, I've devoted a lot of myself to Crestwood Logging. And I love this area. I came here on vacation and decided then that I wanted to live here. I even had *The Paper* sent to me at home. I love the river and the state park and the ocean. And I remembered the forests. I've seen poorly managed logging, Vejay; I know what it can do to forests like

these. I decided then that they needed to be handled
by someone who cared about them—by me." He
took a swallow of coffee, grimaced, then added
cream. "One of the reasons I opted to work for
Crestwood was because, with them, I could get back
here. And I'll tell you—I hope I don't sound like I'm
bragging—but I run their most ecologically sound
logging operation, and not without the promise of
profit. Why, right now, even with the small stand of
trees I can harvest, I've got three dozen carriers and a
flotilla of tugboats ready to carry the logs to a Japanese vessel waiting at sea. Japan is a big market for
lumber. My wife is Japanese, you know."

I nodded.

"Well, Japan's a big market, but the import duties
are a killer. So, for most companies the profits are
marginal. What you need to do with the Japanese is
make the right gesture. They're the people who cut
off all but one chrysanthemum, so that the perfect
flower can be appreciated. One beautiful thing is
worth a hundred—no, a thousand—ordinary ones.
Most Westerners don't understand that. Certainly
Western businessmen don't. It's a way of thinking
they can never really grasp. But with the right gesture, and with my connections in Japan, even this
small cut will turn a good profit."

I had seen the site of his operation. I said, "Aren't
thirty-six carriers rather a lot for so small a tree harvest?"

He smiled. "It sounds like it. But you see, Vejay,
the Japanese ship is on a tight schedule. It can only
stay here one day, so that means that I can't count on
more than a few runs per truck, a few trips for each
of the tugboats. Speed is the key. And in a way, the
river area benefits. Most logging operations are an
eyesore and a nuisance. They wreck the hillside. The
trucks plod along the roads, blocking traffic for days.

But with this, it will all be over in one day. And you know my site is far enough off the main road that you have to be going there to see it."

"I've heard you run a careful operation," I said. He had already told me twice himself. Curry Cunningham, despite his protests, was not one to hide his light under a bushel. "I'm sure you have to file Environmental Impact Reports—"

"Reports!" He sighed. "Actually, for us, they're called Timber Harvesting Reports. But we do tests, surveys, file page after page of report. You wouldn't believe the paperwork. I've had to hire an extra woman just to keep up with it. But I'm not complaining. I'm all for protecting the countryside. Where can you drive along a river and see anything as magnificent as the Nine Warriors?"

I nodded. The Nine Warriors—Edwina Henderson's beloved redwoods that she had convinced the county to protect—were said to be over a thousand years old. They were eleven feet in diameter and reached nearly two hundred and fifty feet into the sky. Some older or larger redwoods could be found in Armstrong Woods State Park, or farther north in Humboldt County, but as a group, the Nine Warriors were in a class by themselves. These trees were so alike, it was said, that one day in the tenth century all nine cones had dropped to the ground; from these, the Nine Warriors had grown. Now they stood between River Road (and North Bank Road in Henderson) and the river itself. Some were within a few yards of each other, others miles apart. They were so cherished that River Road had been built to curve around them.

"This is where I live, where my son will grow up," Curry continued. "I plan to be around for a long time. That's why I joined the historical society, and the Knights of Columbus, and the city council. You

know, you don't get paid for that. And it's a lot of
work, particularly for someone who's not interested
in politics."

"They say the main qualification for a council
member is a willingness to serve."

He laughed. "Just about. You wouldn't believe the
petty stuff that comes before the council. I doubt I've
ever gotten home from one of those meetings before
midnight. Still, I'm not complaining. I'm just saying
that I don't want my image blackened because I was
in the wrong place." He lifted his cup and took a
drink, this time looking satisfied with the mixture.
"You want a doughnut or something?"

"No, thanks."

"You don't mind if I do?" When I shook my head,
he caught Marty as he passed by and ordered a bear
claw.

The café was half empty. Outside, the morning fog
was still thick. People whose lights had stayed on
would be home in front of their fires, drinking their
own coffee and grumbling. Those who had no power
might still be asleep, or have driven to Santa Rosa,
where they could be sure of finding light and heat.
Or perhaps the power had come back on by now.

From Curry's assessment of his own operation,
worthy of any press release, I grabbed onto the one
point that could be of use to me. "You were in the
river area when you were younger?"

He smiled. "I was in high school."

"Did you know Leila Katz?"

Marty arrived with the bear claw. Giving it his full
attention, Curry bit in hungrily. When he had swallowed, he said, "I met a lot of kids that summer. I
dated a beautiful girl named Estella. I thought she
was the most exotic thing I'd ever seen. After her,
everyone else faded into a blur. I may have met
Leila." He shrugged.

"What happened that summer, beside your great romance? Were there any big events, or maybe scandals? This area is full of those, and they're so fascinating when you're a kid." I took a swallow of my coffee, glad Leila Katz couldn't hear me.

"I don't remember anything but Estella and our picnics and the canoe trips, and the walks in the state park, and all that 'great romance' stuff. The earthquake could have come and I wouldn't have noticed. Besides, I was really an outsider. The kids here had gone to school together from first grade. They were friendly to me, and we all did things together, but I knew I wasn't really one of them. If there was any scandal, they wouldn't have told me about it. Only Estella would have told me." He took another big bite of his bear claw. "In any case, there was no scandal like this one now."

I hesitated. Did that hedging afterthought mean that he *had* heard of a scandal, Leila's scandal, that summer? But even if he had, he obviously wasn't going to admit it. Changing the subject, I said, "You're a member of the historical society. You must have known Edwina Henderson through that."

"Essentially Edwina *was* the historical society. It was amazing the zeal that woman had for preserving every fact, every event that happened in this town. If she found a letter, or a dress, or a door latch from before nineteen hundred, it went up on the wall of her museum. Have you been in there?"

"Not recently."

"You can't see the walls any more. There's barely room for the data cards. Edwina really needed to expand. She knew that herself."

"That would be into Fischer's Ice Cream Store?"

"Oh, she wasn't thinking of pushing them out. They'd been there almost as long as the Tobacconist's."

If she hadn't expanded in that direction, the only other way was into the Women's Space Bookstore. "Do you think," I asked, fingering my coffee cup, "that Edwina could have discovered something in her historical research that threatened someone enough to make her kill them?"

Curry laughed. I must have looked shocked, for he said, "I'm sorry. I don't mean to belittle your suggestion, it's just that Edwina had been over every fact about every family in town so often that her big discoveries now were that the Langstons put in inside plumbing in nineteen-eleven, or there was a fire in the old railway depot. I don't mean to sound like Edwina was an ineffective woman. When it came to protecting the town, to getting a court order to prevent Zitter Chemical dumping waste into the river, or an injunction for who knows what, she was unstoppable. It was just with the museum that her obsession overcame her common sense." He finished his bear claw and downed the last of his coffee. Glancing outside, he said, "I think this is a good time to make my escape."

He motioned Marty over and handed him a five-dollar bill. "Either I have to drive to Guerneville and see about my dimmer switch, or go home and hope the lights have come on so I can forget about the whole project."

Marty returned with the change. Then, moving behind Curry, he looked at me and winked. I would hear about this tête-à-tête later.

Once outside, Curry made a dash for his Jeep. I stood on the sidewalk, staring up at the still-foggy sky. This might be one of those days when it never cleared.

If Curry had known who Leila Katz's adolescent lover had been, then my half hour wouldn't have been wasted. As it was, I was already wired from all the coffee, and at nearly eleven in the morning, I had learned virtually nothing.

Still, I thought, as I climbed into my truck, I did know that Leila Katz had had a lover, someone whom Edwina objected to, and someone Leila felt she had to protect. A man who finally had a good job. Curry Cunningham? He was about her age. He had been here at the right time. But there was nothing to make him objectionable to Edwina. No, the man Leila was talking about had been unsuitable, unworthy even when in high school. What was it about him that Edwina objected to? Was he from a notorious family, or was he a delinquent, or was he merely not Catholic? Or . . ."Of course," I said aloud, "was he a she?" Was it a woman to whom Leila had turned for comfort that summer of the scandal? Had Leila 'sneaked' to Angelina's house not just to protect her from guilt by association with her? Had she sneaked there because Angelina was the object of Edwina's wrath—and Leila's affection? I recalled Angelina's remark to Curry Cunningham at the Slugfest: "I wouldn't do anything to help that old witch out of a bind."

I started the engine and headed for the fish ranch.

CHAPTER
10

The Russian River Fish Ranch occupied a manmade island at the mouth of the river. A jetty protected a dock that ran well out into the deep water. The island had been constructed high enough to ride out floods, by a man who had planned to build a hotel overlooking the dock where the fishing fleet would unload. Building the jetty and the dock was as far as he had gotten. The main structure that housed the growing fish was a windowless pre-fab affair. It could as easily have been a giant chartreuse storage shed. About forty by a hundred, it stood with its shorter side so close to the Pacific that its doors opened onto the dock, and waves splashed against the sides of the building in stormy weather. Its only natural light came from the twenty skylights that virtually filled its roof space.

Looking down from the Jenner hill, the Russian River Fish Ranch building sat like a blotchy green stomach in an anatomical drawing. From it fanned out the "intestines" in narrow cement ditches looping back and forth around its sides, ending in one long arc that circled back to the start. Now the ditches were just three-foot-deep ruts, but I understood they were to be given a bedding of pebbles and then the water from the river would channel through them. And when the fish fry were older, they would be moved from the incubators inside the building out into this tightly winding channel to swim through its endless loops for months until they were large enough to be released into the ocean. The whole island couldn't have been more than two acres. But I recalled reading that if human intestines were stretched out, they would go on for something like a mile. So, although the ranch looked like a small operation, there was plenty of distance for an ambitious young fish to cover.

At the far side of the property was an aluminum tool shed and an emergency generator. I had been surprised that the generator was there, rather than next to the main building. But the oddest things in the complex were the rosebushes that surrounded the main building. Anywhere else, those standing red roses would have been attractive, but here, between the green aluminum building and the cement ditches, they looked like another variety of clutter.

A hurricane fence surrounded the complex on three sides. The ocean provided the remaining boundary. Outside the fence was the gatehouse and a two-lane drive that led to a small bridge and then to the main road.

I drove down from Jenner and across the bridge. As always, the gate was closed. I pulled up by the gatehouse, rolled down my window, and took a deep breath of the salt air.

I recognized the guard, Maxie Dawkins. He was a squat man, with thin carrot-colored hair faded by gray. His skin was rough but sallow, and his amber eyes hung back deep in their sockets. Each month he escorted me to the meter. But I wasn't surprised he showed no recollection of me. To many people, meter readers were simply bodies that filled out the tan PG&E uniforms. He leaned on the windowsill and said, "Can I help you?" It was one of those "Can I help you?"s that could have been translated as "What are you doing here?" When I had been here to read the meter, Maxie was always friendly, eager to talk, if not to listen. Now his stiff, guardlike stance took me by surprise.

I decided not to explain who I was. I said, "I'm looking for Angelina Rudd."

"Off."

"She's not here?"

"Nope."

"When will she be back?"

"Maybe Monday."

"Monday! It's only Saturday morning."

"Might be"—he wheezed—"tomorrow night." Getting his breath, he paused, then favored me with a nodding half-smile. "She's got the weekend coming. Hell, she's got a year of weekends coming, but she won't take them. I didn't believe she'd really go. A couple of times she said she was taking a day off, but she's never done it. Never could bring herself to." He wheezed again, as if the long pronouncement was too much for his lungs.

"Allergies?" I asked, glancing at the rose bushes.

"Who knows?" he said in disgust. "Allergies, asthma, bronchial distress, call it whatever you like. That's what the doctors do. But the end's the same: I can't breathe worth a damn. I gotta use these nose drops—cost a fortune, twenty bucks for a tiny little squeeze bottle no bigger than a pair of dice. I gotta take them every four hours. I keep one bottle at home and one out in the shed so I think to take them when I make my rounds. Every hour I make my rounds, I turn the box around so the next side comes forward. Then, when the front panel, the one that says Estrin, is in front, I know to put a drop in, see?" he explained proudly.

"Clever system."

"You gotta have a way to remember. I couldn't do that out in the water. Couldn't breathe enough even with those damned drops to fish." He looked out at the Pacific beyond the dock. "That's why I'm here babysitting the salmon fry instead of out there fighting fair."

"This isn't fair?"

"It's like shooting deer in a game preserve. We hatch the cohos here. We'll raise them for a year, imprint them with the smell of the fish ranch, then turn them out to sea to grow. And when they reach the end of their cycle, they'll swim back, right up our chutes and into our pools. They might as well swim into the grocery trucks. Ain't no sport in that."

"But a lot of profit?"

"More than fishing with the fleet. But I'll tell you, that profit, when and if it comes, won't be trickling down to me. I'm a straight salary man. And for what she pays me, it hasn't always been easy working here. I took a lot of heat from the guys when I signed on here."

I knew from experience how easy it was to keep Maxie Dawkins talking. I might be the only human being he saw all day. "The guys from the fleet?"

"And how. When Angelina started this place, she made a big deal telling everyone how she was going to change the way the whole fishing industry worked. No more men against the sea, she said. She was going to turn fishing into a safe, reliable business. She said it would be like a Chevrolet plant, and you could count on one crop of salmon coming off the assembly line every fall." He wheezed, caught his breath, and went on. "Even Angelina knows there have been fish ranches north of here that haven't turned a profit, but she figures that was because the management wasn't paying attention when they should have been, not that the system is wrong. And she plans to make this place work. She's here every day, in the winter before light. And even when she's off, I see her and her husband drive down at night

just to check things out. I got a buzzer in here so I
can buzz her house directly. If there's a problem,
don't matter how small, or how big, she's the one
who's going to handle it. If something happens and I
don't buzz her, there's hell to pay." He wheezed
again. "But like I was saying, the guys gave me a
hard time at first. They wanted to know if Angelina
was going to build an assembly line out into the Pacific. They kept asking me if my car was a Salmon
Impala. They gave Angelina a bad time too. The guys
all know her because of her father. But she gave it
right back. She didn't back down. She really put her
money where her mouth is. I'll tell you, she'd lose
plenty more than a job if this place went under."

"So this is really her baby, huh? She's in charge?"

"As much as anyone is when the place is run by
Crestwood Industries." He grinned, exposing a space
where a lateral incisor once had been. "Drayton's the
big boss, out of Baltimore. He came through here a
few months ago. You should have seen Angelina
scuddle. You would have thought her mother-in-law
was coming to stay for a week. I'll tell you, this place
got scrubbed inside and out. She sent me out to buy
this uniform." He fingered the dull brown wool
jacket. "She even told me what to say, and more
important, what not to let on."

I waited. But when he didn't explain, I recalled
what Chris Fortimiglio had been telling me about
James Drayton last night—no liquor, sex, or dancing. "Pretty conservative, isn't he?"

Maxie snorted. "Conservative is a polite word.
With him you better not admit nothing. He never has
a beer, never smokes. Don't even say 'damn' when
he's up against it, and don't let his workers neither.
Angelina warned me not to let on that my daughter
lives with a guy. She said Drayton'd fire me in a minute if he knew that."

"That was good thinking on Angelina's part," I said.

Maxie nodded. "She's a smart girl. I've known her since she was a kid. That's how come I have this job. I used to fish with her father. She knew that no one knows salmon better than Maxie Dawkins." He tapped his brown-coated chest. "I may not get around like I used to, but at least I'm not a hoodlum like the guy who works here nights. Angelina's lucky he hasn't been hauled in for brawling. Beat a guy senseless a couple years ago. They didn't think the guy'd live."

"Was he another friend of her father?"

Maxie nodded uncomfortably. "One of Mario's crew. They were a tight bunch, those three. Even now Dutch—the night guy—is still friends with the other crewman. You know Bert Lucci?"

I nodded.

"Nice guy, Bert Lucci. He even let Dutch use him as a reference on his application form here. Needed two references. Angelina couldn't get around that. And I'll tell you, there aren't many guys in this area who'd put their names on the line for Dutch. He was lucky to get two. And grateful. Nothing he wouldn't do for them, so he says."

"Who was the other one?"

"The priest." Maxie shrugged. "But how could he say no, huh? Dutch is Catholic." Then, changing the subject, he said, "You're a friend of Angelina's, huh?" Not pausing for an answer, he said, "That's good. She don't have time for friends much. All the time I've been here I've only seen one girlfriend of hers come here. She said Angelina used to babysit her when she was a kid. Angelina wasn't pleased to see her this time. No, sir. All pushed out of shape, and huffy. That's no way to treat a friend. I was going to tell her . . ." He let the rest of that thought hang while he took a deep breath. "Angelina's here every waking hour, though God knows why. As long as the water keeps running through the tanks and we're on schedule with feeding, there's not much to do. I'll tell you, but don't you tell her." He winked. "I thought when I took a job from her, from little Angelina, that I would have myself an easy berth. I always thought of her as Mario's kid. Didn't realize she was a woman now, and a slavedriver at that."

"Really works you hard, huh?" I asked with a straight face. Sitting in the guard booth eight hours a day was not too taxing.

"She don't work me no harder than herself. I'll tell you, I don't know how she found time to get married, much less to get herself pregnant. But then, that don't always take long." He laughed.

I would have liked to know about her family, but I couldn't reveal my ignorance by asking. I said, "I thought she'd be here. I drove out from Henderson. Do you think she's at home? I could stop by there."

"Fort Ross," he said. "Whole family went up, camping. She wanted Gordon to see the old Russian fort."

I waited, hoping he would indicate whether Gordon was her husband or son. But he didn't. "How is Gordon?"

"Brightest little smolt you'd ever want to see." He smiled.

Were smolts one-year-old salmon or two-year-old salmon? They couldn't be much more than that. Salmon didn't live very long. "His first trip up to Fort Ross?"

"Knowing Angelina, he's lucky to be going now. I never thought she'd take the day off. But, like I say, she surprised me when she married. She kind of surprised everyone—don't know why she bothered—if you know what I mean."

"After that affair." I nodded. When Maxie didn't pick up on that, I said, "The one she had in high school, or was it right after?" Leila had been in high school. Angelina was older than she. Angelina could have been home from college the summer of the affair.

Maxie looked like he was trying to recall it.

"I guess maybe I shouldn't have mentioned it after all these years," I said. "I just assumed you'd know. It's not really a secret anymore. The scandal died down years ago."

When he still didn't say anything, I made my final stab. "I mean, it's not such a big thing to be involved with another woman nowadays."

Now he did respond. His sallow skin turned bright red. He flung open the gatehouse door, banging it into the side of my truck. He grabbed hold of the window, and thrust his head inside. "I don't want to hear that kind of trash about Angelina. No wonder she's huffy, if you're the kind of friend she has. You're no friend of hers, carrying on with lies like that. Filth. Lies and filth. Now you just get yourself out of here before I do what I feel like doing. You hear me? Only 'cause I'm on duty, I'm holding myself back. But if you show up here again, I won't. And don't try coming round here when I'm not on duty, neither. I'm going to give Dutch the word. He's just been waiting for the chance to smash ass. Now you get out."

I considered arguing, but a look at his crimson face and his fleshy fists pressed against the side of my window decided me otherwise. I wanted to get out of his sight before he realized he'd seen me before, or before my face seared a mark on his memory so that he recalled the incident the next time I came to read the meter. He pulled his head back out of the window. I made a U-turn and headed back for the road.

I wished I could be sure the friend whose visit had pushed Angelina out of shape was Leila Katz. A girl she babysat certainly suggested Leila. Now that Angelina was married, did she want nothing to do with Leila, nothing to bring up the past?

CHAPTER

11

I drove back, passing the light green hillocks that rose from the river. Small flocks of sheep and cattle grazed, and the occasional bull, whose main interest in life was likely to be threatening meter readers. Driving by St. Agnes's Roman Catholic Church, I glanced at Father Calloway's vegetable beds. Unlike the flourishing rose bushes at the Russian River Fish Ranch, these beds were bare. Whatever Father Calloway had planted either had died a lingering death at the hands of the elements or a sudden one at the mouths of deer or raccoons. No plant in that garden made it to maturity; Father Calloway admitted that. His gardening taught him nonattachment, he said.

Father Calloway would know about Angelina's past. He had surprised me more than once by the extent of his awareness of the seamier side of Russian River life. But, alas, he was another person I couldn't ask about Angelina. Not straight out. No, on a matter like this my chances were better with Rosa. Rosa would hate to think Angelina had seduced the girl she had once babysat. She wouldn't want to believe that her daughter Katie's high-school friend could be a poisoner. Rosa would be uncomfortable with it all, but she'd tell me.

I drove on, pausing briefly to glance at the first two of the Nine Warriors. The giant redwoods stood a hundred yards apart. Once, when I had stood between them and looked up, they had appeared to be identical. "The Lord's candles," Father Calloway had called them.

The fourth of the Warriors was opposite the For- timiglios' drive. I pulled into the driveway, parked next to the kitchen steps, and got out.

But Rosa was not home. Rosa, Donny informed me, had gone to Steelhead Lodge.

But when I got to Steelhead Lodge, she wasn't there either. I was beginning to wonder if anyone was where they were supposed to be today.

"You just missed her," Bert Lucci told me. "I kind of hoped she'd come out to help me. I had the sher- iff's men here all morning, and they didn't make things any better. Now I've got to do something with this place." Bert leaned back against the veranda rail- ing. He was dressed in his usual work clothes, but today they seemed too big, as if he had withered within them.

"It must have been a hard night for you," I said.

"Worst I can remember. You know Edwina and I had our outs. But I would never have wanted her to die like that."

"Did the sheriff tell you what kind of poison it was?"

"The sheriff didn't *tell* me anything. He and his men just barged around like I wasn't even here. They looked over this; they eyeballed that. After all the dusting and picture taking they did last night, there was nothing in the whole place they didn't get some kind of picture of."

"Well, what were they looking at today, then?"

"They took everything in the kitchen for starts. I don't know how they expect me to eat. The spices, I could see that. But the chopping board and the spatulas, and my own dishes that Edwina wouldn't allow on the table! What are they going to do with those?" He pushed himself up and began to pace.

"Then they went over the table on the stage like they were looking through a microscope. And they were just about to start on the podium when I told them that no one used it." He swallowed. "Edwina didn't live long enough to make her great pronouncement."

Edwina's announcement! I forgot all about that. And that was the whole point of her bringing the Slugfest here. "Bert, what was she going to say?"

"Damned if I know." He continued to pace in a halfhearted way. It was obvious that the subject of Edwina's announcement didn't interest him at all. Her death and the lodge's mess seemed about all he could deal with.

"Surely they must have looked at the podium." I couldn't imagine Sheriff Wescott letting something like that pass unchecked.

"They looked, but they didn't find anything. Sheriff seemed mad. I guess he doesn't have any leads."

"Did the sheriff tell you what Edwina was going to say?"

Bert stopped. "How'd he know?"

"Well, if Edwina was going to make an announcement important enough for her to go to the trouble of getting television cameras here, she must have wanted to be sure of what she would be saying. She wouldn't just speak off the top of her head."

"She did that plenty," Bert said, from habit. Then he looked away. "No, you're right. I've seen her give speeches for her historical society. She always had notes."

"Then those notes must have been in her pocketbook."

"Nope." Bert headed toward the door.

"They weren't? How do you know?"

"Because I saw her put something in the podium drawer and lock it. That was in the afternoon, before you came to check the meter. I wasn't about to ask her what. And then, what with all her orders, and you coming, and then Hooper coming to help me set up, I just forgot about it."

"But how come the sheriff didn't find the drawer?" We were at the old podium now. It was a standard oak piece, with the slanted paper stand, a three-inch panel beneath it, and then a space that went down to the floor. I looked at the panel, but other than the seam where it attached to the slanted stand, there was no break in the wood. And there was certainly no visible lock. "Are you sure there's a drawer here, Bert?"

"Oh, yes. Edwina's had this podium for years. It was her father's. She carts it around if she can, or if she can find someone like me to cart it for her." He bent down, poking his head under the panel. "Look. See, here's the lock."

"I suppose the key was in Edwina's purse," I said with a sigh.

"She wouldn't be about to leave that around. Not after she locked it up."

Eyeing the lock, I said, "Bert? You can get it open, can't you?"

He hesitated.

"We could call the sheriff and have him come and open it."

Still he didn't move.

I knew I should insist on calling the sheriff. But having to deal with him about Edwina's murder was not something I wanted to do right now. And if the podium drawer held nothing more than notes on Edwina's discovery of another nineteenth-century photo or a previously unknown grave marker, I didn't want to face Wescott's derision. I said to Bert, "Do you want the sheriff's whole entourage back out here?"

Without pause to think, he pulled a screwdriver

from his pocket, stuck it into the crack, and hit the end with his hammer. It took only three blows to break the lock.

Bert pulled open the drawer and stared in. It was nearly a minute before he moved far enough back that I could see over his shoulder. I had expected to find notes or even a handwritten draft of a speech, but what the drawer held was several sheets of parchment. The first was headed "Treaty between the State of California and the Pomo Nation." It was dated 1851.

Lifting it carefully, I put it on the paper stand, and Bert and I read it together.

"Son of a gun!" Bert said. "Old Edwina really had a find here."

"You mean she discovered this treaty?"

"You see here"—he pointed to a sentence in the middle of the page—"where it mentions a Pomo rancheria on the river?"

"What's a rancheria?"

"A little reservation. Sometimes real little."

"So the treaty sets up a little Pomo reservation on the Russian River. I don't remember any reservation."

"That's because there isn't one," Bert said triumphantly. "That means that Edwina must have discovered this. No wonder she fussed around for days about how the lodge looked. No wonder she got that television cameraman out here, thinking he was going to report on the Slugfest. This treaty will put her on the map of historians."

"But Bert, why didn't she just call a news conference? I mean, the treaty is way more important than the Slugfest. She could have gotten coverage from San Francisco, maybe Los Angeles, for that."

"Yeah," he snorted. "She should have got that kind of news. But she wouldn't have. Edwina didn't

have a good record with these people. I'll have to
admit it wasn't all their fault. See, she'd been calling
news conferences for years. Every time she unearthed
the foundation of a pioneer house or the remnants of
one of the old railway cars abandoned in the under-
brush along where the tracks used to run, she'd call
the papers and the TV people. Got so that if she'd
found the hundred-year-old remains of General Kuskoff from the Russian settlement up at Fort Ross, she
couldn't have gotten a photographer." He leaned an
elbow on Edwina's podium, carefully avoiding the
treaty. "They thought she was a joke, a crank—the
newspeople and the historians. Makes me damned
mad. Even when she found legitimate historical stuff,
no one paid any mind. And the real kicker is that
Edwina was sure there were rancherias up here. Every year she'd give one lecture on the Indians of the
river area, the Pomos, and she always said that there
had to be more than just the big reservation up at
Stewart's Point."

"Why did she think that?"

"You know, she gave pretty much the same talk
every year. I've probably heard it fifteen times. If you
want an answer to that question, you're asking the
right person. Edwina said that the Pomos didn't live
like one big tribe. They were more like separate village groups, real loosely joined together. She said it
made sense that one of the settlers who aimed to
open a mine or log the area would have been em-
powered by the government to deal with the Indians.
That would have saved the government the trouble.
And Edwina was sure that one of these guys probably bought off the Indians—got some local chief to
sign some treaty. Probably the local chief had no idea
what he was signing—how could he, it's in English.
And"—he raised a finger—"Edwina figured that before there was any question of rounding up the

Pomos and putting the whole village on a little scrap of land like this, the Pomos cleared out anyway. After eighteen-seventy the Pomos were all but gone."

I nodded. "It's a good theory. But if Edwina was so sure, why didn't she go to wherever it is they keep treaties and check it out?"

Bert snorted again. "There's another slap for you. Edwina got cards to the university libraries. She went right in there and did her research. But treaties like this, you know where they were kept?"

"No."

"In the secret files of the United States Senate in Washington, D.C.!"

My look of amazement must have been sufficient, for Bert nodded three times and said, "Edwina told us. It seems that when the main batch of Indian treaties were signed in the eighteen-fifties, they got sent to Sacramento to be ratified. But by that time there was plenty of opposition, and the guys there didn't want to deal with them so they passed them on to Washington. But the senators in Washington didn't want to be bothered either, so they plunked the whole batch into their secret files. Not a one of them came to light until after the turn of the century."

"If they weren't ratified, were they valid?"

That stopped Bert. "Don't know. Since none of them were local, Edwina didn't go into that."

"Do you think this was one of them?"

"Could be. But maybe because the rancheria is so small, it got taken care of in Sacramento. Maybe there wasn't so much opposition to this little one." He picked up the last page of the treaty and put it on top. It was a map showing the river and the rancheria. "See, it's just big enough to put a couple houses on. You'd hardly recognize the river from this."

The gently curving line didn't begin to resemble the tight, sharp angles of the river, and the only

names on the map that corresponded to those of today were Fort Ross, where the Russians under General Kuskoff had established the southernmost settlement of their North American explorations, and the
Russian River itself. The rancheria was a rectangle
spanning the river. On that rectangle were drawn
two trees, close together.

"Do you have any idea where this is?" I asked.

"Oh, yeah. Those trees, they're the last two of the
Nine Warriors. See." He pointed to markings along
the river on the map. "Here are the other seven Warriors. They were giants a hundred years ago. Good
landmarks. But you can tell this spot where the rancheria is—it's the only place where there are two
Warriors that close together with a curve in the river
like this. You know where the W curve is, don't
you?"

"Sure. But are you certain there was never a rancheria there?"

He stepped back from the podium. "Vejay, I grew
up here in Henderson. I had to take California history in school. If there had been an Indian reservation right near here, don't you think they would have
told us about it in school?"

"Maybe—"

He put a hand on my arm. "You're going to say
maybe it lasted only a little while, or my teachers
weren't very well educated. Could be. But listen, I've
known Edwina Henderson since I was in school.
She's been crazy about Henderson history and anything in this area that affected Henderson since she
was a kid. You can believe that if there was anything
written about a rancheria, anywhere, Edwina would
have found it. She would have taken the news down
to her Indian support group and they would have
had a big powwow together."

"If she'd announced it here last night," he went

on, "by today there would have been reporters on the phone to her. But she wouldn't even be here to answer. She'd be on her way to Sacramento; she'd be showing the treaty to all those historical bigshots who couldn't be bothered with her before. It's not every day someone discovers an Indian treaty. I remember Edwina telling us at one historical society meeting a year ago, when she gave her Pomo talk, what she'd do when she discovered her rancheria. She got kind of carried away. You could tell she'd spent a lot of time day dreaming about her big find. She said there'd be a lot of publicity, but she wouldn't be able to stay here to see it. She said if she found something like this treaty here, she'd have to get it up to Sacramento pronto, to the experts there. She said as soon as people knew about it, there would be people out to destroy it." Inadvertently, he glanced toward the kitchen. "She was close on that, wasn't she. Just a little off. Didn't destroy *it*, it destroyed her." He swallowed. Recovering his composure, he went on quickly. "From what Edwina told us, you can bet that if she'd announced that treaty here last night, she wouldn't have been in town today. She'd have been up in Sacramento, keeping guard while those big experts went over it. She told us she'd never trust a treaty out of her sight. Said she'd stay up there as long as it took. She said, 'Bert, if I can ever prove there was a rancheria around here, you better be prepared to come in and take over the Tobacconist's for as long as I'm gone.' I remember we all laughed then and said that all her Asian refugees, Indians, and even the Nine Warriors would have to get along without her. But that comment of hers, it was even quoted in *The Paper* when they wrote up the meeting. Edwina wasn't any too pleased about that. Like I said, she'd gotten carried away. She didn't need the whole world to know it."

Suddenly Bert swallowed hard and looked away from me. "Biggest find of her life and she has to die before she can announce it. I'll tell you, Vejay, if there's a heaven, Edwina's looking down from it now, and she's furious." He swallowed again. "And if there's such a thing as the dead having power, I wouldn't be the person who robbed Edwina of her chance. Edwina wasn't one to forget. When she held a grudge, she clutched it hard and long, and she made her victim pay plenty."

I thought of Edwina's ongoing pique over Donny Fortimiglio's experience with her tobacco, and of her not speaking to Leila for months. I wondered what she had done to the "unworthy" person who Leila had had the affair with. "How did she make them pay?"

Bert looked at me quizzically. "In the past? That's gone now. Edwina's gone." He glared down at the treaty. "All because of this. Just not fair."

I could see I wasn't about to get any more lucid comments from Bert. Either he was just what he seemed—too disheartened to be bothered with the past—or he was putting on a good show, to cover his unwillingness to answer. If Angelina had been Leila's lover, and Bert had been her father's close friend, he wouldn't be about to tell me how great Edwina's retribution had been. He wouldn't give me Angelina's motive for the killing.

With a sigh, I said, "I guess I'd better call the sheriff."

"I might have known!" Sheriff Wescott had made excellent time getting to Steelhead Lodge. As he strode toward me, with his photographer and print man, he glared. "I don't know why I bother to tell you anything."

"Look," I said, "we are giving you a document you never would have found on your own. The natural response to that should be 'Thank you.'"

"You were tampering with evidence—fooling around with that podium."

"It wasn't evidence until we discovered the treaty. Till then it was just another piece of furniture to be carted back where it belonged."

"If you hadn't been poking around here, in a murder case I just warned you to keep clear of, you wouldn't have been anywhere near this podium, right?" He was standing in front of it. "And you wouldn't have been wrenching the drawer open!"

"And *you* wouldn't have the treaty now."

With a silent shake of the head, he turned his gaze to the podium. This was as close as I would get to an admission that I was right. It was probably the only time I'd get the last word. But a victory over the sheriff has its drawbacks. I decided a low profile would serve me best now. So I stood back and watched the print man work. I listened as Bert recounted an edited version of how we came to find the treaty. Either Bert was still subdued from the reality of Edwina's loss, or he was on his best behavior. He didn't end each sentence with "sir," but he might as well have. It was a very un-Bert-like performance.

After the print man finished, Sheriff Wescott turned to me and said, "Of course there won't be any good prints now, after you two have been over it."

"There never would have been good prints," I retorted. So much for lying low.

"Do you know something I don't, something else you've been holding back?"

In the past I had withheld information. It was a sore spot with him. I said, "It's nothing you couldn't figure out yourself, if you took the time instead of badgering me. The reason you wouldn't have found the murderer's prints on that podium is that the treaty is still there. If the murderer's prints were on the podium, he would have found the treaty and it would be gone."

"That's fine for speculating in a vacuum, Miss Haskell, but have you considered that maybe the murderer did try to get into that drawer? Maybe there were marks of attempted entry that you have now destroyed. If you had thought . . . If you had called us before breaking in—"

"Sheriff Wescott, we didn't know there would be anything in the drawer," I said in exasperation.

"You suspected or you wouldn't have forced the drawer open."

"Did you want us to call you every time we had an idea or opened a drawer?"

"I want you to do as I told you and stay out of this. How much clearer do I have to make that?"

I shrugged theatrically. It would have been hard to keep a higher profile than I was. I knew that, but I was too angry to rein myself in. "Is that all, Sheriff?"

"Just a final warning. I don't want to see you near anything to do with this case. I don't want you within ten feet of this podium, or of Edwina Henderson's house, and unless you have a lighted cigar in your mouth, don't go anywhere near the tobacco shop."

"Then I assume I can leave."

"Yes," he snapped.

I strode out, too angry to close the door softly even though I knew how adolescent it was to bang it. I climbed into my pickup, backed it up, and screeched out of the parking area. I was all the way to North Bank Road before I realized that I didn't know where I was headed.

I turned toward town. Though the day was still overcast and windy, traffic built up as I neared the commercial block of North Bank Road. This wasn't anything like it would be in summer, when the tourists in their campers, station wagons, and pickup trucks filled every parking space along the street and down by the town beach. Now traffic slowed as drivers considered whether to turn up Zeus Lane or eyed parking spots by Thompson's Grocery or Gresham's Hardware. I slowed too, and when a car pulled out across from the café, I scooted in.

I might have been headed home, for lack of any other destination, but the sight of the café reminded me that it was nearly two in the afternoon and it had been a long time since breakfast. Meter reading brought with it a big appetite. I'd seen former meter readers who'd been promoted to office jobs balloon into Humpty Dumptys. But considering Mr. Bobbs's opinion of me, that was a problem I was unlikely to face. Right now, my days of climbing up and down the hillside or walking a quarter of a mile up a driveway too potholed for the truck to handle made three hefty meals essential.

As I settled at a table, Marty came over. "Well, don't be a stranger. It's been a couple hours since

you were here last. You ready for our new Special—
coffee without a doughnut?"

I laughed, at first softly, then too loudly. Leave it
to Marty to dissipate anger. That, of course, was
why he'd gotten this job. In summer, dealing with
the frustrations of customers lined up to get into the
only eatery in town required a high level of diplo-
macy. "One a day's my limit," I said. "Give me a
tofu scramble sandwich."

"On black bread?"

"Of course. Do you serve it on Wonder?"

Marty made a show of grimacing. "Coming up."
Marty was a vegetarian. Given the slightest encouragement he would announce the vitamin content of
every ingredient in your meal, and if that particular
meal should be a hamburger, he'd expound on the
carcinogenic effects of high heat.

I walked past the counter to the bathroom. No line
—a sure sign it wasn't tourist season yet. Then I settled at the table, sniffed at the enticing aroma of garlic and soy sauce as Marty mixed them with the tofu,
and pondered Edwina's treaty.

Surely Edwina had been killed to prevent her an-
nouncing her find. If she *had* made her declaration,
what would have followed?

For one thing, the local Indians would have been
pleased. Of course, not many of them could have
lived on a rancheria as small as that one. On either
side of the river, no more than one family could have
lived in comfort. The Pomos weren't Pueblo Indians
like those of the Southwest. Historically, they built
comfortable wooden tipis near the rivers in winter
and spring, and temporary shelters in summer when
they went in search of food. They also built large
round brush houses for village gatherings. But they
didn't live on top of each other.

Actually, the only Pomo I knew was Hooper, who

worked for Edwina in the tobacco shop and who had guarded the food table at the Slugfest. Hooper had long hair and habitually wore jeans and a plaid woolen shirt. There was little about him or his house to distinguish him from any other Hendersonian of limited means. Hooper had taken on the role of Pomo leader of the area, possibly because there weren't any other Pomos here, or because those people who had some Pomo blood didn't care. In any case, Hooper was certainly one person who wouldn't have killed Edwina Henderson.

My tofu scramble arrived. It smelled even better close up. Taking a bite, I muttered, "Delicious."

But what else would have happened if the rancheria had been announced? The Pomos could eventually have opened a business on the land. Depending on what that was, it could have benefitted or harmed the Henderson and Guerneville merchants. But I doubted that any commercial endeavor there would have affected Leila Katz's Women's Space Bookstore. And even if the Pomos had put up a hotel, the clientele would have been entirely different from the guests at Steelhead Lodge. The Placerville Anglers Association wouldn't be likely to change allegiance.

Regardless of what the Pomos might have done, Edwina's announcement of the treaty would have brought the historical society a lot of attention. Its members, including Curry Cunningham, would have been interviewed by the press. I couldn't see him objecting to that. Curry was out to avoid annoyance, not attention, particularly when it put him in the role of town benefactor.

I took a swallow of natural lime soda. (Marty refused to serve Coke with tofu.)

Angelina Rudd? How could a Pomo rancheria affect her? Her fish would swim out, spend a couple years in the ocean, and then, as Maxie Dawkins had said, they would battle right back up the chutes. Whatever happened upriver couldn't affect that.

And Chris? I supposed the Pomos might fish in the river. There might be a few hundred less steelhead trout and a smaller percentage of the Russian River salmon making it into the Pacific. But the salmon that formed the basis of the fishing fleet's catch came from the north. Those that originated in the Russian River were negligible.

I finished my sandwich.

As far as I could tell, the only change made by the discovery of the rancheria was a potential one: benefit to Hooper. Unless there was something about that land that I didn't know.

I downed the rest of the lime soda, paid Marty, and headed out to the one place that the sheriff had forgotten to warn me away from.

The sky was darkening. At two-thirty in the afternoon, it looked more like dusk. The air was getting colder. There was no question but that a big storm was lurking beyond the breakers, waiting for those strong Pacific winds to blow it in. Tonight, again, I'd worry about that bathroom window.

As I drove toward Guerneville, it occurred to me that the rancheria, small though it was, would be a valuable piece of property. For years the Russian River had been a sleepy summer resort area. Twenty or thirty years ago, a week at the river was really getting away. But now, people in Sebastopol, just a few miles south of the river, commuted into San Francisco daily. The Russian River was no longer suitable only for vacations. And land, any land near Guerneville, was valuable.

I passed the near end of the W on the river. It was a popular spot with canoeists, one of the few that called for any semblance of skill. Occasionally, at the center hump of the W, the paddlers swerved too fast and their craft overturned. But since the river in summer was rarely more than two feet deep, the biggest danger they faced was exposing their bare bottoms when they swept downriver au naturel.

Coming to that point, I slowed down. The last two Warriors were visible from the road. I pulled my pickup off the road and got out.

Hooper was already there.

"**W**hat are you doing here?" There was a proprietary quality in Hooper's stance and his voice. He was not a tall man, but he was solid. One day that solidity would spread to fat. Whenever I saw him as I read his meter on my H-2 route, his long dark hair was pulled back in a ponytail. And his clothes—plaid wool shirt, thick brown sweater, and jeans—had, as always, the look of Salvation Army issue. It had struck me more than once that, in spite of his garb, he bore what seemed an internal resemblance to Edwina Henderson. Perhaps it was the suggestion of pent-up energy, or the very tobacco brownness of the hair and eyes, that warned you to be on guard. With Edwina, you had a good idea what causes she would be pushing or what groups she'd be protecting, and her nicotine- and caffeine-spurred intensity had followed fairly set lines. With Hooper there were no such boundaries. It was impossible to tell from a glance what extreme of mood he might be in. Now, as he stood under the branches of the two giant redwoods, he looked at home—and ready to fight for that home.

His attitude was understandable. Hooper lived in a tiny rented cabin on an unpaved road above town. He had no phone, probably no indoor plumbing, and his electricity usage was so minute that Mr. Bobbs questioned my read every single month. In contrast, the rancheria was magnificent. The river curved in toward it, and now, in spring, the water lapped at the bank. The deep green of the ground ferns was broken by the tiny blue oxalis flowers. And above it all, standing like Olympian sentries, were the two huge redwoods. The two Warriors stood a mere fifty feet apart, so close that their branches intertwined. On foggy days the heavy sky seemed to hang between them. On days as densely overcast as today, their topmost branches pricked through the clouds to the hidden sunlight beyond. There was no softness about these coastal redwoods, no gently sloping branches, no thick, pendulous leaves. They were aptly named Warriors. Their strong branches thrust out firmly from the massive trunks. And those trunks led up to the sky straight and sure. I had sometimes brought guests here, to stand between the soaring trees and let their gazes climb to infinity. There was something so primevally commanding about these trees, which were growing tall when Europe was still in the Dark Ages, that even the most cynical of my guests had stood silent.

But the fact that I could sympathize with Hooper made his fiercely possessive stance no less unnerving.

Hooper had worked in the tobacco shop since before I moved to Henderson. I had heard tales of a few flare-ups between him and Edwina. But unlike the reciprocal grumbling Bert had carried on with Edwina, which was nothing more than the natural result of their personalities, the amiable-appearing tolerance that had existed between Hooper and his employer seemed to be solely the product of his own determination.

Now, as he stood between the two giant redwoods, he looked at me.

"Hooper," I said, "how do you know about this land—the rancheria?"

"How do *you* know about it?"

"You first."

His face was completely still. He neither pursed his lips in thought nor narrowed his eyes in suspicion. But that completely blank expression suggested not emptiness but a careful shielding of emotion behind it. "Edwina knew about the treaty for a long time," he said. "She first got word of it maybe six months ago."

"How did she find it?" I waited, but he didn't answer. "Was it with the treaties in the Senate's secret files?"

He shrugged. Behind him, I could hear the river splashing on the bank. Its dampness seemed to have been caught under the interlaced branches of the trees. Even in boots and wool socks, I could feel the penetrating cold.

"Hooper," I said, "you *know*. As concerned as Edwina was about Henderson and the Pomos who lived here, she had to be excited when she got ahold of this treaty. I can't picture her keeping totally silent about it. And if there was anyone she would tell, it would have been you."

Slowly, he nodded. But he didn't speak.

"She obviously told you when she heard about it six months ago."

Again, he nodded.

Exasperated, I said, "This is important. Edwina's dead. She was probably killed over this treaty. You can't keep what you know to yourself. You don't *have* to tell me, but the sheriff isn't going to accept your silence."

"And since I'll have to tell him, I might as well let you in on it?" Hooper was grinning.

"Yes."

It was a moment before he said, "Okay. She told me her niece gave it to her."

"Her niece? You mean Leila?"

"No. Not Leila. Edwina said it was a niece who had worked in Washington, D.C."

"Are you sure she said niece, not nephew?"

Hooper's mouth tightened, then went slack after a moment. "Edwina talked about her *niece*. Her name is Meg."

I recalled Rosa telling me that Edwina had had two sisters. One was Leila's mother. Leila was an only child. Rosa told me the other sister had come to the river once with her *son*. Perhaps the sister had a daughter Rosa had forgotten—unlikely as Rosa's forgetting a person was—or maybe she hadn't brought the little girl with her. Or perhaps she was older than the son and working, and couldn't get time off to travel around visiting an eccentric aunt in the country. I would have to ask Leila about her cousin. "What did Edwina say about Meg?"

"Sit down," he said, indicating a large stone beneath the trees. He settled on another, and said, "The impression I got was that her niece used to work for some government agency, or some concern connected with the government, like a lobbyist or a consulting firm. From what Edwina said, I don't think she was still working there at the time she first talked about the treaty."

"So they talked. In person?"

"I don't know."

"Well, did the niece come here to visit, or did she call Edwina?"

"I said I don't know. I'm really just assuming they talked, because Edwina never mentioned a letter." His round face revealed nothing, but his fingers tightened against his leg.

"So what did the niece say?"

"At first I think she was pretty vague. Edwina said her niece thought a Pomo treaty existed. At that point Edwina didn't sound as if her niece herself had actually seen it. But, maybe a month later, Edwina came in all excited. Her niece knew where it was, and she thought she could get access to it. It sounded like the treaty would be in Edwina's hands in a couple of weeks. But then there were holdups, a series of them—her niece couldn't get access, and once she'd missed an opportunity, the next one didn't come up for a while. I don't think she got to Washington, or at least to wherever the treaty was kept, all that often. I didn't think Edwina could stand the strain much longer."

"But then, finally, the niece did get it to Edwina?" I prodded.

"Right. Edwina brought it to the shop in a manila folder. She was almost dancing off the floor." His mouth widened into a smile. "But, you know, after all that build-up, I was expecting something fancier. I mean, the treaty is just a few sheets and a map. It doesn't look like anything special. And frankly, I'd given the idea of our own local Pomo land a lot of thought, and I was expecting more than this."

I nodded. Although as beautiful as any land in the area, this parcel was small, in part because it was divided by the river. "Doesn't it strike you as odd," I asked, "that the niece would steal this treaty to give to Edwina?"

Hooper's smile vanished. "Odd? I'll tell you what's odd—that this treaty has been around for over a hundred years, that I—my people—have been entitled to this land all that time, and that the government—your government—has hidden the treaty away somewhere in Washington so they could keep our land. That's what's odd. Or maybe if you knew as much about Native American history as I do, and as Edwina did, you wouldn't find it that unusual."

I hesitated to press Hooper any further. Still, I said, "But the niece presumably didn't care about the

Pomos. From what you say, she just knew that Edwina did."

"Edwina didn't question that. What difference does it make whether her niece gave it to Edwina because they both cared about justice, or simply because she knew Edwina did? This much I'll tell you, if her niece wanted to put that treaty in the hands of someone who would make sure it got attention, and would fight till we Pomos got our land, then she did the right thing."

"True. There was no one like Edwina in that regard." I shifted on the cold rock. The river dampness had penetrated my jeans and sweater. I felt a shiver start up from the base of my spine. "Hooper, where is Edwina's niece now? Do you have an address or a phone number?"

"No," he said quickly. "Believe me, I've thought about that since Edwina died. As old as that treaty is, and as mysterious as its arrival here was, someone is bound to claim it's a phony. And what they'll say is that I'm behind it. Makes sense, doesn't it?"

"Can you be certain it's not a phony?"

"I can't think why it would be. *I* didn't create it." He smiled suddenly. "There's never been an instance in the history of Native Americans where the white man's gone to the trouble of forging a document to *give* us land."

We sat in silence a minute or so. The wind from the Pacific fluttered the fern fronds, but the branches of the redwoods hung still. I said, "Hooper, as long as Edwina's murder is unsolved, this treaty is going to be in doubt. You've got a real stake in finding her murderer."

"Dammit"—he slammed his fists into his thighs—"the woman was my friend. She gave me a job. She taught me about my heritage. Don't you think I want to find the guy who did that to her?"

"Then tell me who came near the food on the table at the Slugfest. You were watching it."

"No one."

"Not even Bert?"

"Well, of course Bert did."

"And the cooks?"

"Oh yeah. And the judges. They all circled around eyeballing each dish. Curry and Father Calloway were making cracks and laughing. Edwina looked preoccupied. I figured her mind was on the treaty. She'd been so excited about it for days that by the afternoon of the Slugfest she couldn't even wait on customers without spilling the blends all over. I tried to catch her eye, you know, to show my support, but she never even looked over."

"All the judges were there. They did the Grand Promenade around the table, right?"

"Yes. Even that Bobbs wimp. I was afraid he was going to faint away right into one of the plates. Hey, he's your boss, isn't he?"

I nodded.

"Bet you'll have something to say to him, come Monday."

I smiled. "He's probably the only person, besides the murderer, who will benefit by Edwina's dying. If she hadn't been killed, Mr. Bobbs would never have heard the end of the Slugfest. But let me be clear about what happened at that table. Are you saying that at some point every one of the judges had his back to you?"

"Right. So you think one of them could have poisoned the food then?"

"It makes sense. Did you notice anything suspicious?"

He leaned forward, elbows on knees. I had the impression he was rerunning the film of that time in its entirety. It was fully two minutes before he said,

"There's nothing I can recall. The best I can say is that one of those little pizzas looked darker than the others, the one in the corner."

"Which corner?"

"If you stood, facing the tray, it would be on your near left."

Edwina's pizza. Hardly a surprise. But it did suggest that the poison was sprinkled on, or dropped on, at that table. While that was interesting, what it did was to put the administering of the poison at the one time and place where every suspect had an opportunity.

The wind was picking up. It felt thick, sodden. The branches of the redwoods quivered. The rain could start again any time. I pulled the sleeves of my sweater farther down over my wrists. "You grew up here, didn't you?"

"No."

My mouth was already open, ready to ask my next question. I closed it instead and sat silently a moment. Hooper had been a fixture on the Henderson scene when I moved here. It hadn't occurred to me that he could be a slightly less recent arrival than I was. "How long have you been here?"

He shrugged again. "Four years? Twenty years? Take your pick."

"That's a pretty sizable range."

"Well, I've lived here on my own the last four years. But when I was a kid we moved around a lot and a couple of times it was here."

"How come?"

"My stepfather kept needing to move on." Hooper smiled and shook his head. "He was pretty small time as a lawbreaker, so in a couple of years the sheriffs had forgotten about him and it was safe to come back."

"Did you ever live at Stewart's Point?"

"The reservation?" He looked down, brushing the leaves aside with his foot. "No. My stepfather was too grand to be a reservation Indian, as if racing out of town an hour before the sheriff came was a freer way to live." He didn't look up. And from the anger in his voice, I was glad.

I wanted to leave, but I asked, "When did you live here? When you were in grade school?"

"No, later. My mother didn't acquire George till I was fourteen."

"Did you know Leila Katz then?"

"In high school? Sure. She was two years ahead of me. But she was a rebel, kind of an outsider. I liked that. For her it was a choice; for me it wasn't."

"So you were friends then?"

"No. I was too much younger. I wasn't her friend. I just knew who she was."

Leila lived across the street from Hooper now. But I didn't know if they were friends now. "Did she ever mention an old lover to you?"

His face closed into that blankness.

"It's important. I'm not just asking for gossip. Leila told me she had a lover in high school whom Edwina disapproved of, and there was a big family hubbub about it. Did she tell you?"

"No." His voice was very soft. It sounded like an old man's voice. I didn't believe him.

"Edwina's dead. Secrets don't count any more."

Without moving, his fingers tightened.

"The treaty is going to be suspect till her death is cleared up."

"Do you think I'd sell a friend for this scrap of land? This isn't big enough to build a house on, much less share it with every born-again Pomo in California. Lay off."

I didn't need to be told twice, not by a man that tightly controlled. I pushed myself up and started toward the road. At the edge of the copse, I stopped. "Hooper, one more thing: Who else, besides you, knows about the treaty?"

"Before now? No one."

"Edwina told you. She could have told—"

"She didn't. She swore me to secrecy. She told me she didn't yank the Slugfest out of Guerneville, get Bert Lucci to clean up Steelhead Lodge, and commit herself to eat slugs, just to have word of her announcement leak out before. And in case you're thinking I spilled the beans, believe me, I didn't. If the news had gotten out, Edwina would have known whom to blame."

I made my way back across the undergrowth to the road. Getting into my pickup, I headed back to town. Maybe Rosa would recall something about Edwina's mysterious niece, Meg. If not, she could find someone who did. In the meantime, Hooper had left me with more questions than he'd answered. Who was Leila's lover? Was it just loyalty that kept Hooper from telling me? For that matter, who was Hooper? I had been assuming that he was a long-time Hendersonian. But as a transient, what did anyone know about him? It could be that he wasn't even a Pomo. Hooper could be his stepfather's name, or even a made-up name.

And the poison, was it added to Chris's pizza during the Grand Promenade? Was it a poison that easy to deal with? What was the poison? There were a lot of questions I needed answers to, and Rosa was the person to start with. I stepped harder on the gas.

The redwoods and laurel trees formed a canopy over this part of the road, and it wasn't till I got into town that I realized it was raining. It was a gentle rain, but the dark clouds hung low in the sky, as if preparing to pounce. The wind was blowing the rain eastward, in from the ocean, against my windshield, and in my side window. I rolled up the window, and almost immediately the windshield fogged. Choosing the lesser of evils, I lowered the window.

The rain had thinned the traffic downtown, and it was only a couple of minutes till I pulled up in front of the Fortimiglios' house.

I wasn't out of the truck before the kitchen door opened. Rosa, whom I had almost always seen wearing an apron over old pants and a sweater, was dressed in a wool skirt, white blouse, and low stacked heels. She looked like she was going to church. But her face wasn't made up. She had neither eyeliner or lipstick, not even a spot of powder. Indeed, she looked paler than she had last night.

"What's the matter?" I asked as I hurried up the steps.

But Rosa didn't invite me in. She stood in the doorway, and unlike last night, this time she did meet my eyes. She stared at me in anger. "It's Chris. The sheriff arrested Chris. Because of the treaty you found."

CHAPTER
14

Rosa pushed past me down the stairs to her truck.

I ran after. "Rosa, why should Chris be arrested because of the Pomo treaty?"

She climbed in and started the engine.

At the closed window, I yelled, "Finding that treaty should have taken the sheriff's attention *off* Chris."

Behind the window, she shook her head.

"Once Bert and I found it, I couldn't keep it from the sheriff, even if I had suspected it would cause Chris problems, which I didn't."

The idle shifted down; the truck was ready to go. Rosa reached for the gearstick, hesitated, then rolled the window halfway down. "Vejay," she said, "I know you didn't mean Chris any harm. But it seems like you're just bad luck for us." She didn't look angry any more, just resigned. She rolled up the window, shifted into first, and drove to the end of the drive at North Bank Road. I stood in the rain, watching, as she turned left onto the road. I watched the truck slow, then pull harder as she shifted to second. Then she rounded the curve and was gone.

I walked back to my truck, climbed in, and turned the key in the ignition. I could go home. I *should* go home, shower, and wash my hair. In the warmth of the cab my scalp felt gummy and the wet wool cap was beginning to reek. It wasn't yet four o'clock. I had just enough time to get ready for Harry Bramwell and our early dinner date.

But even as I drove along the commercial block of
North Bank Road, I knew that I was kidding myself.
I couldn't let go of Edwina's death, not with Chris
Fortimiglio in jail and Rosa accusing me of produc-
ing the evidence that put him there. But the treaty?
The creation of the Pomo rancheria? I couldn't see
any connection between either of them and Chris
Fortimiglio.

I glanced at the Women's Space Bookstore. It was
closed. Odd, at this hour. Leila had assured me that
she would be there till six. I wanted to stop, to check
for a note on the door that said she'd be back in five
minutes. But I had to catch up with Rosa.

I came to my house, stopped, scribbled a note to
Harry Bramwell and stuck it on the door. I'd meet
him at his room at seven. He seemed to be an easygoing man; I guessed I'd find out how easygoing.

I jumped back in my truck and hurried toward
Guerneville, passing first a station wagon, then a line
of cars. Rosa had insisted I come to her house after
midnight last night.

I had spent all day trying, however vainly, to give
her the help I had promised. At the least, Rosa owed
me an explanation. I pulled around a camper, barely
making it back into my lane before a car whizzed by
in the other.

Rosa drove slowly in her old Ford truck, I knew
that. But it wasn't till I pulled into the parking lot of
the glass-and-metal sheriff's department building
that I spotted her, already headed in the door. I ran
across the lot, splashing water from the potholed surface onto my legs.

Inside, Rosa was standing by the ersatz wood
counter that ran the width of the building. Behind it,
the desk man spoke into the phone. I recognized him
—Joey Gummo, a distant cousin of Rosa's. As I hurried toward them, he glared.

Ignoring that, I said to Rosa, "I don't under-stand."

I couldn't tell whether her surprise was at my statement or my presence.

"How can that treaty incriminate Chris?" I asked.

"Vejay," she said, as if talking to a particularly backward grandchild, "Chris is a fisherman."

"So?"

"He's ready to see you now, Rosa," Joey said. He opened the half door in the counter and held it for her to pass through.

"Rosa," I said, "you *asked* me to help. Don't leave me hanging."

She started through the opening, stopped, stood unmoving but for her neck muscles pulling tighter. Turning abruptly to me, she said, "Let Chris tell you."

I followed her through the half door, again ignor-ing Joey Gummo's scowl, and into a long, narrow room. It was bisected by glass and had a counter and chairs on either side. There was a round mesh hole in front of each chair. The room was painted muddy blue. There could have been twenty people seated on either side, along the dividing glass, if the river area had ever had twenty prisoners at any one time sober enough to talk to their friends or families.

Rosa swallowed hard and sat down. I took the chair next to her. We both looked at the empty space on the other side of the glass.

The door opened at the opposite end of the room from where we had entered.

Rosa gasped.

In here, the jeans and workshirt that Chris wore most warm days looked like prison clothes.

"Chris," she said, leaning so close to the mesh that her breath fogged the glass around it. "Are you okay?"

"I'm fine, Mama. It's not so bad in here. Joey's going to bring me dinner in a while. Then I'm going to watch television. It'll be just like sitting around the living room at home, except for Stan Kelly's snoring. He's in for drunk and disorderly again. I was hoping Stan's wife would come and bail him out, but I guess she doesn't want to listen to him any more than I do."

"Are you sure she knows he's here, Chris?"

"They call, Mama."

"Maybe she wasn't home."

"Maybe, but when Stan doesn't come home, this'll be the first place she thinks of. You know, Joey told me that Stan's been in here thirty-seven times. He said that's nearly a record. You remember Buddy Griggs?"

Rosa nodded.

"He had the record. Fifty-two times, Joey said."

They were talking just as they might sitting around the kitchen table while the spaghetti sauce simmered. I bit my lip and felt my face flush as I watched them try to weave their own familial security around Chris's situation.

But the small talk died. There was only so much Chris could offer of his experience here that didn't lead back to the reason for his being on that side of the glass. In the silence, my unwanted presence seemed even more intrusive.

I started to say I was sorry if I had caused him to be here, but before the words were out, I realized how pointless that was. Taking a breath, I said, "Chris, I thought finding the treaty would send the sheriff's investigation in a different direction, after someone else. What is it about this treaty that you and your mother and the sheriff think implicates you?"

Chris stared at me, as if he found it difficult to

believe I wasn't joking. He slid into the chair across from me and leaned toward the mesh, even though it hadn't been hard to hear him before. "I know you didn't mean to make things worse, Vejay. You were trying your best to help me."

"But what is it about the treaty?"

"Haven't you heard of the Boldt Decision?"

"No."

"Really?" His eyes widened. "Well, every fisherman knows it: the Boldt Decision was handed down in Washington State in the seventies. There, the Indian tribes had rivers running through their reservations, and they claimed that they should be able to fish in those rivers the way their ancestors did, because it was part of their religion, or something. Anyway, what they said was that their ancestors had gillnetted the fish on the rivers. You know what gillnetting on the rivers does, don't you?"

"Catches all the fish."

"Pretty much. Some fish get through. But when you string a net all the way across the river, you catch a lot."

"But, Chris, you fish in the ocean. So what if the Pomos net every steelhead and the few salmon there are in the Russian River? You've still got the whole ocean. Why would you kill because of that? Bert Lucci would be hurt a lot more than you would."

"That's not the end of the story, Vejay. When that happened in Washington, the sports fishermen and the commercial men went to court, and the state decided—the Boldt Decision—to divide the fish between the Indians and the non-Indians, fifty-fifty."

"Still, that's not so bad. It's better than having them gillnet all the fish in the rivers."

Chris leaned closer to the mesh. His face was getting red under his tan. "That's still not the end."

I waited.

"Then they decided that that fifty percent included the fish in the ocean, because they had been spawned in the rivers."

"You mean the Indian tribes got half of all the fish?"

"Right." His face was redder. I had never seen easygoing Chris this angry.

"But surely that couldn't happen from one little two-acre rancheria here," I said.

"It doesn't matter how big it is if it crosses the river."

"But, that was Washington State. This is California. Maybe the laws aren't the same here."

"They're not," Chris said grudgingly. "But that's because the tribes don't have the same power here. It hasn't gotten to a court case. It probably won't, not for a while anyway, but that's not the point."

"It's not?"

"Geez, Vejay. The point is that once the government gets a hand in deciding who can have what fish, they can do whatever they want. They can decide there aren't enough fish to go around and that the Indians have first right to them, for religious reasons. They can decide we don't get any fish at all."

"But, Chris, the government already sets the salmon season."

He glared at me.

Even I recalled how angry the fishermen had been when, the year after a freak warming of the ocean— El Niño—had ruined the salmon season, the Pacific Fisheries Management Council voted to close the coho salmon season two months early. And when that second season had turned out to be a boom one, the ban remained enforced. The bountiful salmon swam out in the Pacific, mocking the fishermen. With two catastrophic seasons in a row, many of the men had lost their boats. As Chris had pointed out to me then, the bank expects payments whether the boat is out in the ocean or sitting at dock.

"But, Chris," Rosa said, "you didn't know Edwina had the treaty, did you?"

"No."

"So then it doesn't matter what the treaty said. You didn't know, so you wouldn't have had any reason to want to kill her. The sheriff will understand that."

I sat silent, hoping I wouldn't be the one who had to disillusion her. But Chris didn't say anything, and finally, I said, "Rosa, the sheriff won't believe Chris didn't know about the treaty. Edwina might have told anyone. Hooper might have said something."

"Hooper knew?" Chris asked. "He didn't tell me that."

"Why would he tell you?" I asked, with a sinking feeling.

"He was helping me fix the manifold on the boat last Sunday. He was there all day."

I wanted to say, "Don't mention that to the sheriff," but this was hardly the place for that type of comment. It was just as well I didn't say anything at all. Rosa was right: everything I found, everything I even asked about, made things look worse for Chris.

Joey motioned to Chris from the door.

"I've got to go, Mama," Chris said.

Rosa swallowed hard.

"I'll be okay," he added. "It's only Joey, Stan, and me. Don't worry."

Rosa swallowed again.

"Mama, nothing's going to happen to me. The sheriff will find the person who killed Edwina."

Joey walked up beside Chris. Bending so that his mouth was near the wire mesh in front of the next seat, he said, "Rosa, the sheriff wants you in his office."

Rosa's neck muscles tightened. She looked as if she
would have swallowed yet again, but there was nothing left to swallow. "Now?"

He nodded uncomfortably. "It's official—his request."

"Oh, Chris."

"It'll be okay, Mama."

I could tell from their faces that neither of them
believed that.

To Joey, Chris said, "She can have a lawyer or a
representative with her, can't she?"

Joey nodded.

"Mama, you'll feel better not seeing the sheriff
alone, right? You take Vejay with you."

Facing the sheriff in this kind of interview, on this
case, was not something I wanted to do. Being connected to me wasn't likely to raise the Fortimiglios in
the sheriff's estimation. I wasn't even sure that Rosa
found my company better than going it alone. But
taking me with her was Chris's parting request, and
she didn't argue. She turned and walked to the door,
stood staring out, her back to me, until Joey came to
open it and led us through the rows of plexiglass
cubicles to Wescott's office. It was on the inside of
the aisle. Once Wescott had told me that it didn't do
for the sheriff to have his back to the windows.

The office was as I remembered it from a year ago
when Wescott had had me in here for an interroga-
tion. Then, as now, papers were stacked on the
muddy blue desk, on the blue bookcase, and mixed
in with heavy binders atop the blue file case. From
some place in the center of the building came the
plastic clack of a typewriter, its electronic pips mark-
ing the end of each line. Overhead, the air grate
buzzed softly.

Sheriff Wescott was standing behind the desk. His

blue eyes were pale, his rough skin drawn. I wondered how late he had been at Steelhead Lodge last night. When he looked at Rosa, it was with sadness. "Mrs. Fortimiglio." He started to indicate the chair but stopped halfway, as he spotted me. He eyed me with annoyance. "Mrs. Fortimiglio, is it your wish to have Miss Haskell with you?" he demanded.

Perhaps it was the sheriff's tone that got to Rosa, or his implication that she was too timid to say no. "Yes," she snapped, "it is my wish."

I moved the box of files from the other chair to the floor and sat. When we had left Chris, I wouldn't have thought it was possible for me to make things any worse for him and Rosa, but already I had.

The sheriff sat, pulled out a notepad, and said, "You cooked those pizzas, didn't you, Mrs. Fortimiglio?"

"Yes."

"Why?"

Rosa had looked nervous before. Now her eyes widened. She had the same expression of amazed disbelief Chris had had when I told him I knew nothing about the Boldt Decision. "We wanted to win the fifty dollars."

The sheriff pressed his lips together. It was clear from *his* expression that he figured she had misunderstood the point of his question. "Let me approach it from the other end. Why didn't *you* take those pizzas to the Slugfest? Why did Chris?"

Rosa leaned forward, resting her fingers on the edge of the desk. "Oh, well, you see, Edwina was still piqued at me. My grandson, Donny, bought some tobacco from her last fall. He was only sixteen then. He has bad asthma. I'm not excusing Donny, Sheriff; he had no business there. But Edwina should have known better than to sell it to him. I know you don't speak ill of the dead, but truth is truth. We had to take Donny to the emergency room. His face was all red, he was trying so hard to get the breath in. He was scared to death. It was a good lesson for him. He'll never go near tobacco again. But, I'll tell you, we were all scared."

"So you told Edwina Henderson that?" Obviously the sheriff had heard of the incident.

"I went down to the store the next day. I figured she should know."

"And what happened?"

"She got all up on her high horse about Donny being old enough to look out for himself, and her not being responsible for the illnesses in my family." A flicker of a smile broke through Rosa's taut expression. "Edwina realized she was wrong. She just couldn't bring herself to say so."

"Did you think Edwina Henderson would have barred a Slugfest entry with your name on it?"

"Well, no. But I knew this was a big event for her. I wouldn't have considered making an entry, but Donny made such a fuss about it. He said it would pay for his nose drops. They're prescription—Estrin —and they're expensive. So I agreed to cook the piz- zas. I just didn't want to create more turmoil for Edwina by turning up myself. But really, everyone who knows us knew that I cooked those pizzas. Chris doesn't cook."

"Sheriff," I said, "are you telling us that the poi- son was definitely in the pizzas?"

"Everything suggests that." The lines around his mouth had softened as he'd listened to Rosa. Now they stiffened again.

"But you don't *know*."

"No, I don't have *evidence*. The pizzas were eaten completely."

"Then why have you arrested Chris?"

"Because," he said with deliberateness, "the poison was almost certainly in his dish."

"Any of the judges, or Hooper, or Bert Lucci had access to that dish when it was on the table. Hooper told me that when they circled the table, every one of the judges had his back to him at some point. Why not arrest them?"

The typewriter stopped. The buzz from the air grate seemed louder.

"Miss Haskell, Chris Fortimiglio had strong reason for wanting to keep that treaty secret." He paused to see if I could rebut that, then said, "He had access to the poison."

"What was the poison?"

"Liquid nicotine."

"Nicotine!" Rosa and I said together.

"Chris doesn't smoke," Rosa said.

The sheriff nodded to her and shifted his gaze back to me. He seemed to be balancing between the sympathetic tone he would have chosen had she been here alone and the supercilious one he'd been using with me. "Nicotine, as you ladies may know, is a pesticide. In the past it was very popular in dealing with aphids and flying insects. Chris helped his father when he worked in town, cleaning people's yards and doing repairs, didn't he, Mrs. Fortimiglio?"

"In off season, when there were no fish, he did, and before the floods, when there was a lot of work needing to be done."

The sheriff nodded. He made a notation on his pad. The typewriter started again with a rush of electronic pips. "So then, Mrs. Fortimiglio, Chris knew where local people kept pesticides."

Rosa seemed to crumble from within. I put my hand on her arm. "Rosa, it's okay. Everyone knows Chris helped his father. You didn't tell the sheriff anything new." Glaring at Wescott, I said, "All sorts of people have pesticides. Saying Chris is the only one with access to a pesticide is ridiculous, particularly when you're talking about nicotine. For Christ's sake, Edwina ran a tobacco store."

"Miss Haskell," he said, with ill-concealed triumph, "the only reason to have pure nicotine in a tobacco store is if you want to kill someone."

"You can boil down smoking tobacco," I said.

"If you have the time and are willing to run the risk of being discovered with the evidence burned into your equipment. Why would you do that, Miss Haskell, when liquid nicotine is already available?"

"That still doesn't point to Chris. They've got pesticides at the fish ranch, for instance."

"Are you suggesting the killer drove all the way out to Jenner and back?" he asked.

"I'm just saying that access to nicotine is widespread. It's not reason enough for arresting Chris."

"True."

"Then why?" Rosa asked in a barely audible voice.

Still looking at me, Wescott said, "We found the container the nicotine was in. It's a tiny plastic squeeze bottle. An Estrin bottle."

I told the sheriff that Maxie Dawkins, the guard at the fish ranch, and probably any number of other people, took Estrin, but he cut me off with the remark that Maxie had not been at the Slugfest. When I suggested someone could have used his bottle, the sheriff actually laughed, then caught himself and stopped abruptly. Did I, he asked, as he stood up, assume the killer had somehow discovered the treaty in the locked drawer of Edwina's podium, then excused himself from the festivities at Steelhead Lodge, driven half an hour to the fish ranch and half an hour back, for the pleasure of using an obscure nose-drop bottle? The bottle, he pointed out, was a convenience. It was not the entire focus of the crime. And it was easily accessible only to someone like Chris, whose nephew, Donny, used Estrin. With that, the sheriff took a step toward the door.

At least, I thought, standing up, this discovery was not my fault. Or so I assumed, until Rosa asked Wescott where he'd found the Estrin bottle. He'd uncovered it in a garbage can that he'd spotted at the lodge when he came out to examine the treaty!

I walked out of the building with Rosa, waiting for her to say something. But her silence was as total as it had been before, and now it seemed final. I waited as she got into her truck, and only moved on when she shut the door.

Without bothering to avoid the ankle-deep puddles, I walked slowly across the parking lot to my

truck, and climbed in. The cab was cold. I didn't
touch the ignition. I sat staring into the rain. It was
heavier now, blowing across the parking lot in
waves. I looked through it at the building. Glass and
metal, it had the appearance of the bottom two stories of a skyscraper, suitable to Los Angeles, not
Guerneville. The old sheriff's department was a beige
stucco building that slumped back against the beach.
It had looked like a place you could feel safe explaining why you hadn't paid your parking tickets. But
this razor-edged building was one you would be
called to by a computer notice; where, rather than
being presumed innocent until proven guilty, you'd
be held until you could show the computer had
erred. It was a building where innocent men were
held for murder.

I didn't consider going home now. I didn't consider whether to keep clear of Chris's dilemma. The
sheriff hadn't handled the interview professionally or
fairly. He'd let his anger with me overwhelm the
sympathy he'd felt for Rosa when she walked in. He
was a decent man, and by now, I felt sure he was
even angrier with himself, and me. He wasn't out to
get Chris. In the twenty hours since Edwina's murder, he probably hadn't done any more active seek-
ing for clues than to interview those of us who had
had access to the food. He probably hadn't looked
for evidence against Chris per se. It had just piled up
in front of him—thanks, in large part, to me. Regardless of what Rosa wished, by now I was too cul-
pable to just walk away.

Nicotine, I thought. Anyone could get it. But for
someone to bring it to the Slugfest meant that that
person was planning to kill Edwina. And if the motive was to keep the treaty secret, that meant the
killer knew about the treaty. And according to Hoo-

per, the only one besides Edwina who knew what she was going to say was himself.

Why would Hooper admit to knowing about the treaty? Surely he would realize how incriminating it was. But with moody, volatile Hooper, the normal logic didn't hold. I couldn't predict how Hooper would react. All I knew of Hooper was what he had told me—assuming that was true—and that he alone benefitted from the treaty. As I would have admitted to the sheriff, had he asked me, that was hardly grounds for an arrest.

I turned the key in the ignition. I needed to know more about Hooper—background that Rosa could give me. But I couldn't ask her now.

Leaving the lights off, I stared into the empty parking lot. Then I noticed it wasn't empty. A man in tan rain gear was making his way toward a beige sedan. As I focused on him, I realized it was Mr. Bobbs.

Mr. Bobbs! What was he doing at the sheriff's department today? Sheriff Wescott himself had told me they'd interviewed Mr. Bobbs last night. Why had they called him in for a second go around? Was he a more serious suspect than I had imagined? Or did he know something I hadn't considered?

He got in his car and drove toward the exit of the lot. He hadn't even warmed his engine. How rattled was he to forget or forego that? I had seen him sit in the PG&E lot for ten minutes warming the engine of a vehicle that had just been used. Now his car sputtered as he pulled out of the sheriff's department lot. I followed.

He drove slowly. I had never ridden with him, but I wasn't surprised that he kept the car exactly at the speed limit. If he had been on company time, he would have been intent on upholding the unimpeachability of his position, lest anyone should suggest that the manager of the Henderson PG&E office

was a scofflaw. Now, after five, on Saturday, with
the office closed and the week's route books safely
on their way to the computer in San Francisco, there
was no reason to rush. He was just filling time till
Monday morning.

He slowed as he passed the curve by the W in the
river, where the Pomo rancheria would be. I looked
to the left, but if Hooper was still there, he was invisible from the road. There was no car or truck parked
there, but that didn't mean anything. Hooper didn't
have a vehicle.

The rain hit sharply on the windshield. Overhead,
the California laurel branches hung low. The redwoods pushed up above them. This patch of road,
right before the Henderson line, where River Road
became North Bank Road, was one of my favorites.
The canopy of trees reminded me of being a child, of
suspending a blanket over the tops of folding chairs
and making a secret passage. The redwoods and eucalyptus and laurels didn't quite meet across much of
River Road, but they crowded to the sides of it all
the way to St. Agnes's, well beyond Henderson. The
charm of the road, its unspoiled quality, was one of
the things that had clinched my decision to move up
here. "Nature's high-rises," my ex-husband John had
called them on his one unexpected visit after I settled
in Henderson. He had looked appraisingly at those
redwoods that had been standing longer than the
white man had been on the continent, and said,
"Someone could make a fortune from this lumber."
When I had reminded him that stripping the riverbanks would create a public outcry, he had smiled
and said, "And someone else could make a fortune
with a good PR campaign. Of course, it would have
to be very good."

After John had left, I had been angry, but more
than that, puzzled by his reaction. John was the per-

fect public relations man. He knew how to assess what customers wanted. He knew how to adapt it into a workable and appealing campaign. He was a master at getting along with people. His ability to appear agreeable had so permeated his views and re-actions that I had found it increasingly difficult to ferret out any substance beneath his smile. In the end, I had felt that I was living with a facsimile of a husband, created from public opinion polls. We hadn't argued; John hadn't been offensive; he simply hadn't, in reality, been there at all. And that day when he arrived unannounced in Henderson, his atti-tude had been so unlike anything I'd seen before that I'd been more stunned than irritated. But I hadn't wanted to dwell on John's character—the time for that was long gone. Instead, I had focused my con-cern on the redwoods, and had been comforted by running into Curry Cunningham and having him as-sure me that no one could come along and decimate miles of river bank. "You need a Timber Harvest Permit for anything over three acres," he had said.

Ahead, the Henderson traffic light was green. I stepped on the gas. It would be a long wait if the light turned red. Mr. Bobbs slowed. In my rearview mirror I counted six trucks and cars. The light turned yellow. Mr. Bobbs stopped. I jammed on my brakes. A red Mustang screeched to a stop inches from my bumper. The truck behind him looked like it was coming through my rear window. Obviously, all six of them had planned on making it through the light.

My fingers were pressed white against the steering wheel. Deliberately I flexed them. As we sat, waiting long after the cross traffic had passed, the Mustang driver raced his engine. When the light changed, Mr. Bobbs continued straight on North Bank Road, at exactly twenty-five miles per hour. The Mustang driver honked. I threw up my hands. He honked

again. In the heavy rain, the sidewalks were empty.
The doors to the shops were closed and the lights
were on inside. I knew Mr. Bobbs didn't live out this
way—I read his meter. Where was he going?

He slowed down to twenty.

The Mustang driver hit the horn and the gas, and
pulled around me into the left lane in front of an
oncoming semi. I hit the brakes. The semi swerved
right. Behind me tires squealed. The Mustang barely
squeezed back in front of Mr. Bobbs.

Mr. Bobbs put on his righthand turn signal and
pulled into the lot of Davidson's Plant Shop.

I found a spot at the other end of the lot, and sat
till the blood stopped throbbing in my head. Then I
turned off the engine. Should I go over and see if Mr.
Bobbs was all right? After being interrogated at the
sheriff's department, maybe this near miss on the
road was too much. He might be much more upset
than I was. Still, I hesitated because, among other
reasons, having tailed him for six infuriating miles, I
didn't want him to pull himself together and drive
off while I was walking across the parking lot.

But he didn't. It was he who got out of his car and
trotted across the lot into the plant shop, as if nothing had happened. I hurried after him.

The oblong building was divided into three sections, with the counter by the glass door at one end,
potted house plants in the middle, and bags of fertil-
izers at the far end. There, Mr. Bobbs was hoisting a
two-cubic-foot bag of potting soil onto his shoulder.
It was far and away the most athletic thing I had ever
seen him do.

As he turned toward the counter end of the building, he spotted me. "Miss Haskell." He gave me a
small, acknowledging nod and kept walking. Drops
of water fell from the brim of his tan sou'wester. If
the near accident he'd caused distressed him, he gave

no indication. He merely looked irritated and preoccupied—normal for him.

Not bothering to mask my anger, I said, "I saw you coming out of the sheriff's department. What did he want with you today?"

"Miss Haskell?"

"The sheriff had a man talk to you last night. Why did he need to see you again today?"

He glared at me. This was hardly the kind of demand he expected from an employee. But my relations with him were so strained normally that this couldn't make them much worse. And despite my near-the-limit Missed Meter count, I did my job too well for him to find reason to fire me.

Mr. Bobbs's normally sallow complexion took on a tint of orange as he nervously looked around the shop. There was a woman behind the counter, an elderly couple assessing a fern in the middle of the room, and Grant Quistle, a lawyer from Guerneville, looking at fish emulsion. Mr. Bobbs lowered his voice. "It's none of your concern, Miss Haskell."

I stepped in front of him, blocking the aisle. He moved back quickly. The potting soil bag jerked with the motion and looked for an instant like it was going to fall and carry him with it.

"Mr. Bobbs, what do you know about Edwina Henderson's murder? She died an awful death; Hooper may not get his Pomo rancheria; and Chris Fortimiglio is in jail. What is it you told the sheriff?"

Mr. Bobbs swallowed; his neck was as orange as his face. "I have no knowledge of Miss Henderson's death. I was not aware that she had died until the sheriff's deputy arrived at my door last night."

"But you were at the judges' table. You walked around the food table in the Grand Promenade. You saw what the other judges did before any of you ate a bite. What do you know about the judges, or Bert Lucci, or Hooper?"

Mr. Bobbs rebalanced the plastic bag on his shoulder. Had he been in the security of the PG&E office, he would have stalked by me. But here, amidst strangers, in the ungainly position under the potting soil bag, he looked around warily. The white-haired couple was at the counter paying for a four-inch potted fern. Grant Quistle had abandoned the fish emulsion and was reading the back of a box of snail pellets.

I wanted to grab Mr. Bobbs by his orange neck and shake his secret out of him. Instead I took a breath and said, "You've been in Henderson for years, in a position of importance. It's only reasonable that you would be aware of things that others might miss." For a moment, I wondered if I had laid it on too thick, but Mr. Bobbs only nodded. And just when I thought that nod was all I was going to get, he said, "Hooper had his power on four years ago."

That was hardly the type of disclosure I had hoped for. But it was just like Mr. Bobbs to recall the month a customer—an "account," as he called them —had the electricity turned on, and to find it significant. I waited, hoping there was some connection between this bland fact and Edwina's murder.

Lowering his voice, Mr. Bobbs said, "He complained about the deposit. Said it was a hardship."

Aha! I knew Mr. Bobbs's opinion of accounts who didn't want to pay a deposit—low-lifes who would suck the wires dry and skip town, leaving months of non-pay on the records of the Henderson office; deadbeats, who would ruin the office statistics and nullify all Mr. Bobbs's efforts in fighting us over Missed Meters.

"He must have had a record of deposit somewhere. Did he have previous service?"

"Not in his name."

"His family was here when he was in high school. That wasn't so very long ago—maybe fifteen years. He wouldn't be able to use that deposit, of course, but—"

"Made no deposit."

I stared. "Hooper's family didn't have to pay a deposit?" Hooper had described his family as transients, with his stepfather escaping a couple of yards ahead of the sheriff. They were hardly people Mr. Bobbs would trust without a deposit.

"It was paid for them," he said.

"Closing," the woman at the counter called. "Please bring your purchases up here."

Mr. Bobbs pushed around me and trudged toward her. Coming up by his side, I said, "Who paid the deposit?"

He put the bag on the counter.

"Six forty-seven with the tax," the woman said.

Mr. Bobbs handed her a ten-dollar bill.

I stood between him and the door.

He took the change, pocketed it and the receipt, hoisted the bag on his other shoulder, and took a step forward.

I didn't move.

But my trick didn't work twice. He shifted around me and headed out the door.

I ran after him. "Who, Mr. Bobbs?" I demanded as we crossed the parking lot.

He lowered the plastic bag next to the back of his car. "Edwina Henderson."

"What? Edwina Henderson paid his family's deposit? Why did she do that?"

"I don't know, Miss Haskell. It seems to have escaped you that it is not the function of Pacific Gas and Electric to inquire into the motives of accounts when they remit their required fees." He opened his trunk, hoisted the bag, and set it in. The trunk was otherwise empty, and spotless.

"Well, did she make a habit of helping poor people with their deposits?"

"No, she did not. The Hooper family was the only deposit she ever paid."

"Mr. Bobbs—"

"Miss Haskell, I've told you company business. I shouldn't have. But having done that, I'll tell you now that that is everything I know about the Hooper family. If it is your intention to keep yourself standing in my way until you drown, you can do so, but there is not another thing you'll be able to ascertain from me. Is that clear?"

"Just one more thing, Mr. Bobbs."

He shook his head in disbelief.

"It's not about that. It's about your garden. Do you use liquid nicotine to kill your aphids?"

"Certainly not." He slammed the trunk.

"Why not?"

"Miss Haskell, nicotine is a poison. I don't want that near my vegetables. The only place you can safely use that is where there's no danger of it getting into the soil, at least not unless you're sure there'll be a good month for it to wash out. And, Miss Haskell, the aphids aren't so accommodating as to move on a month before I'm ready to harvest my lettuce." He opened his car door and got in.

I was still thinking about those odd little beds of roses at the fish ranch when he pulled out.

After Mr. Bobbs had driven out of sight, I wondered why the sheriff had called him in for questioning again today. Had it just been a double check? Or was the sheriff zeroing in on Hooper's visit here years ago? I could have gone after Mr. Bobbs. I knew where he lived. But I couldn't face that any more than he could. Instead I drove across North Bank Road and onto the town beach.

In summer, the beach was two levels. The lower tier was near the river where the sunbathers shared the sand with beached canoes and paddle boats, and grandparents and grandchildren grouped around the wading pool the town made by shovelling a U back into the beach and allowing the river water to fill it. In summer that area was thirty yards wide. Now, with the river almost at flood stage, it was under water.

The second level, where I was parked, was used for cars in summer, too.

I sat, watching the brown water tumbling toward the ocean. Each spring the summer dams were erected. Without those dams, the water wouldn't be deep enough to swim in. In places it wouldn't cover your knees. But now it tossed whole branches like they were twigs. The rain smacked down on my windshield. Suddenly, I realized how cold the truck was. I reached for the heater, but didn't turn it on. The damp cold was fitting.

What I had found out, after an entire day devoted

to Edwina's murder, was nothing more than a slew of questions. Who was Hooper? I had wondered why Edwina chose to hire him to work in her store. Now I had the answer: she knew him before. She had paid the family's PG&E deposit. Why did she do that? Nothing suggested that Edwina was financially generous. From what I had heard, her commitments were limited to time and enthusiasm only; her money was reserved for herself. I recalled Bert Lucci complaining that she wouldn't even pay for the cleaning service at Steelhead Lodge. So why would she come across for a transient family's utility deposit? Because they were Pomos? If so, why, in all the following years, had she never helped another Indian family? Or an Oriental family? But she hadn't. On that, Mr. Bobbs's recollections were the word of God.

And nicotine. Again, I trusted Mr. Bobbs. There was no reason for him to lie. If it wasn't applied near vegetables, then one place it was safe to use it would be at the fish ranch. The outside area of the fish ranch was all cement, all except the flower beds. Even the ditches where the young fish would swim were cement. Maxie Dawkins had explained to me once, at length, that they would be filled with a layer of pebbles before the little fish were allowed out in them. So, beyond the flower beds, the nicotine had no soil to spread in.

And that brought the question back to Angelina Rudd. Even if she had access to nicotine, it still meant that she had to have known about the treaty long enough in advance to stop at the ranch and pick up the poison. And Hooper had said Edwina told no one but him.

But if Edwina had gotten the treaty from her mysterious niece Meg, mightn't Meg, who was Leila's cousin, have told Leila, and Leila have told Angelina?

It all pointed back to Leila. It was time she gave up protecting her lover and told me if that lover was, indeed, Angelina.

I put the truck in reverse, swung around, and headed back for North Bank Road.

The Women's Space Bookstore was dark. No one was visible inside. Where was Leila? She had insisted she had to be here all day. The store had been closed when I drove by two hours ago.

I pulled into a parking spot in front, got out, and walked to the door. I had hoped to find a note saying "Back at 6:00," but there was nothing tacked to the door. I reached for the handle. The door was unlocked!

For the first time I was more worried than annoyed. I tried to think of a reasonable explanation for her absence. Could she have run across the street to the café to fill her thermos? But she wouldn't have turned the lights off in the bookstore for that. Could she—

A car door slammed. A woman—tall, blond—ran across the sidewalk toward me. She was carrying a camera bag. "Hello. Are you Leila?" she called out. "I'm Anna Martin." Looking at her watch, she added, "Right on time, too."

"You're from the *Chronicle*, aren't you?" I asked. "Doing the feature article?"

"Yes." She eyed me skeptically. "Aren't you Leila Katz?"

"No. I'm Vejay Haskell, a friend of hers. She was planning to be here now. She told me this morning how much she was looking forward to seeing you. It was very important to her. But her aunt died last night. Leila was up all night. She was exhausted this morning, but she was still determined to see you at six." My words rushed out. Somehow, in my increased worry about Leila, it seemed essential that I make this woman understand that Leila hadn't just stood her up.

Anna Martin nodded slowly. "I've got to be back in San Francisco at nine. I'll have to leave here by seven-fifteen at the latest."

"I'm going to Leila's house now. She probably was falling asleep this afternoon and went home for a nap and forgot to set the alarm. Look, the door to the store is open. Why don't you go on in and check it out, take pictures."

"Okay, but like I said, I've got to be home at nine."

I ran for my truck, started the engine, and hung a U on North Bank Road. At Zeus Lane I turned right. The road was steep and dark. Before I came to Leila's house, the pavement ended. From that point the street was mud. In a more cosmopolitan area the top of the hill would have been a plush location. It would have boasted half-million-dollar homes with imposing decks. But the apex of Zeus Lane looked like a scene from the Ozarks. Dim lights came from the windows of tiny ramshackle cabins, and herds of maimed vehicles, many on blocks, were parked where front lawns might have been.

But Leila's little house was well maintained. It was also dark. And worse, there was no car in front. I knocked on the door.

No answer.

I knocked again, loudly. Then I leaned over the porch rail and rapped on the bedroom window.

No response at all. She couldn't have slept through all that banging. She wasn't there. Now I was really worried.

I walked back to my truck. What could have made her forget Anna Martin and the publicity that might thrust the bookstore into the black financially? Why would she have left the bookstore unlocked? What could have been so important, so surprising, so compelling?

I looked across the street at Hooper's cabin, hoping he could tell me something. But his place was dark, too.

Turning the truck around, I headed back down the hill. I parked in the same spot on North Bank Road, and ran across the street to the café, and then back to Fischer's Ice Cream. But neither of the clerks had seen Leila leave. Neither had even realized the bookstore was closed.

I pushed open the door to the bookstore. All the lights were on. Anna Martin was standing by Leila's chair, next to the table that held the thermoses. "Did you find . . . I guess not," she said.

"No. I'm a little worried," I said, in understatement. "Can she call you?"

"I guess. But I can't drive back up here. I'm on a tight deadline. I had the flu last week and I'm really behind. I took some pictures of the store. I've got a good idea of the stock. Here's my number at home. She can leave a message on my machine if I'm not there." She handed me her card. Her home phone number was pencilled in.

After Anna Martin had left, I stood in the empty store. The bookshelves looked undisturbed. On the table were three empty cups, one with lipstick marks and one half full of black coffee. Leila had been drinking her coffee black this morning. But that didn't mean anything. I sank into the chair where I had sat this morning, asking Leila about her lover, listening to her refuse to reveal his or her identity. Now, as I looked at her chair, I saw it wasn't empty. On it lay a book, lying face down—a tall thin book, a children's book. I turned it over. *For Bear Lovers Only!*

Bear Lovers! Leila had explained about Bear just

this morning. She'd expected me to stop here this
afternoon. She was telling me she had gone off with
Bear. With a shudder, I realized that if Leila had left
with an easy mind, she wouldn't have put the book
on the chair for me. She left a trail because she was
worried, or frightened. Had she gone with Bear to
protect him, or her?

Maybe Leila had dropped everything to help Bear.

Maybe. No one but Leila knew Bear's identity. *If*
Bear had killed Edwina, then Leila was a threat.

Who was Bear? According to Rosa, Angelina was
the only adolescent girlfriend Leila had had. She was
the person to whom Leila turned the summer of the
scandal. Leila went to her house secretly, to protect
Angelina from Edwina's wrath. Angelina had access
to whatever nicotine there was at the fish ranch, and
to Maxie Dawkin's Estrin. It all pointed to her. But I
wanted to be sure before I committed myself to going
to the fish ranch for the evidence—before I took the
chance of coming up against the violent night guard.

I couldn't be sure Angelina was Bear, but she was
more likely than anyone else. And with Leila gone, I
had to do something.

Perhaps I was jumping to conclusions about Leila
being worried. Maybe the book was a coincidence.
Maybe she'd just gone off. But she wouldn't have left
the shop unlocked. She wouldn't have forgotten
Anna Martin.

Not believing for an instant that it would do any
good, I looked up Angelina's phone number and
used Leila's phone to call. There was no answer. Angelina and her family could still be up at Fort Ross.
They could be pitching the tent right now. Angelina
might be innocently vacationing, but . . .

It didn't leave me much choice. If Angelina had
lured Leila away from here, if she was keeping her
captive, assuming she hadn't already killed her, she

wouldn't be likely to do that in her own house, with her husband and child there. She'd be holding Leila at the fish ranch, where she had a guard who had said there was nothing he wouldn't do for her.

Turning out the lights in the shop, I closed the door and headed for my truck and the fish ranch.

But as I started the engine, I thought of Maxie Dawkins's description of the night guard who had almost killed a man. One more check at Leila's house, I told myself. I would feel like a fool if I raced out to the fish ranch and ran afoul of the guard, only to discover that Leila was home in front of her fire.

By now—seven-twenty on a Saturday night— North Bank Road was too crowded to allow a U-turn. I drove east to the traffic light and waited. The sidewalks were filled with groups of fishermen making the most of their last night before the salmon season. Tomorrow night they would be on their boats, ready to head out into the black Pacific at two A.M.

I turned left, and then left again onto Zeus Lane, and then up through the mud to Leila's house.

I ran through the rain to her door and banged long and hard. But there was no answer. I started to bang again, as if the force of my fist could bring her here to safety. Then, realizing the futility, I stopped.

There was a light on in Hooper's cabin. I ran across the muddy street to his door and pounded. But although the cabin was tiny, I heard no steps toward the door. Hooper wasn't the type to leave the light on and go out. The part-time work at the tobacco shop was his only income, and knowing Edwina, that was no more than minimum wage. In the two years I had been reading his meter, Hooper consistently had the lowest usage on the hill.

"Hooper. It's Vejay Haskell."

Moody as he was, it was more likely that he was inside and didn't want to come to the door. I knocked again.

The door opened. Hooper looked as he had this afternoon. He had on the same worn work clothes. His eyes had that same wary look. From behind him came the smell of wood burning. "Are you still nosing around in Leila's life?" he demanded.

That was the question and the attitude that had forced me off the Pomo rancheria this afternoon. But now I stood firm. "Leila's not home. Do you know where she is?"

He glanced over my shoulder in the direction of her dark house. "Maybe she's at the store."

"The bookstore was closed at four this afternoon."

"Are you sure?" He sounded worried.

"She wasn't there to meet the *Chronicle* reporter."

His eyes widened. It was clear he understood the significance of that.

"And the store door was unlocked. Can I come in? It's pouring out here."

"Yeah, sure. Leila should be home. This isn't a part of town you leave your place dark. If Leila goes somewhere, she tells me. If she's going to be gone overnight, I stay in her place. Her house is a lot better than this." He indicated the room behind him.

It was warm and somewhat smoky inside, the smell of burning wood filling the tiny room. Beside the fireplace was a stuffed chair that could have been the companion piece of a Steelhead Lodge sofa. The floor was covered with pieces of rugs, some remnants, some clearly rejects. They were piled haphazardly one on another so that ends curled upwards at odd places on the floor and every step required thought. An archway led to another room that was divided, half covered with a pile of blankets (similar to the rugs in here) that must have been Hooper's bed, and the other half holding a miniscule kitchen. I saw no sign of a bathroom; there was probably an outhouse out back. Behind him was what appeared to be Hooper's one extravagance—his books. The bookcase ran from floor to ceiling and covered the entire wall. There were clothbound volumes on California law, hardbound and paperback books on gardening, native California plants, and organic vegetables. And on the two top shelves, Hooper must have had every book written on American Indians.

"Leila's got stuff worth stealing in her place. When I stay over there I figure that if anyone is dumb enough to break in here, they'll be so mad that they'll wake me up slamming things around."

I must have looked surprised, because he went on. "Leila and I are friends. Up here there's no one else. This part of the hill, it's all little places like this. Most of the people live in them because they can't get it together to pay for anything better. Me, I choose not to. There's a difference."

I nodded.

"But Leila, if she says she'll bring you something from the grocery, you can warm your oven. If she borrows a book, she returns it and the binding isn't broken. With the rest of these people, I'd never think of lending one of my books." He laughed. "Of course, it's not like they read. When you're that zonked out, a label on a can of chili is like *War and Peace*."

This part of Zeus Lane was well known in the PG&E office. It got more fourteen-day notices, three-day notices, and shut-offs than any other part of town. And there was barely an account that hadn't merited an "R" in the changes column for tampering.

"Could Leila have decided to spend the night with a lover?" I asked.

Hooper's face shifted into that ominous blankness. I glanced down at his stocky, muscular body. How sure was I that it wasn't he who'd killed Edwina? I really didn't know anything about him. He had come through town one or two summers, years back. Then four years ago he had turned up again. I didn't know from where. I didn't even know for sure he was a Pomo. I, and everyone else, had only his word for that.

He took a breath and motioned me toward the one chair. I sat on the edge. The fire warmed my right side. Squatting on the rug pieces, he said, "Leila doesn't have a lover now."

"Are you sure? Could she have met someone new?"

"Anything could be. But it would have to have been since Thursday night, because she spent that evening here complaining about how long it had been since she'd been with anyone."

"How about the old lover from the past? Would she have gone off with him or her, for any reason?"

His eyes tightened. "Listen, I told you—"

The heat of the fire made my scalp feel gummier than ever under the wool cap. Exasperated, I leaned forward. "Hooper, look at me. Do I look like a woman who's been sitting around sipping sherry all afternoon and pondering people's love lives? Leila's my friend, too. I'm worried about her. There's already been one woman killed in Henderson this weekend."

He hesitated.

"Tell me about that affair Leila had in high school."

"I don't know."

"Come on, Hooper. Leila's in danger."

"No, really, I don't know about it. I asked Leila, just like you're asking me. And I was just as angry when she didn't tell me. After all, Leila told me about all her affairs. We sat around a lot of nights and talked about life. Then, all of a sudden, she's got this big secret that's too special for her to divulge." He pushed himself up and began to pace, placing each foot carefully on the pile of rug scraps.

I believed him. But that didn't make the prognosis for Leila any more hopeful. "If she didn't tell you, who would she have told?"

"No one. Leila's learned not to trust people, even lovers, maybe especially lovers."

"Because of that high school affair?"

He nodded. "I had the feeling that that set the tone for her love life since. Pity."

"When she talked about it," I said slowly, "did you have the feeling that the lover was someone older?"

"Maybe. I don't know if older was it. But the lover was someone who knew a lot more than she did, someone who showed her something she hadn't seen before."

"Man or woman?"

"Don't know. She was real careful not to say. It was one of the things that got to me then."

I sighed. I had been hoping for some bit of information, however small, to lead me away from the fish ranch. "You know, Hooper, this isn't much help."

He glared. "What do you expect me to do? I can't make her have told me things she didn't." He moved to the window in back, stepping carefully through the pile of blankets. There was no spot on the entire floor of his place where he could put a foot without thinking about it first. It made his pacing more deliberate and controlled.

He might have told me everything Leila confided to him. Even if he hadn't, there was nothing more to ask about her. I stood up. "Hooper," I said, "when you were here years ago, Edwina paid your family's PG and E deposit. Why did she do that? Charity?"

"Charity!" he exclaimed, "Is that what you think? Is that what the people of Henderson, the *white* people of Henderson, think, that Edwina out of the goodness of her heart took pity on three indigent Indians?"

I said nothing.

"She didn't *give* us the money for that deposit. She bought a basket cup, for the price of our deposit. Do you know how much a double coil Pomo basket cup was worth even then? We Pomos were known for our baskets. The coiled baskets were woven so tight they could hold boiling water without leaking. Edwina didn't do us any favor, she took advantage of our poverty." He walked to the front window and back. His face softened. "Edwina felt bad about that, though. She never let on—Edwina never admitted she was wrong. But it's why she hired me at the store. And when she got ready to announce the treaty, she rearranged the museum and moved that basket cup to a special stand. That's what she was doing yesterday afternoon, right before she left to go over to the lodge and nudge Bert along." He swallowed. "She was so excited. She dropped the basket twice."

"But she certainly wasn't happy when she got to the Slugfest. She looked awful then."

Hooper nodded. "I couldn't even catch her eye."

"What happened in those two hours?"

He leaned against the bookcase. "I don't know. Edwina went over to the lodge. And by the time she came back, I only had a moment to tell her that her visitor was there, and then I caught a ride to the lodge to help Bert."

Edwina's visitor! Harry Bramwell! I'd forgotten all about him. He'd expected me at his room an hour ago! "Hooper," I asked "did Edwina say anything when you told her he was there?"

He shook his head.

"She knew he was coming. He had an appointment. Did she seem pleased?"

"Pleased? No, that's not it. She seemed excited—nervous-excited. She was holding the basket cup when I told her Harry Truman Bramwell was there. She dropped it."

"Did she know him?" That wasn't the impression I had gotten from him.

"Just by name, and reputation. I've heard enough of Edwina's lectures. Even I recognize his name. It's not one you'd forget. He's pretty well known in the field of Native American history."

I drove down Zeus Lane, slamming on the brakes at North Bank Road. Traffic was heavy, even for Saturday night. I turned right and drove the eighth of a mile to Genelle's Family Cabins. The blue Volvo was parked in front of a cabin at the back. I felt rather like Edwina had—nervous-excited—but mostly apprehensive. I was tempted to check in the rearview mirror, to see how I could touch up my appearance, but I knew it would be a mistake. After an entire day under a wool cap, my hair would not only be greasy, it would be pressed into odd curlicues. Letting it down now would only change my appearance from unappealing to ridiculous. I jumped down from the cab and ran across to Harry Bramwell's door and knocked.

Harry Bramwell opened the door. Behind his rimless glasses his dark blue eyes widened in a double-take. He was dressed as he had been when I first saw him in Edwina Henderson's driveway, in a brown herringbone jacket and a black turtleneck. He was dressed for dinner.

"Apparently, I had in mind something more formal than you did," he said.

"I can't go. I'm sorry. I just stopped by to tell you that."

He lifted an eyebrow.

"I'm not as flaky as this looks. I really wanted to have dinner with you. I just can't."

"You could have let me know earlier, instead of leaving that note about being here at seven."

"I planned to come. I really thought I could get ready by then. Look, I'm really sorry. But when I left the note I was on my way to the sheriff's department."

The eyebrow lifted again.

"When I got to the sheriff's department I found out they had arrested one of my friends for murder. And now another woman in town is missing."

"One person was murdered, one's in jail, and another's missing? Some town you've got here!"

"I know it sounds crazy. Right now you're probably thinking that you had a narrow escape from having to spend the evening with a lunatic." The water was dripping off the porch roof onto my back.

"It wouldn't have been dull." He smiled—a noncommittal smile.

"If you get up here another weekend . . . I'm not like this when things are normal. But this is a small town, and when a woman is murdered here, it preempts everything."

He nodded. "Well, either you're telling the truth, or you're loony enough to have been a judge at that Slugfest of yours." He stepped back, then he smiled. His beard wriggled. Anxious as I was, I almost laughed. And I wondered how many coeds (if Harry Bramwell was indeed a professor) had been charmed by that odd little twitch. He put a hand on my wet shoulder. "Come on in and tell me what you've been doing."

I stepped in, feeling the welcome warmth after the rainy night outside. There was a sweet, rather homey smell to the room. It took me a moment to place it—witch hazel. The cabin was almost as large as Hooper's entire house, with a double bed and a single bed, two chairs, and a coffee table. The walls were pale blue, the carpet tweedy blue, and the bedspreads a dark blue flowered print. On the table was a vase of daffodils—Genelle's special touch. Taking off my slicker, I sat in one of the chairs. "Let me ask you one thing first. When you saw Edwina Henderson yesterday, was it about the Pomo treaty?"

"Right." He took off his jacket, laid it on the single bed, and sat in the other chair. "It was one of the best works I've seen."

"The treaty?"

"I get a lot of calls about documents of that sort. I did my dissertation on the litigious relations of the Hoopas and the State of California. While I was involved in that, I studied a number of other Native American treaties, and the court briefs that followed. Now when someone has a question I'm the one they call."

"You sound important."

"You're not just buttering me up now?" He grinned; his curly beard quivered infinitesimally.

" 'Fraid not. Hooper, the guy who works for Edwina, recognized your name. He said anyone who had heard her lectures would. So, if you're famous here in Henderson, you must be a star in the larger world."

His grin grew larger. "I'm an expert in a rather

small field. There's not much cause for people to question treaties anymore. Most of them have been tested in court well before now. And new treaties don't just pop up."

"Except in the case of Edwina's."

He laughed, then looked embarrassed. "I shouldn't laugh. She was so appalled. I don't even think I've seen historians that abashed, and their careers depend on their work."

"What do you mean?"

"Didn't she admit it?"

"She didn't say anything. She's dead."

"What? Do you mean Edwina Henderson was the woman who was murdered?" He jerked forward in his chair. He must have been the only person in Henderson not to know about Edwina's murder.

I told him what had happened. I answered his questions. Then, I said, "What was it Edwina didn't say?"

"I suppose this could be important," he said. "The treaty, it's a beautiful job, one of the best I've seen. But it's a phony."

"Are you sure?" I asked, amazed.

He nodded slowly. "No question. I've spent years in the field. I would have loved to be in on the discovery of a new treaty, to go through the setting up of a rancheria firsthand. I can't tell you how fascinating that would have been, to say nothing about what it would have done for my career—papers to write, lectures, consulting, a full professorship. I wanted it to be real, but it wasn't."

"How do you know?" I insisted.

"Specifically? Well, the paper wasn't quite right. It was close. If *you* looked at it you'd never know the difference, even if you had a real treaty from the same period right next to it. Forgers are pretty sophisticated about aging paper, but it would have taken a real craftsman to manage this. The thing that tipped me off, though—it's a classic failure with forgers like this—was that he preserved everything that would make the treaty appear to be legitimate, but he put age marks over the things he couldn't be sure of copying right, like the chief's mark. He probably couldn't find a copy of it. So far as I know, none exists for many of the village Pomo chiefs. But the forger couldn't be sure, so that's the place that has a brittle age hole in it. You see?"

I nodded. "Are you positive about this?"

"No question. I'm the authority. If the newspapers need an opinion, I'm the one they call. That's probably how Edwina Henderson knew my name."

"Did she believe you?"

"She didn't want to. But she had a good background in local history. When I pointed out the flaws in the document, she understood."

"What did she say?"

"She said she guessed I had to be right."

"Was that all?"

"Pretty much. Then she just went on about the television cameras. It seems she planned to make an announcement of the treaty at some function that night."

"The Slugfest."

"The one you were telling me about Friday?" He raised the eyebrow. "Well, it would have made an interesting juxtaposition."

"Didn't she say anything else? Like something about how the treaty could have been a phony? Or who could have made it? Or why?"

"I asked her, before I looked at the treaty, how she came to have it. She said she had a niece in Washington, or maybe Virginia, I don't remember. In any case, she worked for a senator, maybe in connection with a consulting firm. But the story Edwina got was that she had to check something in the senate files and came across the treaty."

"And didn't mention it to anyone but Edwina?" That was what Hooper had told me.

He nodded. "Even as she said it, it sounded peculiar, but I was so anxious to see the treaty that I didn't ask about it then. And afterwards, since the thing was a phony anyway, it didn't matter."

"But it does matter. Edwina's dead. She was poisoned before she could announce the treaty."

"No. She was poisoned before she could *de*nounce the treaty. The one thing she did tell me was that she would have to go before the television cameras and explain that she had been boonswaggled—her word."

"Edwina was going to tell them that the treaty was a phony," I said, mulling over the thought. "Was she going to say who the perpetrator was?"

"I think so. She seemed to know."

"Who was it?" I held my breath.

"She didn't tell me. By that time I'm not sure she even remembered I was there. She was pretty much muttering to herself. She was carrying on about not being surprised, that she shouldn't have been surprised, that she had no one but herself to blame, and that at least she'd had the sense to check, so it wasn't any worse than it was, but that she should have known. It went on like that."

"Did she say anything else," I asked, barely able to conceal my disappointment. "Even something that didn't seem important to you? Maybe something that you didn't connect with the treaty?"

He ran his fingers down his beard. Outside, a car drove by, then stopped several cabins down. Harry Truman Bramwell continued to stroke his beard. "The only other thing I can recall is Edwina Henderson snorting"—he snorted in imitation—"and muttering, 'And Lyle protecting her!' "

CHAPTER

18

"And Lyle protecting her!" Of course that was Harry Bramwell's interpretation of Edwina's lament. What she really had said was, "And *Leil* protecting her!" So, again, it all came back to Leila. And to the person—the woman—who was responsible for the phony treaty. There might have been many women who could have come up with a fake treaty, but only one, besides Leila, who could have sprinkled the poison on Edwina's pizza. Only one whom Leila was in the habit of protecting. And Angelina, Leila's former babysitter, might have met Meg through Leila, or, failing that, found out enough about her from Leila to impersonate her in letters to Edwina. Maybe she even knew Meg well enough to convince her to help out in the scheme herself.

So I had been right about Angelina all along. "I have to go," I said to Harry Bramwell. I jumped up, raced to the door, and stepped out onto his stoop.

"What?" He followed me to the door.

"Time is vital. I can't stay. I'll explain later."

"Don't bother," he said in disgust. "Do you think I have nothing to do but hang around? Like you said, there may not be much to do here at night. But there have to be better things than waiting for you."

"I—"

"Forget it." He slammed the door.

I wasn't even tempted to knock again. Harry Bramwell was the most interesting man I had met in months. But I'd blown whatever chance there was, and in high style.

I didn't have time to hang around and mope. I ran to my truck and started the engine. As sorry as I was about losing Harry Bramwell as a potential lover, I was almost more frustrated at not having anyone to tell about his key discovery.

I drove the truck over the gravel to North Bank Road and waited for a chance to turn right, toward the ocean, and the fish ranch. In the rain, the traffic moved slowly. I could see a logging truck at the head of the line, moving like a Slugfest contestant.

In my excitement, I had almost forgotten my fear that Leila was in danger. I had lulled myself into thinking that Angelina was her friend. But for someone who had gone to the trouble of obtaining a phony treaty, of stringing Edwina along as Hooper had said, and then killing her, friendship wasn't likely to be a deterrent to another murder. Cutting off a sportscar, I pulled onto North Bank Road.

I drove with my hand poised on the horn, hitting it at each straight stretch of road. The rain slapped the windshield. I turned the wipers on high, and blew the horn again as we came to a straightaway. I pulled around the car in front, and the truck in front of that, and back into line as we came to the next curve. The overhanging redwoods and laurels made the road darker. I passed another car, and two more, and finally the logging truck itself, then hit the gas and raced ahead.

The wind gusted stronger as I neared the ocean. I clutched the wheel tighter. Even with the wipers on high, the rain curtained the view half the time. The occasional passing car seemed to come out of nowhere, hit me with its blinding lights, and be pulled back into darkness.

As I neared the fish ranch bridge, I shivered. In this

storm, the isolated fish ranch was the perfect place to imprison Leila Katz.

Looking across the bridge, I could make out a light in the gatehouse. I followed the road another quarter of a mile into Jenner and pulled into the first street that led to the houses on the hillside. I parked next to a clump of juniper, got out, and made my way back down to the main road. At the foot of the hill were a couple of bars. Should anyone pass me, they would assume I was headed there. After that, there was nothing before the fish ranch.

At the fish ranch bridge, I paused. The only things on this side of the river were tall grass and one utility pole. There weren't even trees this close to the ocean. Across the narrow, forty-foot bridge was the drive to the gatehouse, the ditch, and the hurricane fence that ran around three sides of the compound. On the fourth side of the compound was the water. Even in the dark, I could make out the dock that led out into the inlet and the water hitting against the building.

I could still go back. In all likelihood, the electricity had come on in my house. I could take a shower, make myself presentable, and call Harry Bramwell and try to explain. If I hadn't been so frightened, I would have laughed.

Crouching next to the railing, I ran across the bridge, then kept behind the hedge of pampas grass till I was nearly to the gate. The ocean wind blew strong here in the open. The tall strawlike stalks of grass bent back away from the water, slashing wildly in the wind. Bending low, I kept on the far side of them till I was nearly to the gatehouse.

The gatehouse was a six-foot-square building. The guard could keep an eye on the entry road through a window in the upper half of the Dutch door. Each of the other three walls had one window. The light was on, but from this angle I couldn't see the guard inside. There was nothing to do but spring up and look. If the guard spotted me . . . I didn't want to think what this violent man, penned up night after night, waiting for interlopers who never came, would do if he caught the one interloper Maxie Dawkins had told him to watch out for. "Just waiting to smash ass," Maxie had said of him.

Still partially screened by the pampas grass, I sprung up, looked, and dropped back down to all fours. The guard fit Maxie Dawkins's description of him. He was big, and thick. Everything about him was thick: his neck, his shoulders, his arms, his chest, even his nose. He looked like a man who would enjoy smashing the woman who had called Angelina a lesbian.

Protected by the noise of the wind and rain, I might be able to crawl right next to the building, under the windows. And hope the guard didn't decide to look down. The gate was open. Why? Did such an ominous guard feel no need to keep the gate locked? Or was there a more practical reason for its being open—someone coming in, or being taken out?

If I could make it past, the wooden backing of the gate would hide me from the guard. Then there would only be those intestine-like cement ditches between me and the building itself.

Bunching up the front of my slicker, I crawled forward, listening with each move, hoping that the wind would cover any sounds I made but not muffle those of the guard. I edged up to the building, my right shoulder nearly touching its side. The sandy ground squished under my hands; my jeans were soaked from the rain. My mouth was so dry I couldn't swallow. The light from the windows shone down on the road beside me. I wanted to push up off my knees, to race forward, but I forced myself to keep down, to move slowly, to listen. I passed under the door and

came to the edge of the gatehouse. The gate was two
yards ahead—two yards with no cover. If he looked,
the guard couldn't miss me no matter how low I
kept. I pushed off my knees and raced, crablike,
around the gate.

My heart pounded under the plastic of my slicker.
The rain smacked my face; my sopping cap clung to
my head, and under it my hair was becoming wet.
The briny smell of the ocean filled the air. There was
no sound from the gatehouse. Squatting, I leaned
back against the gate. The fish ranch building was
thirty feet away, with its door on the far side. The
rain shrouded the lights, but I could make out the
rosebushes next to the building and those looping
cement ditches, waiting, empty, for the salmon fry.

Behind me, the wooden covering of the gate extended up four feet. It would cover me for maybe
two yards, if I kept low. Beyond that, I was back to
luck. But now I had no choice. Dropping my hands
to the ground, I raced forward and flung myself into
the ditch.

The ditch was three feet deep, its bottom rough
cement. Lying flat out, I inched toward the building.
The wind slapped wet against my face. Looking back
at the light in the gatehouse, I took a breath, pushed
myself up, and raced behind the partial cover of the
naked rosebushes.

The door to the gatehouse opened.

I didn't wait to see where the guard was headed. I
ran behind the flower beds and around the corner of
the building to the water. Behind me, through the
whipping of the wind, came a thud—the guard leaping heavily across the ditch. I spun around. He was
huge. He could break my arms, ribs, back, neck. He
could leave me a mass of pulp in the ditch.

There was nothing to do but take my chances with
the ocean. Even if it was twenty feet deep, my odds

were better there than with the guard. Grabbing the side of the dock, I swung under it. My feet struck hard against the bottom. The storm-driven waves crashed in from the sides. Momentarily I saw the guard's feet on the rocks. I let the waves push me under the center of the dock. The water smashed against me on both sides; it struck the aluminum building and slapped back into my face. It swept my cap off. I tried to get a foothold, failed, and sat heavily, my head dragged down under the swirling water. Salt water shot up my nose. I slammed my feet down into the sand and pushed up. My head hit the dock hard, but my feet held. I gasped for breath, then braced my hands against the dock above me and listened. But the crashing of the waves blocked out any other noises. I saw the flashlight beam pass over the water.

Was the guard certain someone had gotten into the complex? Or was he just checking? Had he seen me behind the rose bushes, or had the darkness shielded me? Or had I left footprints in the rose beds? If the guard spotted one, he surely wouldn't stop till he found me, no matter how well hidden I was. The unlikeliness of my hiding place would only mean it would take him longer to discover me, and he'd be in a rage by the time he did. If I hadn't drowned first.

I pressed my hands harder against the dock, and waited. The flashlight beam shone on the other side of the dock and disappeared. The waves tossed the water up against my neck. I shivered. The water pulled at my boots. Still, I waited.

I tried to count, to change the unmoving time into minutes, but the waves kept knocking me to the side and I never got beyond twenty. After what seemed like hours, but was probably no more than ten minutes, with no sight or sound of the guard, I pulled my feet loose, trudged to the far side of the dock, and, grabbing thankfully at the edge, raised myself up.

The guard was nowhere to be seen. I flung myself at the rocky bank next to the building, crawled up, and lay back against the aluminum wall. My sopping clothes clung icily to my body. I shivered violently. Vainly I tried to listen for alien movements through the whirling of the wind and the crashing of the waves.

Bracing against the building, I stood up and moved to the corner. Ahead of me was darkness. I forced myself to survey the area—the side of the building, the rose bed, the looping ditches, the shed with the auxiliary generator beyond, and a veritable mountain of large crates piled against the fence beside it. But nothing moved; no guard.

There were also no windows in the building.

"Damn!" I muttered aloud. I knew that. I had been in here often enough to read the meter. How many times had Maxie Dawkins led me to the meter, complaining all the while about the skylights that had to be scrubbed clean monthly, grumbling that Angelina Rudd insisted on having them for natural light. "She would have had a convertible dome if she could," he'd insisted. Now, I remembered all too clearly: the building had a slew of skylights, but not one window!

The wind blew my slicker tight around my legs. The rain splattered on my shoulders and hit hard against my back. Water from my soaking sweater and jeans ran down my body. I tried the doorknob— locked. There was no way in but through the skylights. Climbing up on the roof in this weather, with that guard nearby, was the last thing I wanted to do. But it was the only thing to do. I couldn't even use the excuse of not knowing where they kept the ladder. I had seen Maxie put it away the last time I read the meter.

With a sigh, I glanced around at the dark yard. There was nothing to keep me from walking beside the ditch, leaping the curve at the end and taking a few steps to the rear fence, and picking up the ladder that lay against it. Once I had it, I could only hope that the guard didn't check the grounds again.

I hurried to the shed. This little building, the one I *didn't* need to get into, did have windows, and a light on inside. Standing on its protected side, I glanced in. Despite the rain veiling the window, I could make out gardening supplies on the shelf. The nicotine wasn't even hidden! It stood innocently in a half-pint bottle next to a bag of snail pellets. But Maxie Dawkins's bottle of Estrin was gone. And the ladder, too long to fit inside, leaned against the fence.

Picking it up, I headed back across the open space. It was aluminum—light—but the wind seesawed its ten-foot length back and forth, and when I jumped down into the ditch, I had to hold on with all my strength to keep it from banging to the ground. Reaching the side of the building, I leaned it against the roof, with a bang. I froze, trying to make out the sound of footsteps above the noise of the rain and wind. But I could hear nothing.

I pushed the ends of the ladder hard into the muddy rose bed, hoping they would hold against the wind. My balance was good from my two years of standing tiptoe on the edge of walkways, looking up to read the five dials of the meter. But if the wind knocked the ladder over, balance wouldn't help. I would land flat on my back, with the ladder on top of me and the guard glaring down. I pushed harder. Climbing to the first step, I bounced on it, jamming the feet into the ground. It still didn't feel sturdy, but it would have to do.

I moved up to the second step. The ladder shim-
mied, but held. The wind caught my slicker, flapping
it forward against the ladder. I climbed on, pausing
with each step, listening. But there was only the sear-
ing of the wind and the taste of salt in my mouth.

The roof was peaked, but the slant gentle. I pulled
myself up and over the edge. The prefab roof was
smooth. My knees slipped and banged into the gutter; pain shot down my shins. I turned, braced my
feet against the gutter, and reached for the nearest
skylight. The roof was full of skylights. There were
five rows of four each. They took up at least half of
the roof space. Surely, it wasn't too much to hope
that one of the twenty would have a faulty latch.
Every skylight I knew of had some problem. Why
should Angelina's be the exception? I reached for the
latch on the one next to me.

Brakes squealed.

I peered over the peak of the roof. There were
headlights at the gate.

There was no time to get down off the roof. With
my feet braced against the gutter, I grabbed the top
of the ladder and pulled. The uprights banged
against the edge of the building. I moved my hands
down the slippery metal. It banged again. I froze,
listening for the slamming of doors, the slapping of
running feet. I could hear nothing through the whirl
of the wind, but that didn't mean that nothing was
happening. I could still picture the guard as he'd
been, standing by the ditch. Taking a breath, I lowered my hands, pulled again, and on the fourth pull, I
turned the ladder on its side and yanked it up over
the edge of the roof and lay it against the gutter.

Crawling to the peak of the roof, I peered over.
The vehicle at the gate looked like a pickup, from the
height of the headlights. I waited, hoping it would
make a turn and leave. The wind blew my hair into

my eyes and mouth. The rain beat my back. My feet, wedged against the edges of two skylights, cramped. I pressed them hard against the skylights and willed myself to outlast the cramps. Then the truck started up and crossed the parking area.

I flattened myself against the roof. Below, I could hear the truck coming around to the side of the building. I pressed closer to the roof. The brakes squealed again. A door opened. I listened for voices, but I could hear only the wind slapping the aluminum building and flicking the edge of my slicker. Stiffening my legs, I let go with one hand, grabbed the hem of the slicker, and held it down.

The truck door slammed shut. I held my breath. From the ground came paired thumps. Footsteps? Was the driver coming to investigate the holes where I had pushed the ladder into the ground?

I pressed harder into the roof; strained to make out voices; failed. Footsteps thudded again. Closer? Farther? I couldn't tell. The truck door opened and slammed. The engine started. The truck pulled away. I held my breath, waiting for it to stop, for the driver to change his mind.

But it didn't. I pulled myself up to see over the peak and watched as the truck drove out the gate.

Had the driver not noticed the holes, or was he going to get help?

I didn't have time to consider that. I checked the latch of the nearest skylight. It held firm. The one next to it was no more promising. I must have tried seven or eight before I found a broken latch. It was in one of the side rows, probably ten feet above floor level. If I lowered myself over the edge, and hung on, the drop shouldn't be more than four feet. I pulled the window back, laying it against the roof. I looked down. The interior of the building was black. It might be warm and quiet down there—safe, relatively speaking. Or it might hold the guard. But I couldn't stay up here.

Clinging with both hands, I lowered one foot over the edge, then dropped the other, just as the wind gusted. The skylight cover bounced. The hinges creaked. It slammed on my fingers.

I let go and fell.

CHAPTER
19

My feet struck cement. I sat down hard on the floor. My hands hit a split second too late to break my fall, but soon enough to push my wrists back the wrong way and send stabs of pain through my fingers. The room was black. It reeked of fish and chemicals. I stayed as I was, listening for the heavy, angry breath of the night guard.

Lights flashed from the ceiling. The brightness blinded me. And when my eyes finally focused, I could make out Angelina Rudd by the door. She was alone, and she was holding the biggest pistol I had ever seen.

"Get up," she demanded.

"I can't." Pressing on my wrists sent another wave of pain into my fingers.

"Get up."

I looked behind her at the door, expecting the guard to burst in, but the door stayed shut. Thrusting my weight forward onto my feet, I swung up.

"Over here." She pointed the pistol toward the office door. Despite the size of the gun, she held it steady. She had big hands, muscular for a woman.

I moved into the office. It was a six-foot-square room—without windows, of course—in the southwest corner of the building. Next to it, in the middle, were the double doors to the dock. On the far side was a door to another tiny room, probably the lab.

The tiny office was barely big enough for a metal desk, chair, and a two-drawer file cabinet. All were gray. There was nothing on the desk but a phone at the far corner—no papers, no pens, no photo of spouse and child. The wall above held a bulletin board with schedules tacked on. I propped myself against the file cabinet.

Where was the night guard? Why was it Angelina who was here, pointing a gun at me? Why did she have a vicious guard, if she didn't use him to trap interlopers? Why, unless she couldn't afford to let him in the building, because she was holding a captive—Leila—here?

Angelina looked like I felt. Her hair hung in wild, knotted clumps. There were dark circles under her eyes. And her naturally olive complexion looked khaki green. Her jeans and jacket were wet. When she leaned back against the office doorway—blocking any chance I had of making a run for it—she seemed to need the support of the wall.

But there was no note of weariness or weakness in her voice, or in the hand that held the gun. "Just what are you doing in here?"

I shivered violently in my soaking clothes. Pushing my wet hair off my face, I stared past her into the main room. There should have been wall-to-wall fish vats with water gurgling through them, maybe a bench in the middle loaded with supplies. I had expected to find Leila Katz tied up between them. But there was none of that; no vats, no fish, no Leila. There was nothing. The room was entirely empty! Only the smell of fish and chemicals remained. If Leila was being held here, she was either in the lab or behind the doors that led to the dock, ready to be dragged to a boat and dumped out in the ocean.

Angelina could easily shoot me now. Deep-sixing two bodies wouldn't be much harder than one. But if she did plan to shoot me, tempering my questions wouldn't save me. "Where are the fish?"

"Be quiet!" she snapped.

"This place is supposed to be filled with tiny fish. Where are they?"

She tightened her grip on the gun. The veins in her hand stood out. Her teeth pressed together; she was thinking, deciding. I held my breath. Finally she said, "They were diseased. I had to dispose of them."

I sighed, then asked, "Nicotine poisoning?" It was a long shot.

"What? I don't use nicotine on the fish." She looked at me like I had suggested she fed it to her son. "They had IHN—Infectious Hematopoietic Necrosis. Once they've got it there's no way to save them. You have to dispose of them. Then all you can do is disinfect and be more careful the next time."

Knowing how hard Angelina had worked, I could see why having lost her entire crop of salmon would put her in this state. Still, I didn't believe that was the cause. If the salmon had been lost due to unavoidable circumstances, she would have been discouraged; if they had to be destroyed because she hadn't taken the proper precautions, her job would have been in jeopardy and she would have been frightened. But she was neither; she was angry and frustrated. There had to be something else going on here. Taking advantage of Angelina's turmoil, I said, "You were Leila Katz's lover, weren't you?"

Her eyes widened.

"When she was in high school, right?"

She laughed—the forced laugh of someone for whom humor is not familiar. Her eyes remained tired and hard. Again, her hand tightened on the pistol. "Just what are you doing here?" she demanded.

If she were going to call the sheriff, she would have done it by now. Whatever happened would be between us here. That meant that the stakes were higher, a lot higher, but maybe that my chances were better. I said, "Leila is missing. And Chris Fortimiglio has been arrested for Edwina's murder."

Her whole body seemed to tighten, but I couldn't tell whether the reaction was surprise or fear, whether she was alarmed at Leila's disappearance or my discovery of it, or Chris's having been arrested.

In the main room, a skylight banged against its frame.

"Why Chris?" she asked.

"Edwina found a treaty from the eighteen-fifties giving the Pomo Indians a rancheria. It extended across the river."

Her long narrow face scrunched in from the sides. It was clear that she understood the implications Chris had explained to me. She nodded slowly, deliberately, as if checking off the various effects of the treaty.

I said, "He told me it could endanger the entire fleet."

The skylight banged. She barely reacted. She looked like she was trying to restrain her urgency. But something, some intention I couldn't make out, or perhaps pent-up anger, pushed her on. "Maybe that's what that fleet needs," she said bitterly. "Cowboys, these men riding out to sea in their little boats. Half of those boats are so old they shouldn't be floating around the inlet, much less out at sea where the waves can be fifteen, twenty feet high, coming three directions at once, and the weather can change from sun to fog so fast you can't even check which direction shore is."

I wanted to keep her talking, not considering the advantages of disposing of Leila and me together. "They take care of their boats. I've seen them at the docks."

"They do what they can. But they can only do so much. They can't make fifty-year-old planks new.

They can't stretch a twenty-six-foot Monterey into forty feet. And nothing they do will change the fact that every year one or two, and some years eight or ten fishermen, will be washed overboard. Do you know what happens then?" She glared at me. The gun rested in her rigid fingers.

"They drown?" Could I surprise her and knock that gun out of those stiff fingers?

"Oh, a few are saved," she went on, "if they happen to be lucky enough to be fishing near a friend, or sensible enough to keep their radios going. A few. Most of them drown. But they don't just fall into the water and die and have the waves carry their bodies to shore. Sometimes it's weeks before their bodies are found. They wash up miles down the shore."

The gun barrel had dropped a little; it pointed at my stomach. "Is that what happened to your father?"

"Oh, no. His body didn't wash in at Bodega Bay or Point Reyes. We waited, my mother and I. At first we hoped he'd been picked up by some boat heading north or south, that we'd hear from him any moment. Then, slowly, we realized that we wouldn't hear at all. Then we waited, dreading the time when we'd get a call to come look at some body so bloated that we wouldn't be able to say for sure it was him."

At the far side of the desk, the phone was out of reach. I had seen the cord lying behind it—it would reach across the room. "And?" I said.

"Even that didn't happen. His body never turned up. A lot of bodies don't. The currents sweep them out to sea. Maybe they sink to bottom. Maybe the crabs eat them." She shivered in the unheated room. "We'll never know what happened to him. But I'll tell you what it did to us. He was a fisherman— macho. He didn't want his wife working. My mother had never worked. And when he died, we didn't have

any money. We didn't have any boat. All we had was
the bank wanting their money for the payment on
the house and the truck."

"Didn't he have insurance?"

She laughed, bitterly. "Without a body the insurance company doesn't have to admit he's dead. And
they don't. They don't pay a cent until seven years go
by and you can get a court to declare him legally
dead. By that time, the house was gone, and it had
been so long since we'd had a truck that we'd forgotten what it was to leave town."

I shifted nearer the phone. My water-logged
sweater hung heavy on my shoulders. The smell of
wet wool battled the stench of fish and chemicals.

"And you think I was spending those years screw-
ing around with little Leila Katz?" she said.

"You were her babysitter."

"She was a child, for Christ's sake."

"She trusted you then. She trusted you later."

"I never touched her." Her face was red.

"You were just home for the summer then, a college student, full of new ideas, exciting experiences."

Angelina laughed. The gun shook. "So you assume
I went off to seduce women at San Francisco State or
U.C.L.A.? Off to the wild life? I'll tell you where I
went when I got out of high school. I'll tell you how
much I hated the macho way this town was, how
much I hated my life here. I went to a convent."

"A convent!"

For the first time, she gave me a smile with a flicker
of pleasure in it, as if she was comforted by the fact
that I could see the ludicrousness of that move. "I
stayed two years. Long enough to get college credits
to transfer to Sonoma State. Long enough to try for
loans and scholarships, and plenty long enough to
see that I'd jumped from one form of slavery to another. But don't misunderstand me, when I went

there I was sure I'd be in that convent till I died." She adjusted her grip on the gun. "And when I got out of there, I worked like the devil to prepare myself for something like this, this fish ranch."

I shifted my feet again. The phone was still out of reach. "So," I said, "if the Pomos were to string gill-nets across the river and trap every steelhead and salmon in the Russian River, it wouldn't bother you?"

She shrugged. "Hardly. They can catch everything that moves upstream."

"What about government control of the fish in the ocean?"

"You're thinking of the Boldt Decision?"

I nodded.

"If that happens, I'll have records of how many smolts I sent down my chute. If I had to go to court, I'd get my share."

I stood, then sat back full against the desk. One more move and I'd be able to reach the phone. "Still, it's hardly advantageous to have your fish caught by someone else, even by the fleet."

She sighed, the sigh of a businesswoman at the end of a long, fruitless meeting. "There'll be plenty of fish to go around. If every smolt I send out were to come back up my chute, this building wouldn't be able to hold them."

I hadn't believed her when she told me about the disease of the fish fry, but I couldn't zero in on why. I stared past her into the empty room. "You start with the fertilized eggs, right?"

"We fertilize them here."

"Then where do they go?"

"In trough incubators."

"How big are those incubators?"

"About four foot square. Look, why are—"

"Well, where are those incubators? You just

flushed all your fish fry and suddenly you don't have any equipment either? Where are they?"

Her hand tightened on the gun. "Outside." But her voice had lost its authority.

"Outside?" The pile of crates by the fence. "Why would you take them outside?"

"To disinfect them."

"With the river this high? Come on, you couldn't find more germs and bacteria and just plain mud than you'll get if it washes up here."

From the distance came a whine.

"What are you using this place for?" I demanded. "What have you emptied it out for?"

The whine outside was louder, clearer—a sheriff's car. I had worried about the guard. No wonder he wasn't here. I'd thought *I* was keeping Angelina talking. I wasn't making her talk; she was holding me for the sheriff. Lunging to my right, I grabbed the phone and slammed it down on the gun. Angelina screamed. The gun hit the floor. It didn't go off.

She grabbed her hand in pain. I fell to my knees and scooped up the gun. It was cold, heavy. I put my finger over the trigger, hoping it wouldn't release easily.

"Where's Leila Katz?" I demanded.

"What?"

I didn't have time for that. "Open the lab."

"It's not locked."

I ran past her, past the doors to the dock, and pushed open the lab door. The room was empty.

The siren shrieked, then died. The sheriff's car would be stopped at the gate. I pushed open the doors to the dock. There was nothing behind them.

I ran back to Angelina. "Turn off the electrical system."

She laughed. "You're not going to shoot me. Not with the sheriff right outside."

"You're right. But if you let the sheriff get me, I'll make sure everyone in the Russian River area knows this building is empty. I'll call the *Bodega Bay Sentinel, The Paper,* and the *Russian River News.* I'll tell them your fish died."

She didn't say anything. She didn't have to.

"Come on," I said. "Either you get me over that fence, or when salmon season starts Monday, the fishermen will be laughing so hard they won't be able to get to their boats."

She reached for a switch. The room went dark. I followed her to the outer door and across the yard behind the cluster of overturned incubator boxes. She slapped her hand on the deadened electric wires. I climbed on a box. As I jumped down outside the fence, I could see the sheriff's headlights come around the building.

I took off my yellow slicker and stuffed it up under my sweater. The wind stung my skin. The rain splattered on the soaked wool. But my sweater and jeans were dark. I wouldn't make the same target I'd have in the slicker. The gun was like concrete; I shifted it to my left hand.

The fish ranch complex was surrounded by the electrified fence and a four-foot-deep ditch. Keeping down, I ran along the ditch, behind the fence to the corner that would lead back to the guardhouse. I kept straight on, forcing my wet, cold-tightened legs to push harder, sinking with each step in the sodden ground, racing for the bridge, crossing it, hurrying along the road, no longer at a run, up the hill to Jenner.

It was an even bet whether Angelina had had second thoughts and told the sheriff I had forced her to turn off the power and help me escape.

But the sheriff wasn't at my truck, and once I got inside and started the engine—thankful once more for the snap pockets of my slicker that protected the keys—I realized that the person who had answered the call at the fish ranch was probably a deputy. Even if Angelina had told him who the intruder was, he wouldn't know what my truck looked like. Not yet.

The other thing I realized was that I couldn't go home. Even though I was shivering, every garment I had on was dripping, the cab of the truck reeked with the smell of wet wool, and there was nothing in all of life I would have traded for an hour in the tub, I couldn't go home. If the sheriff was looking for me, that's where he would look.

But spending the night in my truck was out. I couldn't keep the engine idling all night, and in an unheated truck I would have pneumonia by sunrise. Where could I go?

It was not quite ten o'clock—a long time till morning. Could I go to Rosa's house? No, too obvious. Besides, half the town would still be there, including officer Joey Gummo. A motel? Hardly, if I needed anonymity. A friend's? The sheriff knew my close friends, the people I could drop in on soaking wet late on a Saturday night. I shivered. Even though all the windows were closed, drafts of air chilled my skin.

I turned the truck around and headed down the hill, past the fish ranch. Through the rain, I could see the yellow dots of the fence lights, but if the deputy's car was still there, its headlights were off. The road was empty. I pressed harder on the gas and turned right toward the fishing village of Bodega Bay. As I crested the hill, the Pacific wind bounced the truck onto the white line. I yanked the wheel at each curve, waiting for the tires to grab on the slick macadam. The three-building shopping area—more a convenience for fishermen and tourists than a town hangout—was coming up on my right. There was a space in front of the Laundromat. I pulled in.

The Laundromat was empty. Clearly no one else in Bodega Bay had so pressing a need to be either clean or dry that they had been lured out on a cold, stormy night like this. Locking the gun in the glove compartment, I wriggled out of my clothes, and into my slicker, and hurried into the Laundromat, sopping garments in hand.

It was marvelously hot and steamy. The smell of

soap and bleach filled the air. Bursts of laughter and shouting came from the bar next door. Three men—merchant seamen from the looks of them—made their way past the Laundromat to the bar.

I opened the dryer door, jammed my clothes in, and clunked a quarter in the slot. Then, naked under my slicker, I walked to the back of the Laundromat where the candy machine was, bought a Baby Ruth, and sat down.

I had suspected that Angelina was hiding Leila Katz at the fish ranch. But the fish ranch held neither what should have been there—fish—nor what shouldn't have been there—Leila. When I read the meter there Thursday, the fish incubators had not been in the yard. So the fish had been disposed of since then. Could the fish have died, as Angelina insisted?

Outside, two more seamen raced through the rain to the bar.

Maybe the fish had died. I had heard that ranched fish were neither as hardy nor as intelligent as wild fish. There was a tale of ranched fish that were raised for a year or so in cement channels like the ones Angelina had, then turned loose into a river that emptied into the ocean. Instead of swimming to the ocean to mature, the ranched fish had swum upstream, decimating the younger, smaller wild fish that were headed to the ocean. There was a lot of skepticism about fish ranching. If Angelina's fish had succumbed to IHN, every fisherman along the Russian River would be laughing. No wonder Angelina would be angry and frustrated. No wonder she'd toss those useless empty incubators outside. No wonder she'd go to extremes to keep me quiet.

Still, as an explanation for Angelina's decision to help me escape from the sheriff, it seemed weak. But if I didn't accept that, what reason was there for Angelina to toss out fish, stack her equipment in the yard and leave the building empty—and then be panicked when I discovered it?

If I hadn't suspected Angelina of being Leila's lover, would I have found the situation at the fish ranch so odd? Considering her vehement denial of that accusation, could I really be sure she was Leila's lover? What was it Maxie Dawkins had said? "She surprised everyone when she married—don't know why she bothered." Was everyone surprised because she was a lesbian? But if she was, Rosa didn't know about it. And that meant most people didn't know. So that wasn't the reason for surprise. "Don't know why she bothered," Maxie had added. Of course! She was already living with her husband! That had to be it. And that, everyone would have known. Everyone but her boss, the very conservative James Drayton. Had Edwina threatened to tell him? If Angelina had been Leila's lover, perhaps for her it was a collegiate fling, or a rebellion against her years in the convent. But for Leila, the affair would have been the beginning of a new way of life. Then, Angelina's living with a man and her subsequent marriage would have made Edwina all the more outraged.

I put another quarter in the dryer, choosing not to examine my sweater. Skintight and dry had to be better than loose and sopping.

Still, I had no proof Angelina was Bear. If she *wasn't,* then who was? Maybe it was someone who didn't even live in town anymore. Maybe the affair had nothing to do with Edwina's murder.

But even if Edwina's murder had no relation to Leila's lover, I couldn't believe it wasn't connected to the treaty, the fake treaty. Who would go to the trouble of acquiring a fake treaty? And why? Anyone who had been to a historical society lecture knew how enthused Edwina must have been about her "discovery." Anyone familiar with her numerous attempts to call news conferences to present the most minor historical findings wouldn't doubt that she would have gotten television coverage for the announcement of the treaty. She had told the society members that if she ever discovered a treaty she would race off to Sacramento as soon as she had finished the announcement and present her find to the big shots there. Anyone would have known that by the time they declared the treaty false, Edwina would have created enough fanfare to make her humiliation overwhelming.

Who hated Edwina that much? With a warm flow of relief, I realized that one person who could be eliminated was Chris Fortimiglio. He didn't hate Edwina; he merely considered her an irascible eccentric. And as for the treaty, Chris wasn't interested in the historical society or the possibility of treaties. He could have read in the paper about Edwina's plans for the treaty she always dreamed of, but I doubted he had.

That left those who had been to Edwina's lectures —Leila, Curry Cunningham, Bert Lucci, Hooper, and maybe even Father Calloway. But of the five, who hated Edwina enough to contact her niece and convince her to be party to the scam, or to arrange to have phony letters sent from Washington in her name? It was the type of plan that could only be sustained by someone who enjoyed each escalation, who made it a point to be near Edwina and watch each reaction with carefully concealed triumph. Who?

The dryer clunked to a stop. I pulled the door open and grabbed my clothes. The sweater was still damp, but it was also two sizes smaller. One more turn in the dryer and it would have fit only a doll. I carried the clothes back to my truck and wriggled into them.

I reached for the key to start the truck, then hesitated. No one with the possible exception of Leila had a motive for the elaborate deception of the false treaty. No one, except Leila's lover. A desire for revenge would be ample reason. But now I had even less idea who Bear might be than I had had before. Leila was the only one who knew. I felt more certain than ever that she was in danger, but now I had no idea where to look for her.

Suddenly I realized what I needed most right now was a shot of brandy. And for once, in a day when no one had been where I looked for them and nothing had worked out, I was dealing with a need I could fill. I grabbed my purse and headed for the bar next to the Laundromat.

The Seaside Shanty was a shabby rectangular room, with a fish net and a couple of dusty seashells on one wall, a hodgepodge of tables and chairs, and the bar at the other side. As soon as I stepped in, the lay of the land was clear. Tonight's clientele was divided into two groups: fishermen and merchant seamen. I recognized guys from the fishing fleet leaning back precariously on chairs grouped loosely around tables in the rear. Rindo Mercatti, who was as close to what could be taken for a leader of such an independent group, was complaining about the storm outside. "How many days is it going to cut off salmon season?" he demanded of his cohorts. "And do you think Fish and Game is going to say, 'Oh, those hardworking fishermen have missed a week, let us, gentlemen, prolong the season'?" He was greeted by a mixture of laughter and grunts, and a few more personal characterizations of the biologists at the Fish and Game Department.

In front, separated by a bare three-foot strip, were clutches of men, the merchant seamen I had seen

heading in here. There must have been twenty-five of
them. They were bemoaning the rain too.

I made my way past them to the bathroom. Even
through the coating of dust and water spots on the
mirror, it was a shock to see how haggard I looked.
My skin was leaden gray. My hair hung like sea-
weed. I ran a comb through it, but when I moved my
head the clumps glued themselves back together
again. I could have put on eye makeup, but it didn't
seem worth the effort.

Instead, I walked back to the bar and ordered my
brandy.

The mirror behind the bar was almost as crusty as
the one in the bathroom. Reflected in it, the fishermen in their heavy gray sweaters looked rather like a
faded Renoir print.

The bartender slid my brandy toward me. I took a
long swallow, let my eyes close, and felt the warmth
flow down to the bottom of my spine. I had the
whimsical feeling that when I looked back in the mirror, Rindo Mercatti and his buddies would be
painted in bright blues and greens.

What I did see, when I glanced in the mirror, was a
still gray-clad Rindo Mercatti staring at me. A few
times in San Francisco I had made the mistake of
assuming a sixty-year-old man's intentions were pa-
ternal. But I doubted Rindo was considering picking
me up—not on the last night he could spend with his
buddies. He was just trying to remember where he
had seen me. It had been at Rosa's, over a year ago.
Considering how I looked now, I wasn't surprised he
couldn't place me.

I handed the bartender a five, and took another
sip, then finished the drink. Pocketing the change, I
headed back to my truck.

While the engine warmed, I sat back, still savoring
the heat of the brandy and picturing Rindo Mercatti

in a lavender fishing sweater. Maybe he *had* been considering picking me up. In the world of lavender and green he wouldn't have hesitated. An older man . . .

Could Bear be an older man? Could age be why he was "unsuitable for a Henderson woman"? Would that have been enough to ignite Edwina's years of retribution? Bert Lucci was not just older, he was a bedraggled handyman. And Father Calloway—my breath caught. I could barely let myself consider him. I liked him. Everyone liked and trusted him. And priests aren't supposed to seduce young girls. But if he had seduced her young niece, that would be plenty of reason for Edwina to pursue her revenge.

Hours ago, I had intended to go to Rosa's and insist she search the crannies of her mind for recollections of adolescent Leila. Even if she couldn't recall anything more about Leila, she could remember if Bert or Father Calloway had behaved oddly that summer of Leila's affair, or if Edwina had suddenly been on the outs with one of them.

Rosa had refused to talk to me hours ago. Now, surrounded by her family and friends, people who would be calling me plenty worse than "bad luck" for the Fortimiglios, Rosa wasn't likely to be more willing to accommodate me. Joey Gummo would take pleasure in throwing me out. But it was a chance I would have to take.

CHAPTER
21

I parked the truck in a copse just beyond the Warrior opposite Rosa's driveway. Now, nearly two hours since I had jumped the fence at the fish ranch, my fear of the sheriff checking out all my likely haunts seemed slightly ridiculous. Still, I wasn't willing to chance parking right in front of Rosa's house, even if there had been a square foot that wasn't already taken. There must have been forty vehicles left along the side of North Bank Road, parked every which way along the driveway or nosed toward the house. There was barely room to walk.

The windows of the oblong house were steamed from the warm breath of Rosa's friends inside. In spite of the rain, the kitchen door was propped open. I could smell the aroma of garlic and oregano as I neared the steps.

If this gathering was like the ones I had been to at this house a year ago, by now the spaghetti Rosa had made when the first guests arrived would have run out, and rather than face the possibility of someone going without, Rosa would be making more. One night, when she had had an official party, perhaps for Chris's birthday, she had made a third batch and we'd eaten it at two in the morning. In those days there had been bursts of laughter, comradely shouts and claps on the back, and music from a record player Rosa had bought when she was first married. But tonight, as I climbed the steps to the kitchen door, there was no music or laughter, just a steady, deep hum of serious talk.

When I walked into the kitchen, the first person I saw, standing behind the counter, was Joey Gummo. As he looked at me, his eyebrows pulled together in angry disbelief. "What are *you* doing here?" he demanded.

Joey, the desk man at the sheriff's department, could he know about my breaking into the fish ranch? Surely, the sheriff hadn't—

"You've got a nerve after what you did to Chris," he said.

I almost smiled with relief. "I need to talk to Rosa." I started toward the living room.

He grabbed my arm. "She doesn't need to see you."

"We're not at the sheriff's department, Joey. She can make her own decisions here."

He didn't move. Behind him, in the living room, I could see the Greshams, who ran Gresham's Hardware, and Sam Danielson, the soccer coach at the high school, and Heather Howard, who ran the travel agency near Guerneville. The room was packed. Rosa's daughter Katie, the one who'd known Angelina in high school, stood talking to another daughter whose name I couldn't remember. Behind them was a clutch of fishermen, some Chris's age, many his father's. But I couldn't spot Rosa.

Suddenly, in the warm safety of Rosa's house, all the fear I had pushed away while I was climbing around the fish ranch caught up with me. I felt myself shaking, exhausted. I leaned against the doorjamb. "If you want to guard me, Joey," I said, "that's fine. Rosa won't be away from the kitchen long."

Joey released my arm. I pulled out a chair and sank down onto it.

"You don't have any right barging in here," Joey said. But his words sounded like the face-saving growl of a dog as it backs off. I didn't bother to answer.

In the living room, by the stairway that led to the more recently created rooms downstairs, stood Father Calloway and Faith Boord, one of Henderson's resident eccentrics. She had inherited land from St. Agnes's along the river. She could speak at length about the stock market and what her shares of Genentech or General Foods were doing. But her awareness apparently didn't extend to her appearance. Her clothes were ill-assorted, nowhere near new, and none too decent smelling.

The stairway was cut almost to the middle of the living room floor. It, and a few odd nooks created in one of the other remodellings, made the walls as irregular as books on a shelf. It was from those stairs that Rosa emerged. I was surprised; in the last few years the basement rooms had been closed off in winter. Rosa paused to exchange a few words with the priest and his be-caped companion, then, putting a hand on his arm, she propelled him into the kitchen.

Inside the doorway, Rosa stopped dead. She stared.

I pushed a clump of hair back out of my face.

Father Calloway's brow wrinkled with concern.

Seeing that round, ruddy face, the kind expression, the white hair, the portly frame, it was virtually impossible to imagine him seducing a young parishioner. Father Calloway seemed born to deliver forgiveness. The closest he came to evil was betting on the 49ers—and that with Maxie Dawkins. But if he had had a mind to seduce Leila Katz, it would have been so easy. He could have seduced her and absolved her all in one session.

"How are you, my dear?" he asked. "Rosa has just liberated me from a test of Christian patience. We're taught not to speak ill, but Faith Boord moves one to override such injunctions. She must be the most tedious woman in the whole river area. She was just telling me, at great length, that she's come into some money—some more money, she might have said. Sold some timber harvest rights. But apparently wealth hasn't given her airs." He grinned, casting a look at Faith Boord's magenta cape and green rubber boots. When none of us responded, his smile faded. To Rosa, he said, "What's the matter here?"

Rosa glanced at Joey, but didn't speak.

I wasn't about to answer him. I tried to catch Rosa's eye, but she looked over my shoulder at the steamy windowpane. I didn't have time to wait for things to settle themselves, for her to reconsider her decision to avoid me. But I could hardly ask her about Leila's lover in front of Father Calloway. I couldn't even tell her about the treaty being a phony with Joey Gummo standing there. All I would need would be for him to decide I knew something important enough for the sheriff to hear. I said, "Rosa, I have to talk to you."

"No, Vejay."

"Rosa, Leila Katz is missing. She's not at home. She wasn't at her store this afternoon. She was expecting a reporter to come there to do a story about her. When the reporter arrived, Leila was gone. The store was dark, and the door was open."

"Oh, Vejay." Rosa shook her head, but she still didn't look at me.

"Rosa doesn't know where Leila is," Joey proclaimed. "Rosa's been right here after she left the department, after she saw Chris there," he added pointedly.

I waited for Rosa to say something, but she just

stood. She looked like she'd been running on coffee and worry since last night.

"Rosa," I said, "Chris is already in jail. What more harm can I do?"

She swallowed, then turned to look at Joey. Joey concentrated on the tomato sauce cooking on the stove.

"Dammit, Rosa, look at me! I nearly drowned trying to help Chris. Leila may be dead. Edwina *is* dead. Don't you care at all?"

Joey started to speak, but Rosa held up her hand. She sighed, then slowly walked to the table and sat down next to me.

It was too much to hope that Joey and Father Calloway would leave us alone. Joey stationed himself by the tomato sauce, stirring it silently with a wooden spoon and glaring at me. And Father Calloway continued to stand inside the living room door.

I couldn't ask about the treaty, or about Leila's lover. That left the niece Edwina had gotten the treaty from. Leaning toward Rosa, I said, "Hooper told me that Edwina got the treaty from her niece in Washington. That would be the daughter of her other sister, the one who moved away, right?"

"That sister had a son, not a daughter. I told you that."

"Are you sure?"

"Well, let me think. I'm trying to remember how I know. They were here that summer when we drove East, the sister's family. So I never saw the boy. But I'm sure it was a boy, or at least pretty sure. Why do you say it was a girl?"

"Hooper told me that Edwina said so. Her name is Meg."

"Named for her aunt, no doubt; Leila's mother, Margaret," Father Calloway said. He had moved toward the table, so that the three of us were huddled near the window, and Joey, by the stove, was at the farthest point of the small kitchen, where he could listen and observe, but still remain detached.

"I take it you didn't see him or her the summer the family visited," I said to Father Calloway.

"I'm trying to recall. It would have been like Edwina to bring her family to Mass. She never missed. But from what I've heard, that sister was something of a black sheep, the type for whom coming to Mass would not be a habit."

I sighed.

Two of Chris's friends, tanned, dark-haired men in gray fisherman's sweaters, wandered in from the living room. One stared at me.

For a moment I was afraid he would yank me up and shove me out the door.

He looked away, embarrassed. He didn't know me, didn't realize I was the Vejay Haskell who'd gotten Chris arrested. He'd just been taken aback by my bedraggled appearance.

His friend put a hand on Rosa's shoulder. "We've got to be going. But tell Chris we were here. And tell him not to worry about his boat. His friends will see she's ready to go." He forced a smile. "Maybe she'll even be in better shape than if Chris was out there himself, huh, Pete?"

Pete grinned.

"You're not leaving," Rosa said, standing up to face them. "The sauce will be ready in just a few minutes."

"We'd like to stay. I had two helpings earlier, so I'm not going to starve. But if I could stay, I'd have more." Pete smiled at Rosa. "I've got to take another look at the bilges. With this storm, you can't tell what will happen overnight. We may have plenty to do tomorrow."

"Won't hurt us to keep an eye on our slips at the

dock, either," the other said. "When you look at Bodega Harbor, you can't believe there is a boat left
anywhere else. Every salmon troller in California
must be there. There are guys I haven't seen in five
years."

"And those tugboats banging around. They
shouldn't let boats that size in. One of those gets
washed into you and you're in trouble. But we're
keeping an eye out for Chris. Nothing will happen to
the *Rosa*. You tell him."

"He'll be grateful to you, Peter. You're good
friends to Chris," she said, sitting back down.

As they headed out the door, Father Calloway
started to push himself up. "I should be going, too.
My day starts early tomorrow."

"Oh no, Father. You can stay a little longer."

He started to protest, but Rosa hushed him.
"Vejay may need your help. You hear about things
no one else does."

He smiled uncomfortably, and sat back down.
Next to Rosa, Father Calloway was the best source
of information in the river area. He was always embarrassed when people mentioned that. Now,
though, I wondered if his discomfort were solely
caused by Rosa's acknowledgment.

Rosa looked toward me, expecting me to go on. I
hesitated, watching Father Calloway rub his forefinger nervously on the edge of the table. With him
right there, I had avoided mention of Leila's lover,
the person Edwina had consigned to a life of second
best. Now, for the first time, I wondered why Father
Calloway had remained a parish priest outside a little
town all these years. He was a personable, intelligent
man. He could have been a monsignor by now,
maybe even a bishop. Keeping my eyes on his face, I
said to Rosa, "I asked you earlier about that affair
Leila Katz had when she was in high school. Today,

she left something on the chair in her store, to tell me that she had gone with that lover, or had been forced to go. I have to find out who that lover is."

Father Calloway's forehead wrinkled. Rosa sat with her eyes half closed.

"That was the summer of our trip," Rosa said. "If there was any fuss, it must have died down before we got back."

"Did anyone seem to be acting peculiar then? Not being where you'd expect them to be?" I looked from one to the other, but both shook their heads. There was a lull in the conversation in the living room. In the void, I could hear Joey stirring the tomato sauce. The spicy aroma reminded me that it had been a long time since my tofu sandwich.

"What about Edwina?" I asked. "Was she on the outs with anyone after that summer?"

For the first time, Rosa smiled. "Vejay, Edwina was piqued so much of the time that I couldn't begin to recall who she was miffed with and when."

I looked toward Father Calloway, but he merely shook his head.

"Isn't there anything you can think of?" I asked. "Leila is the only person who knows her lover's identity. If that person killed Edwina—"

"But why would he?" Father Calloway asked.

Rosa looked up.

I hesitated. I certainly didn't want to bring up the treaty in front of Joey Gummo, but there was no alternative now, except to tell Father Calloway that I couldn't explain and then slink home. I said, "Edwina's Pomo treaty was a fake. Someone got hold of a fake treaty and gave it to her."

"But how? Why? How do you know?" Their questions all came at once.

I explained about the treaty coming via Edwina's niece, and about Harry Bramwell's assurance that it was a phony. "Someone put a lot of effort into humiliating Edwina. But once Edwina found out about the treaty, she was determined to denounce it and, doubtless, the person who foisted it on her."

Father Calloway nodded. "I heard her talk about finding a treaty like that. She would have been in Sacramento with the experts by now. To have announced it on television, and then have it turn out to be false . . ." He looked truly distressed. Of course, he had had years of practice looking concerned.

Rosa nodded. "You know Edwina didn't have a sense of humor. It would have been awful for her."

I leaned in toward Rosa. "And what she said when she found out the treaty was a fake was 'And Leil protecting her!' Who could that *her* refer to?"

Rosa shook her head.

"Maybe the niece," Father Calloway said.

"But even if she *has* a niece, that niece wasn't on stage at the Slugfest. The niece couldn't have murdered her."

"You think she meant Angelina, don't you, Vejay?" Rosa asked sadly.

"I did. Now I don't know. But I do think that her murder has to be connected with Leila's disappearance, and that's connected with her lover. And I need to know who that is. Think, Rosa, isn't there anything you can recall that seems odd?"

She half closed her eyes, but said nothing.

"Think about the Slugfest judges," I prodded.

For a moment her eyes stayed half closed. When they opened, she looked down at the empty table in front of us, then jumped up. "I should have gotten you some wine. And Father, where is your glass? I'm sorry; I'm forgetting myself."

Before either of us could respond, she rushed to the cabinet and extricated two glasses from the rear of the shelf. Idly, I wondered how many wine glasses she had, if everyone in the living room was drinking, too. As she reached for the bottle, Joey muttered something to her. She smiled tentatively.

The kitchen was steamy warm from the cooking, but a draft from the living room chilled my legs.

Rosa set the glasses down in front of us, stepped back for her own, and sat down.

"What about Bert Lucci?" I asked.

For the first time Rosa flushed. "Bert? Well, Bert is what Bert is."

"Bert knew Edwina for years. He certainly voiced his opinion of her—and it wasn't good."

Rosa nodded. She was definitely flushing now. She looked more uncomfortable than Father Calloway. I wondered what she knew, or didn't want me to know.

"Where is Bert?" Father Calloway asked. "I figured I'd see him here." He meant that, as a relative and friend, Bert would have been expected to be at Rosa's now.

"He had a group of loggers booked at the lodge for tonight," Rosa said. "But he was here this afternoon. He left just before the sheriff came. He'd been here patching the porch roof where it started to leak."

"Good of him to help out," Father Calloway said. "Good man, Bert Lucci."

Rosa nodded, but she added nothing more. I waited. In the living room I could see Faith Boord talking to Jim and Sara Pasti, who owned a small family winery near Sebastopol. The word about Chris had spread fast.

What could Rosa know about Bert Lucci? Bert, as emcee of the Slugfest, had had his opportunity to poison the pizza. But Bert was a distant cousin of Rosa's. I couldn't believe he would choose her dish to put the poison in, even if no other was so suitable.

For Bert to do that, he would have to have been
nursing a hatred of Edwina that was much greater
than the annoyance his carryings-on about her taking over the lodge indicated. And if he had been that
angry, why had he done anything that would make
life easier for her—why had he allowed her to commandeer the lodge? Even though she owned it, there
had to be restraints about her tossing out parties that
had booked a year ahead.

But suppose I had that backwards? Suppose Bert
had planned to kill Edwina. Suppose he decided the
Slugfest was the safest place to do it. If the Slugfest
had been held anywhere else, Bert would never have
had access to the food. He wasn't important enough
to be a judge. Judges were people of influence in the
community, people whom the average citizen would
enjoy seeing uncomfortable. It was one thing to see
your parish priest or the head of a local business
squirming at the taste of slug. It was not so amusing
to see the handyman of a dilapidated lodge eating
something that was probably tastier than what he
threw together for dinner every night. If Bert planned
to poison Edwina, having the Slugfest at the lodge
was essential. It was the only way he could be on the
stage and have it seem natural.

Did Rosa suspect that too? Anyone but Rosa
wouldn't shield Bert, if baring her suspicions would
help her son. But Rosa wouldn't believe Bert could
have killed Edwina, so she wouldn't think whatever
she knew could help Chris.

Rosa glanced back at Joey, but said nothing.

"You've known Bert for years," I prompted her.

"Oh, yes," she said, "he's my cousin's cousin. I've
known him all my life." She started to look back at
Joey, then stopped midway and turned to the window.

Of course! If Bert was Rosa's cousin's cousin, and

Joey was a distant cousin of hers, then Joey was probably related to Bert, too. And whatever Rosa had to tell, she wasn't about to announce it in front of someone who was both a relative and a member of the sheriff's department.

I caught Father Calloway's eye, and glanced at Joey and back. But if he perceived that relationship and its significance, he gave no indication. He continued to gaze idly at his wine glass. He looked like he was settled in waiting for the next serving.

To Rosa I said, "Don't you need more logs for the fire?" In this area that was always a safe bet.

Rosa showed none of Father Calloway's obtuseness. Without hesitation, she said, "Yes. Joey, Father, I hate to ask you to go out in this weather, but—"

"No, no. Of course we'll take care of that." Father Calloway pushed himself up and headed for the door. A reluctant Joey Gummo followed. Rosa took his place stirring the sauce.

Rosa leaned toward me. "Like I said, Vejay, I've been around Bert all my life. You know, when I was a girl, Bert was quite a handsome man. I had a crush on him for a while then. Sounds silly now, after all these years. It's probably hard for you to imagine anyone finding Bert handsome, the way he keeps himself now."

I wanted to hurry her to the point before Joey returned, but I hesitated to disturb her train of thought.

"Bert is ten years older than I am. So when I was fifteen, he was already a man, quite a dashing man. He was working. He could dress well, and go places. There were ladies who had their eyes on him."

"How come he never married?"

Rosa lifted a strand of spaghetti out of its pot and tasted it. "Another couple of minutes."

"Was there some problem with a woman?"

Panting under the weight of two logs, Joey walked in.

"Why are you carrying both of those?" Rosa demanded. "We won't need four."

"Father Calloway had to go. It's after midnight. He said to say good night. He'll see you at Mass." Joey shifted the logs, grunted, and moved on to the living room.

"Rosa," I said, "we don't have much time."

She leaned the spoon against the side of the sauce pan. "Well, Vejay, what I know is in confidence. And you don't think Bert of all people would hurt Edwina?"

I began to see what she was concealing. "Rosa, was there something between Bert and Edwina? They were about the same age." I tried to picture Edwina as a young woman. Could she have been attractive? It was hard to picture that hawklike face softened by infatuation, that tobacco-cured skin still fresh and taut.

"Vejay, Bert would be horrified if he knew I told you this. He promised Edwina he would never tell a soul. But, like I said, I was taken with him then, and I hung around him a lot, and I guess he viewed me like a kid sister, which was the last thing I wanted. But sometimes when he was depressed, he wanted to talk to someone, and I was always there. So he told me."

"Told you what?" I could hardly contain my impatience.

"Bert and Edwina were married in 1944."

CHAPTER

22

Before Rosa could say anything else about Bert Lucci's marriage to Edwina Henderson, Joey Gummo strode back into the kitchen and announced that the fire was blazing and some of the guests were ready to eat again. "Want me to call them in?"

"Walk me to my truck, Rosa," I said quickly. Once the mob in the living room invaded the kitchen my chance to talk to Rosa about anything, much less this sensitive subject, would be over.

Rosa didn't even seem surprised that I wasn't staying to eat. Perhaps she was relieved. Telling Joey to hold the fort, she grabbed a slicker off one of the pegs and followed me out. We hurried past the hodgepodge of vehicles and found shelter behind a camper van. According to Bert, she explained, Edwina loved him, but she couldn't reconcile a Henderson marrying a Lucci. Bert's family were fishermen, but they didn't even own their own boat; they crewed on the boats of relatives or friends. In the caste system of pre-war Henderson, the Luccis were near the bottom. Probably Edwina would never have done anything so impulsive as to marry Bert had it not been for the Second World War. Even Bert had admitted to Rosa that he had played on Edwina's fears, sympathies, and patriotism before he went to fight in the Pacific. She had agreed to marry him, on the condition that he tell no one. And when he came back two years later, her ardor had cooled, but her insistence that he keep his word had not. Why Bert

had allowed the situation to stabilize there, Rosa
didn't know. The time of their (Bert and Rosa's)
closeness had passed. She didn't even know if Bert
and Edwina were divorced.

Both Bert and Edwina were Roman Catholics, I
thought as I watched Rosa hurry back to the kitchen.
If Edwina had viewed Church doctrine with the same
rigidity as she had the Henderson heritage, she
wouldn't have sanctioned divorce. When she made
her decision to be rid of Bert, she would have applied
for an annulment. She would have applied through
Father Calloway.

I ran to my truck, ready to charge out to St. Agnes's after Father Calloway. No, wait, I thought. Father Calloway had been at St. Agnes's only twenty
years or so. If Edwina had sought to annul her marriage, it would have been right after the war, in 1946
or 1947, way before Father Calloway arrived.

In any case, Bert Lucci and Edwina Henderson had
never lived together. It was hard to imagine them
indulging in a couple of nights of passion. Did they
steal away to San Francisco? Or did Bert sneak up to
Edwina's in the dark, maybe on a stormy night like
this?

But that didn't matter. What did matter was that if
they were never divorced, then Bert stood to inherit.
He might not get her house or the Tobacconist's, but
it was fair to assume he would get Steelhead Lodge.

Till now I hadn't given much thought to Bert's job
performance running Steelhead Lodge. If I had, I
would have wondered why Edwina would hire a
man who did so little in the way of maintenance.
Why would she allow him to use the lodge for fishing
parties that apparently didn't pay much because of
the rundown condition of the place? The lodge could
have been revamped for the tourist season and
brought in three or four or maybe more times the

profit. Why? Because she dared not say no lest their marriage be exposed.

I had wondered why Edwina had chosen a seedy place like Steelhead Lodge for the Slugfest and for the site of her announcement before the television cameras. Did she want to force Bert to fix it up? Maybe she just figured it was hers and she was finally going to get some use out of it.

Or maybe, as I had speculated in the kitchen, Bert insisted on holding the Slugfest there so he could poison her.

I shivered, half at the thought and half because the truck was freezing. I couldn't stay here. What I needed was to go home, stand under the shower, and sort things out. I put the truck in reverse and concentrated on the exacting task of backing out between the trees of the copse. At North Bank Road, I turned right toward town and home.

Not only was it hard to think of Bert poisoning Edwina, it was almost impossible to consider him planning that carefully. But, I reminded myself, before last night, I would never have imagined Bert could be so professional an emcee either. Maybe I really didn't know Bert. Maybe none of us did.

Stopping at the light, I thought of Bert, and of Rosa's porch roof. There was something odd about his fixing that. Not just doing it today, in the storm —you can still patch in the rain. I knew that from a stint on my kitchen roof Christmas Day. But why was Bert doing the patching? Why didn't he assume Chris would? It wasn't salmon season yet. Chris was home. The sheriff hadn't arrested him till after Bert left. Why was Bert there? Had he been around enough to know about the leak? Had Rosa asked him to fix it?

The light changed. I stepped on the gas. "Damn!" I muttered. When Rosa had said I was bad luck for

her, she was right. I had thought there was no way I
could make things worse, but if Bert had been at
Rosa's not so much because of the roof as to be with
Rosa—Rosa, who had had a crush on him once, who
had flushed when I asked about him now—then I
was on my way to making things plenty worse for
her.

"Damn!"

My driveway was to the right. I hadn't been con-
centrating enough on my driving to slow down. I
was already past it when I lifted my foot off the gas.

But before I could step on the brake, I spotted a
car parked beside the road, with a man in the driver's
seat—a sheriff's department car!

The sheriff's car was facing my driveway. Easing
my foot back on the gas, I drove on. Had Angelina
reported my breaking and entering at the fish ranch?
How many years could I get for that? Where did they
put breakers and enterers—state prison? I pushed
harder on the gas pedal, knowing it would make no
difference. If Angelina had reported me, the sheriff
had simply to wait, unless I was planning to keep
driving till my money ran out and take up a new
identity in Fresno.

I drove through Guerneville, and Rio Nido, and
along the dark stretches of River Road that led past
the grape orchards. Somewhere in that darkness, I
realized that Joey Gummo had probably called the
sheriff and reported my story about the fake treaty,
and, just as I had feared, the sheriff decided to bring
me in to question. The fact that it was the middle of
the night would have seemed an ironic sort of justice
to him. When Joey Gummo had told him that I had
been back to Rosa's, hunting around for Leila and
probing deeply enough into the treaty to discover it
was a fake, the sheriff was probably just sorry he
couldn't storm into my house and drag me out of my

bed. If a deputy came across me now and took me to the sheriff's department, it would be many hours before I saw the outside again. (Assuming Angelina hadn't reported me. If she had, I'd be inside for a lot longer than hours.) By the time I got out, Leila Katz could be dead.

I thought back through all I had been told during the day.

Suddenly, I didn't want to chance driving into Santa Rosa, or onto Route 101 where Highway Patrol cars would be used to check for fleeing vehicles, and a brown pickup truck would be more unusual than on the truck-laden back roads that led west. I turned south. Bert Lucci. Hard as it was to imagine him having been married to Edwina, it was twice as hard to think of him killing her and kidnapping Leila.

But the person who kidnapped or lured Leila away was Bear. Could Bert be Bear?

Had Leila chosen the name Bear because it was so close to Bert? Was that a flash of bravado? Or a cautious choice in case she spoke his name by mistake?

But Bert as Leila's lover! Even considering that the affair had taken place ten years ago, and that Rosa had said Bert was quite a handsome man once, I couldn't picture him appealing to a young girl. I couldn't imagine Edwina could picture it. But, of course, Edwina was the one person who would be able to picture it. She had married him.

I turned west, toward the ocean. The rain hit the windshield. And though there were fewer trees to cover the road here, it was still dark. The wind hit the side of the truck. I held more firmly onto the steering wheel. Red specks of taillights ahead were invisible till I was almost on top of them. I braked, skidded to the right, nearly off the road. Ahead was another logging truck. I'd have to watch my driving;

counting my driveway, this was the second thing I
had almost misjudged tonight.

Married! If I needed to find a motive for Edwina's
vengeance and for Bert's revenge, I didn't have to
look farther. Bert was not only old enough to be
Leila's father, but he was Edwina's husband. It might
not be incest, but it would certainly be an unforgivable betrayal! Middle-aged Bert seducing adolescent
Leila would be something Edwina would never have
forgiven. She would have held it against him till he
died. She'd have made him pay. She'd certainly have
exerted every ounce of her prodigious effort to
make him take second best. Well, Steelhead Lodge
wouldn't be anyone's first choice. And the Bert Lucci
I had seen emceeing at the Slugfest could have done
lots more with his life than managing a ramshackle
fishing lodge.

It made a good case. Even the fish ranch fit in. I
remembered Maxie Dawkins telling me that Bert was
one of the two people who had given their names as
references for the night guard when he applied for
his job. The night guard had said there was nothing
he wouldn't do for them. Certainly he wouldn't deny
Bert access to the fish ranch.

But still, it didn't quite fit. Why would Edwina
hold the affair against Leila? Why had she, as Leila
said, written *her* off? Would she be embarrassed that
her own husband had seduced her? Or was it the
other way around? Had Leila seduced Bert? Had she
chosen that method to get back at Edwina for all
those years of being treated like a poor relation?

What I needed was proof. And, I realized, the person who might have that proof was Harry Bramwell.

CHAPTER
23

I pressed hard on the gas, racing toward the ocean, slamming on the brakes behind a convoy of logging trucks, then pulling out to pass them even though I couldn't see as far as the first in line. I took curves too fast, and skidded back onto the straightaway, rushing to get to Harry Bramwell's cabin. As if he would find my waking him up at three in the morning more acceptable than at four. As if he wouldn't slam the door in my face again.

I was tempted to turn north, to cut back through Henderson to the motel, but even in my rush, caution—or fear—won out. Henderson was where the sheriff was looking for me. If I intended to get to Genelle's Family Cabins unnoticed, I would have to come from the other direction. I drove on, through Bodega, and Bodega Bay, past the fish ranch, quelling a spasm of panic as I spotted its lights, and turned east on River Road. It was close to four A.M. when I pulled up in front of Harry Bramwell's cabin.

I glanced in the mirror, with the idea that perhaps I could do something to make myself look better. But the hours of clutching the steering wheel and squinting into the dark for slow-moving taillights or speeding sheriff's cars hadn't improved my appearance. My skin was jaundiced gray. There were dark circles under my eyes, and the eyes themselves were bloodshot. I looked like something any decent person would throw out.

I climbed down out of my truck, ran through the rain to the cabin, and knocked.

On the second knock, the door opened. Harry Bramwell stood in the doorway in a blue Japanese robe. His curly brown hair stood out from his head. His eyes were still half-closed. "It's four o'clock in the morning!" He shut the door.

I pounded. "I know what time it is. I haven't been to bed."

There was no response. But there had been no sound of footsteps moving away from the door.

"It's important. I wouldn't be up at this hour if it weren't. I wouldn't wake you up. Just tell me one thing and I'll leave you alone."

"Promise?"

"Yes."

He pulled open the door, looked me over, and shook his head. "Okay, what is it?"

"You told me Edwina said, 'And Lyle protecting her!' "

"Right."

"Could you have misheard her?"

"I don't think—"

"Was it noisy in the shop? Was she muttering?"

He closed his eyes. They stayed closed so long I wondered if he had gone back to sleep standing up. Finally, he said, "She was very upset. I think I told you she had probably forgotten I was there. She was really talking to herself."

"Could she have said, 'And Leil protecting Bert!'?"

"No."

"Oh."

He started to close the door, then stopped, looked at me again, and sighed. "You'd better come in. You can tell me what you've been doing all night. You can even give me that explanation you promised me."

I followed him in, took off my slicker, and slumped into one of the chairs. The room was still warm, but the heat didn't penetrate my skin this time. I felt as icy as I had clambering out of the water on the fish ranch rocks.

Harry Bramwell lowered himself into the other chair. The blue of his robe set off the blue of his eyes. His curly brown hair was still rumpled from sleep, and his just-wakened face had an appealing softness. Here in the warm room, sitting in the padded chair, the tension that had kept me going faded. I stared blankly at Harry Bramwell. Despite his robe and the hour, he didn't look very different than he had standing in Edwina Henderson's driveway Friday afternoon. Then I had been rushing around, irritated about my Missed Meter and the prospect of justifying it to Mr. Bobbs. Part of my annoyance had been at the prospect of Mr. Bobbs being unreasonable. Part had been because the categorizing of Missed Meters was unreasonable in itself. What was an acceptable Missed Meter this year—an M-1, vicious dog—might not be next year. It was all decided when the union negotiated our contract. Maybe next year even a blocked road wouldn't be reason enough.

"So?" Harry Bramwell demanded. "Have you dragged me out of bed just to sit here and stare?"

"I was thinking about seeing you yesterday, and my Missed Meter. Facts can appear entirely different depending on who is doing the interpreting." I realized now that I had accepted Harry Bramwell's interpretation—the interpretation of the one person who knew none of the suspects—and let that mislead me.

He inhaled slowly, irritably. "I'm not even going to ask what a missed meter is. I'd just like to think it has something to do with the murder you were going to tell me about."

I sat up straight. "It does! Of course! It does. 'And

Lyle protecting her!' That's what you thought you heard, what seemed logical to you, your interpretation. But that's not what Edwina said."

"Then what did she say?" he demanded. "Who is this Lyle and who was he protecting?"

"Not he. By Lyle, Edwina meant L-e-i-l, for Leila, her niece. Edwina referred to family members by their first syllables. And the 'her' wasn't a her at all."

"This Leila, was she the niece who sent Edwina the treaty?"

"No, no. Edwina said that niece was named Meg. Edwina had two sisters, and each had one child, Leila and one other. Rosa told me the other was a boy, but Edwina said Meg. Both Rosa and Edwina were right. Leila's cousin was a male, and Edwina got the treaty from her niece Meg."

"Do you mean Meg was another of Leila's names, like she was called Leila Margaret?"

"No, no. Meg is a different person. She made the treaty."

"Did she kill Edwina then?"

"No. She's not even here. It was Leila's lover who killed Edwina."

Harry Bramwell sighed.

"I know it's confusing. It's hard to follow when you don't know any of these people. Try to bear with me."

He sighed again. "That seems to be the nature of our encounters. But you go ahead."

"Look, Edwina had made Leila's lover pay for that affair for years. Now revenge was possible. And the beauty of it was that Edwina's dogged commitment to the history of the area was what made it possible. So Leila's lover gets Meg to tell Edwina about the treaty. This is six months ago. Meg plays Edwina along. First she says she can get the treaty, then she says Edwina will have to wait, then wait longer. It's like baiting a dog. But the six months was important for other reasons. One was that forging a treaty takes time."

He nodded. "A job like this one certainly would. The research alone, and dealing with the paper . . ."

"And Edwina had to be given enough time to make arrangements for the announcement. And to prepare to take the treaty to Sacramento for all the necessary assessment. A proper announcement was important. You see, Leila's lover was counting on Edwina creating a stir with the treaty."

"So, he, or she, assumed that Edwina would accept the document as legit?"

"Oh yes. Edwina trusted Meg. That was the beauty of the scheme. Edwina liked and trusted Meg because of what she was. And when Edwina announced the treaty, there would be a great hubbub. Then she'd leave immediately for Sacramento, just like she always said."

"But surely Meg realized that when the treaty got to an expert it would be exposed."

"No doubt, but that would take a few days at the least. Even if Edwina had left Saturday morning, she wouldn't have seen the experts till the afternoon. And then, if they decided the treaty was a fake as quickly as you did, they would still want to double-check it, wouldn't they?"

He nodded.

"And after making a fool of herself before the television cameras, and the historical experts, Edwina wouldn't kill herself to hurry home. It's safe to assume she wouldn't be home till Sunday night at the very earliest. She might have been gone much longer. But for the scheme to work, the weekend was all that was needed."

"Go on," he said.

"The key here is what would happen with Edwina totally preoccupied over the weekend. And the answer is that the causes to which she normally devoted herself, Native Americans and the environment, would have been left on their own. One thing people have told me repeatedly is that there is no one who could get an injunction or a court order as fast as Edwina." I shifted in the chair. "Have you noticed that there are a lot of strange men in town? There's a group at Steelhead Lodge tonight. They're here tonight because they will start work in the morning—this morning, Sunday. Sunday is one day that even the average concerned citizen would have trouble finding a judge for an injunction. But Edwina wouldn't. She knew the judges, and she had dealt with them before. But with Edwina otherwise occupied . . ."

"Okay, so Edwina's absence is essential to protect whatever scheme is going on. I won't even bother to ask you what. And by the time the treaty would have been exposed, this operation would have been over. Edwina would have been humiliated and discredited, right?"

"Right. The perfect revenge. Of course, she'd know who was responsible: Leila's lover. But since Meg was the one who created the treaty and she's gone, that wouldn't matter."

He was almost leaning off his chair now. "Okay. I follow this as much as I could hope to, except for the major point, which is why was Edwina killed. There's nothing in what you've said that would lead to her being poisoned."

"No. It wasn't in the plan. The murder was a sudden necessity. The reason she was killed is, I'm afraid, you."

His blue eyes widened. "You're kidding."

"No. It's hardly your fault. But when Leila's lover

heard that Harry Truman Bramwell was here, that Edwina had called you here . . . Well, anyone who heard Edwina's historical society lectures would recognize your name. Leila's lover did, and knew that when you saw the treaty you would declare it a phony. Edwina would know who was behind it, and being the type of person she was, would not only proclaim the fraud but would expose the perpetrator. Discovering this fraud would only reinforce what she had thought all along: that Leila's lover was unworthy for a Henderson, or, more to the point, unworthy, period."

He started to speak, but I held up a hand.

"Not only that, but Edwina wouldn't be preoccupied this weekend, and the whole arrangement, with payment for all those men, and boats, and equipment, would be thwarted. So, to save it all, Edwina had to be killed. Fortunately, there was time to drive to the fish ranch, get the liquid nicotine that they keep there for the roses, put it in the nose drop bottle that the watchman put on the shelf in the shed, and drive back to the Slugfest. And at the Slugfest—you'd have realized this if you'd come—it was easy to hold that tiny bottle in the palm of a hand and squeeze its contents on the one pizza that would be left for Edwina. The Grand Promenade around the food table provided the perfect opportunity for a cool-headed murderer."

"Okay, okay. But you said Edwina's niece Leila was in danger. You were looking for her. Because of her lover, right?"

I nodded. "She's the only one who realizes all the connections. She's been on bad terms with Edwina for years. She resented what Edwina had done to her lover. She was always protective. She never mentioned a name or even a sex. But she wouldn't keep quiet about a murder. So, after Edwina was killed, Leila's death became essential."

"So she's dead?"

"I hope not yet. There's been a lot going on, what with all the arrangements to make. I just hope another murder was too much to schedule in. I hope that having been Leila's lover, and having shared the bitterness toward Edwina all these years, created enough of a bond to postpone the necessity of killing her as long as possible."

"Well, where do you think she is?"

"The fish ranch. I thought I had looked everywhere when I was out there. It seemed odd that those four-foot-square incubators had been piled outside. But I hadn't realized then that one could conceal a body, alive and tied up, or already dead." Through the window behind Harry, the sky was still dark. But the first hints of dawn would become visible soon. "I've got to go."

"Again?"

"The whole operation will begin as soon as it's light. When the first truck pulls into the fish ranch, Leila will be dead. I have to get there before that." I stood up and grabbed my slicker.

"I'll come with you," he said.

"No. Someone needs to get to Sheriff Wescott. There may still be a deputy parked across from my house. You can have him call ahead. But you'll have to drive to Guerneville. You'll have to see the sheriff in person and explain all this."

"Why don't you do that, and let me go to the fish ranch?"

"Because it will be guarded, and I'm a meter reader, and I know how to get in there."

The sky was becoming lighter and the rain had let up. That made it better for all those workers, and worse for me. The rain, at least, would have provided me with some cover.

I drove along River Road behind the slow-moving trucks, waiting for the road to be straight long enough to let me pass. As I neared St. Agnes's Church, a van pulled over to the side and men started climbing out. I pressed harder on the gas, taking the curves too fast. When I got to Jenner, it was almost dawn.

I left my pickup on the hill where I had had it last night. Putting my slicker on the seat, I grabbed a coil of rope from the truck bed and raced down the hill. I would have felt more comfortable if I hadn't left the gun in the glove compartment, but I couldn't do what I had to carrying both the gun and the rope. And the rope was essential. Besides, I told myself, a gun you don't know how to handle can get you in a lot of trouble.

At the main road I could see the closed gate of the fish ranch and the light still on in the gatehouse. I wouldn't get in the way I had last night. But I didn't expect to. I kept on, along River Road, passing by the bridge into the fish ranch. The rope hung heavy on my shoulder. The wind that had seared my skin last night was dead still now. The air had that marshy smell of dawn.

The river tumbled brown, hitting high against its

banks. In summer it would be nearly dry here, but
now the water tossed branches into each other as it
raced toward the ocean.

I ran beside the road another twenty yards to the
utility pole. The lowest rung on the pole was ten feet
up. It took me three tries to catch the rope over that
rung. PG&E has a pole-climbing school, a course
where they teach how to manage the hundred-foot
poles. I had never taken it. (The idea of spending
three consecutive days atop a hundred-foot pole,
shifting fifty- to hundred-pound weights, was not
something that appealed to me. I'd heard about the
guys who lost their footing, slipped all the way to the
ground, and landed with a hundred feet of splinters
in their noses.) Now I regretted my ignorance. I
would just have to shinny up the pole like I had as a
kid.

Taking a firm grip on the rope, I clasped my knees
around the width of the pole and pulled on the rope.
It took eight pulls till I could grab the bottom rung,
and then the next one. From there I coiled the rope
around my shoulder and climbed.

The training poles were a hundred feet high. This
one was only forty. At the top was the transformer
tub.

I clung there, catching my breath. I could see well
out into the ocean. A flotilla of tugboats rode the
choppy water out past the jetty. I counted them—
nine—before I jerked my attention back. I tightened
my grasp on the crossbar and looked over the tub
toward the ranch. When the lights went out, either
the guard would stay put or he would head for the
auxiliary generator at the south side of the compound. Either way, he would be occupied for three
or four minutes. I wasn't primarily worried about
him. Edwina's killer was the one I wanted to see.
When I got to the far side of the building, I wanted to

find the door open and that figure running across the looping cement channels to the generator—leaving Leila Katz inside.

Avoiding the wires, I worked my way up till I could reach the fuse cartridge above the tub. I looped the rope around it and gave one sharp pull. It snapped—cutting off all power to the fish ranch. I lowered myself hand under hand down the pole and jumped to the ground.

The gatehouse door opened. The guard rushed to the gate, unlocked it, and locked it behind him.

With the rope on my shoulder, I ran full out across the bridge, along the gatehouse road, past the gatehouse to the fence. Was I fast enough? Once the guard got to the generator and threw the transfer switch, the juice from the generator would make the fence live again. It would fill me with enough volts to light half my H-1 route. I grabbed the mesh on the fence, yanked myself up, stuck one foot on the top, and flung my body over, landing with a thud. I didn't wait to hear the sizzle of the wires as the power came back on. I ran, leaping over the fish channels, racing for the side of the building, and flattened myself against it.

The sky was lighter. My mouth was dry, but I could taste the salty ocean air. The guard would be on his way back now. I ran for the ocean side of the building, hearing the splat of my feet against the cement, picturing that hulking guard as I had seen him last night. If he caught me now—I forced that thought back and flung myself around the corner, onto the narrow rock seawall, onto the dock, and to the seawall on the other side. At the corner, I peered around.

The guard was at the door, his head inside. I pulled back, feeling my throat tighten with fear. I counted to ten, then looked again—he was stepping

back. Flattening myself against the building, holding
my breath, I listened for the sound of footsteps ap-
proaching. The ocean water splashed onto the seawall and against my legs. I peered around the corner
again. The guard was turning the far corner. He was
on his way back to the gatehouse.

The door to the building was shut! I had counted
on the sudden darkness driving the murderer out.
But it hadn't. Now the murderer knew the power
had gone out. A warning? Enough to remove my
hope of surprise? And the door was shut. It was the
worst possible combination.

"And Leil protecting her!"

I hurried along the side of the building, past the
closed door. As I rounded the far corner, I could see
that someone had started to remove the end of the
prefab building. Started, but stopped before there
was any space wide enough to give me entry inside.
The workmen would be arriving to finish the job any
minute now. That siding had to be out of the way
before the first truck arrived. I didn't have much
time.

I looked up till I spotted the wires running in from
the transformer. Following them to the edge of the
building, I found the service drop, halfway along the
side of the building—in full view of the guard. The
weatherhead, where the wires connected, stood up a
foot above the edge of the roof. I looped the rope
over it, braced my feet against the side of the building, pulled myself up till I could catch the gutter,
then clambered over the edge.

Recoiling the rope around my shoulder, I made my
way along the slippery metal roof to the far corner
over the office. The skylight was clouded with sedi-
ment of dirt and salt, but I could see in. Trying to
keep my steps silent, I hurried across the roof and
looked down into the lab.

Leila was there, on the floor. She lay unmoving. I couldn't be sure, but it looked like her hands and feet were bound.

"And Leil protecting her!"

But, of course, that was just Harry Bramwell's interpretation of what Edwina had said. In fact, she had no more said "her" than she had said "Lyle." Harry Bramwell had thought she said "her" because he didn't know Edwina shortened relatives' names, and because he didn't know those names.

But I knew who that "her" was. I also knew that if it came to a fight, I would end up like Leila Katz. I had been up all night; I had been exhausted hours ago.

I looked through the skylight again. I would have only one try at the killer. If I missed . . .

Leaning back away from the skylight, I smashed it with my boot, kicking till the shards from the edges fell to the floor.

Running footsteps slapped the cement. The door opened. I could see the killer standing at the doorway, too far out of range. He looked down at Leila Katz, then around the small room. He stepped forward, under the skylight, and peered up, right at me.

I jumped on his back.

He came down hard on the floor, the wind knocked out of him, his face in the glass. My boots hit his mid-back. I grabbed his hands and pulled them behind him. Gasping for breath, he drew them apart. His feet flailed. I yanked on his arms, jerking them back from the shoulder sockets. He let out a yelp of pain. I lifted up off him and slammed my bottom down on his ribs. He gasped. His arms went slack. I pulled the rope around his wrists and yanked it tight, then hauled his arms up, pushing his face back down into the glass. Once more, I lifted off him and came down hard. When he gasped, I flung the rope around his bent legs, made one more loop around his feet and, getting up off him, pulled his feet toward his hands.

" 'And Leil protecting Curr!' That's what Edwina said, wasn't it?"

But Curry Cunningham, Edwina's nephew, didn't answer.

CHAPTER
25

Curry Cunningham got his wind back. He pulled and kicked against the rope. I braced my feet into his back and hung on to both ends of the rope. It cut into my hands. Curry flailed with the strength of panic. The rope slipped. Where was the sheriff? Grabbing tighter on the rope, I yanked Curry's head up and let it slam down against the floor. I hadn't even had a chance to pull the gag out of Leila Katz's mouth. I wasn't even positive she was breathing.

Those tugboats outside the jetty! The men already out of their transports along the road! They had had plenty of time to assess the trees, get out their chain saws, and start to work. They could be making the wedge-shaped undercuts in the bases of the trees right now. Once those cuts were in, it would be too late to save the trees. Where was the sheriff? Minutes were precious. Harry Bramwell had left the motel an hour ago. The sheriff had to be on his way by now.

Curry kicked. This time I didn't wait. I lifted his head and slammed it down again. "I can do this as long as you can," I said. "It's your chin."

There was blood on his cheek and chin where they'd hit the broken glass. But those slightly bulging eyes that he had inherited from his aunt Edwina didn't look acquiescent. He was biding his time. He didn't know the sheriff was on his way. Rather than expecting the sheriff, he assumed his workmen would be driving in any minute to finish removing the side of the fish ranch building. He figured that it

wouldn't be long till the first of the logging trucks
pulled in and backed into the building, right up to
the double doors. He figured one of those tugboats
would be docking at the jetty any minute, ready to
carry his cargo out to the waiting Japanese ship.

The sheriff would only know what I had told
Harry. He wouldn't suspect this plan. I needed to
call him before it was too late. But I couldn't let go of
the rope. I glanced at Leila Katz. She still lay unmoving. Could I pull Curry across the building to the
office and the phone? Leaving one foot braced
against his back, I stood.

The sheriff's siren seared the air.

Curry started, then flailed with newfound force. I
dropped, my knees in his back. He groaned.

"It's too late," I said.

He didn't move.

I glared down at him, thinking of Edwina as she
lay on the floor in the Steelhead Lodge kitchen, surrounded by her own vomit. "Death—even the awful
way Edwina died—wasn't much worse than what
you had planned for her, was it?"

He grunted.

"You never intended to fell your own trees back in
the hills like you told me. That wasn't what all those
logging trucks were for, and those cargo boats. It
was the Nine Warriors you planned to cut down,
wasn't it?"

His grunt sounded strangely like a chuckle.

"Edwina was worried about kids carving their initials in them; that's what her ordinance dealt with.
But your plan was to send her to Sacramento with
the treaty, to let the experts there expose the fake,
and then to let Edwina, shocked and humiliated,
drive home along River Road and find nine stumps."

Now he did chuckle.

I recalled that one time I had seen Edwina look

peaceful, as she sat staring up into the huge redwood behind her shop. I yanked the rope up one more time, and let Curry's grin smash down into the glass.

Sheriff Wescott ran in. The ambulance men were right behind. One bent down and removed Leila's gag. She groaned. A deputy took charge of Curry. Wescott surveyed the broken glass, the rope. "Vejay, what the—"

"He killed Edwina. He kidnapped Leila. And he's got men cutting down all Nine Warriors right now."

Wescott's tanned face turned red. He yanked Curry to his knees. "That right?"

Curry kept silent, but he couldn't hide a smile of triumph. It was enough for the sheriff. "Read him his rights," he said to the deputy. Then he ran out.

It was a moment before I followed. I tried to run, but I was too exhausted. By the time I reached his car, he had the radio mike in hand and was saying, "Make it fast. Ten-four." He started the engine.

"I'm coming," I said.

I expected him to argue. He hesitated, then opened the back door. I was barely in when the car raced out of the complex, over the bridge, and inland on River Road. He didn't speak. He kept his eyes on the road. The siren squealed above. I couldn't tell how fast he was driving, but it was way faster than I had ever taken these sharp curves. The tires slid on the slick surface. I braced my feet against the front seat. The radio crackled as the dispatcher sent cars to Guerneville, to Henderson, all along River Road and North Bank Road to the sites of the Nine Warriors. Wescott slowed behind a camper, pulled out around it, and cut back in, nearly taking off its fender. He pressed harder on the gas, came abreast of St. Agnes's, and slammed on the brakes, skidding to a stop behind the last logging truck. He was out of the car before it had settled. I shoved open my door and ran past the trucks to the nearest of the two Warriors here.

The drag cables were already stretched in lines between the nearest logging truck and the tree. A group of plaid-shirted men stood beneath it. And in its base was a deep gash—the undercut. The huge tree looked ready to crash down.

Wescott stared, his face flushed with fury. "Sheriff's department," he yelled. "Back off from the tree. Get those men away from the other one. Now! Move it!"

"Hey, man, we've got a contract," one of the loggers said.

"Illegal. There's an ordinance protecting these trees." He looked back at the undercut and asked softly, "Can this redwood be saved?"

No one answered. From the looks that passed between the men it was clear that "saving" was not a term they associated with redwoods.

A car pulled up and two deputies got out. Sheriff Wescott walked over, and I could see him explaining and sending one of them to the far tree, the other to take charge of this one. He took a last look at the gouge in the trunk, let his eyes climb the full length of the tree to where the branches pierced the fog and disappeared. He stood. Then he turned and walked back to his car.

He sat on the seat, his feet in the dirt outside. The wind blew in off the Pacific, but he seemed impervious to its cold damp touch. Without looking at me, he said, "Once this area was a rain forest so thick that even the Indians lived only on the edges. When I was a boy, there were so many trees on the riverbanks you could barely see the houses. The redwoods stood like pillars; they looked like they were lifting the hillside up to the clouds." He swallowed hard. "Every year something is destroyed. The river is filled with sewage, the salmon are killed, assholes set fires . . ." More softly, he said, "The redwoods *are* the Russian River area. They give us distance from each other. They remind us we're a part of nature, swept by the same current as the river. Every year more are gone."

I was stunned by the depth of his feeling. I stood still, unwilling to intrude. Perhaps he would regret revealing his anguish in front of me. He sat, staring into the dirt. I hesitated, then put a hand on his shoulder. He didn't shake it off. Neither of us spoke.

Then he motioned me to the back of the car, turned, and started the engine. With that, he became all business, asking me about Curry Cunningham and Edwina, and Leila. He drove carefully now, occasionally interrupting me to answer the dispatcher or to call in another order. By the time we reached the fish ranch, his questions had tailed off.

A deputy was keeping two workmen at a distance from the end of the building. They were insisting they needed to get it off and out of the way by eight A.M. Beyond the jetty, those nine tugboats were treading water.

Sheriff Wescott told a deputy to take me back to the station in Guerneville to make my official statement, then headed inside the green pre-fab building.

Wescott had never admitted that I was right in my suspicions. It didn't need saying. But after the deputy took my statement, during the time it took to have it typed, have me check it, and retype the corrections, he did stop by the station and tell me that, faced with Leila Katz's accusations and the rest of the evidence against him, Curry Cunningham had confessed. He answered my questions with a patience that came close to blotting out the memory of his patronizing tone Friday night. And he called the café and had them send an order of eggs, chorizo, and kraut, and a pot of real coffee, with real cream.

By the time I had finally finished with my official statement—and my breakfast—it was nearly noon. I walked out to the sheriff's department lobby.

Joey Gummo was at the desk. "Vejay," he called.

I turned. Somehow I didn't connect Joey Gummo with use of my first name. He beckoned me over.

"Rosa called," he said. "She wants you to come by the house."

I nodded.

"Vejay," he said again, uncomfortably. "You know when I tried to keep you from talking to Rosa last night? Well, I was only trying to protect her."

"I know," I said.

"It was nothing personal."

"I know."

"The sheriff, he doesn't dislike you. You just get his dander up."

A rather revolting description. "I know."

Now Joey grinned. It was an unfitting use of his small, pointy features. "Listen, Vejay, I can make it up to you."

How he could do that was one thing I didn't know.

"You work for PG and E, right?"

"Yes."

"For that guy Bobbs?"

"Right. As a matter of fact, I have to face him tomorrow morning. I had a Missed Meter Friday.

First thing tomorrow, he'll want me in his office telling him what I've done about it."

Joey's grin broadened. "No, he won't. Tomorrow morning he'll be making a delivery here. He'll be making a delivery every day till Wednesday."

I remembered Mr. Bobbs had been at the sheriff's department Saturday when I'd seen him in the parking lot. He had never told me what he was doing there.

"What's he delivering?"

"Well, you know he got sick at the Slugfest."

"Yes."

"He said that it couldn't have been caused by . . ." Joey groped for the right word.

"Squeamishness?"

"Right, squeamishness. He said it must have been food poisoning. So, well, we are public servants. We had to be sure."

"So?" I wondered how long Joey could drag this out.

"He's bringing us samples, urine and shit—a paper cup and a bottle. I thought you'd want to be the first to know."

All the tension of the weekend welled up and exploded. I roared. My whole body shook. I braced my hands on the counter. "Thanks, Joey," I said when I could talk again. "We're more than even."

"He's supposed to get here by noon. I chewed him out yesterday for being so late. If you hang around, you can see him carting his sack in."

"That's okay," I said. Despite my amusement, the last thing I wanted to do was to be a visible witness to Mr. Bobbs's latest embarrassment. There was enough rancor between us already.

Before I could turn to leave, I heard the outside door opening behind me. I didn't move, hoping to blend into the background. But the footsteps came right up behind me. A hand touched my shoulder, and when I turned around, Harry Bramwell gave me a great hug.

His beard scraped against the edges of the cuts on my cheek, but it didn't matter. I just let him hold me. And then I let him drive me home, and make himself coffee while I took a hot shower, washed and dried my hair, put on makeup and clean clothes—a dress! —and presented myself back in the living room.

"My God!" he said. "If I'd realized you could look that good, I would have made sure I got to the Slug-fest."

"Why didn't you?" It seemed so long ago now, I had almost forgotten my disappointment. "I gave you good directions. I wanted you to be there."

"I was going to come. I was looking forward to seeing it, and you. But after I talked to Edwina Henderson and I realized she would be humiliated in front of all those people she knew, and the television cameras, I just couldn't bring myself to view that."

"Nice man," I said.

He patted the couch next to him. "Sit down. We'll talk about how nice I am."

I smiled. "Later, at length. But now we have to get to Rosa's."

"Couldn't we skip it?"

"No, this is one occasion we really can't."

He stood up. "Like I kept saying to you last night, I don't really understand, but I guess we'll go there. But while we're on the way, maybe you can explain all those things I didn't understand. Like why did Curry Cunningham kill Edwina?"

I put on my jacket—it was wonderful to leave my slicker on the hook—and we started down the fifty-two steps that led in a Z to the street.

"If you don't brace a few of these, you're going to break your neck, you know," he said.

"I'll add that to my list. It'll come somewhere between reshingling the roof and replacing the bathroom window."

The blue Volvo was at the bottom. I climbed into
the passenger seat. "Straight ahead," I said when he
had started the car. "Okay. Curry Cunningham.
Curry, or Curr, as Edwina called him, was her
nephew. He came here to visit one summer and had
an affair with Leila Katz, his cousin. Incest was definitely 'unsuitable for a Henderson.' And Edwina
never forgave him; she never let either of them forget
it. She controlled the family money, such as it was, so
there was no fancy college for Curry, no possibility
of a stake to open his own business. Edwina had
enough influence with local judges, politicians, and
merchants so that it would be easier for them to say
no to something—or someone—she didn't want than
to go to bat for a complete stranger. Why should
they take on Edwina when they could avoid it? They
saw enough of her petitions and campaigns as it was.

"If Curry had decided to stay back East, Edwina's
ability to thwart him would have been limited. But
he must have been telling the truth when he said he
loved this area and made a point of moving back
here."

Harry looked out his window at the Henderson
Tobacconist's and the redwood that still stood behind, its great branches dwarfing the old shop. He
glanced past me at the high sidewalk that had an
extra step up from the street, and at the café, now
Sunday-lunchtime crowded. Then he turned his gaze
straight ahead on North Bank Road to the end of the
small commercial block where town proper stopped
and the laurels and redwoods and eucalyptus trees
reached in from either side of the road, covering it as
if it were a minor and transient alteration of their

domain. "I can see why he wouldn't let one old woman deny him all this."

I nodded. "Curry's problem was that he was too much like his aunt. He went after her with the same singlemindedness that Edwina devoted to her causes and her vendettas. He told me he had *The Paper* delivered to him out of town. With that, he could keep up on Edwina's various campaigns. *The Paper* reported the historical society meetings and doubtless Edwina's other activities. So Curry was aware of her fascination with the area and the Pomos, and her certainty that there must have been a Pomo rancheria near here. She gave her Pomo talk every year. Who knows how many times he'd read reports of it?

"Curry told me he joined Crestwood so he could get back to this area. His wife, Megumi—Meg—was Edwina's niece. Edwina didn't consider her a niece by marriage. Leila told me that once a person married into the Henderson family, Edwina accepted them as a full-fledged niece or nephew or whatever. So Edwina's niece, Meg, created the treaty. Meg is an artist. Her field is eastern religious art."

"Where the emphasis is on reproducing a copy as close to the original as possible. Aha!"

"Exactly. Meg told Edwina she had access to the treaty. She and Curry had lived near Baltimore, within easy commuting distance to Washington, D.C., and the Senate's secret files. She traveled back East to study the collections at the museums. But Edwina didn't know the purpose of her trips; she only knew what Meg and Curry told her—that Meg was doing consulting work connected with the job she had had back East, and it required her flying back to Washington. So, to Edwina, it was quite possible that Meg had come across the treaty."

"Still, for Edwina to believe her—"

"Oh, but you see that's the beauty of it. Edwina

was captured because of her own biases. She believed Meg because Meg is Japanese, and by now, you know Edwina's predilection for Indians and Asians. She would never have trusted Curry or Leila, but Meg, well, that was different."

"And Meg's gone now?"

"She and her son are in Japan. Curry told me she was there studying. He also said that her being Japanese had opened the doors for him to make his planned shipment of timber."

"While you were in with the sheriff, there must have been ten calls about fights and guys from out of town. Sounds like Curry's lumberjacks are pretty pissed off."

"I'll bet." I laughed. "Crestwood Industries isn't going to be any too pleased either, when they get the bills for all these loggers working on overtime and the tugboats and the logging trucks. And they'll have to pay a fine for the trees he destroyed—not an enormous one, since they were all on private property. But if Curry's plan to corner the Japanese lumber market had succeeded, it would have been more than worth all the expense and bad publicity here. He had an in because of his wife. And he told me yesterday that what a businessman needed in dealing with the Japanese was to make the right gesture. He mentioned the example of the Japanese gardener cutting all the blooms off a plant to leave the one perfect one undiminished by clutter. Curry's gesture was to send them nine huge, matching redwoods—the Nine Warriors." I started to tell him the history of those trees, but he stopped me.

"I know," he said. "And I'll bet he was right. Anyone would be awed by them, by the magnificence of the trees, and the magnificence of the gesture. But surely someone would have noticed. Cutting down a thousand-year-old redwood isn't a quiet process."

"That's why he had all those trucks and men. He had them start work at first light. Not many people are up early on Sunday morning. The crews had two-man band saws; they're pretty fast. They were to cut down the trees, load the boles onto the trucks, and drive to the fish ranch. The back wall would have been removed, and all the salmon fry and the incubators have been cleared out of the building, so the trucks could drive right up to the dock. There the men would drive pegs into the bole, attach the shackles and chains, and push it into the water. Then they'd bring up the next and do the same thing. The sections of the bole would be joined together like five links on a belt. And the tugs could drag each tree out to the Japanese ship waiting out in the ocean."

Harry shook his head. "From what I've learned about Curry Cunningham, I'm surprised he didn't arrange for Edwina to see all nine trees being pulled across the water one after another."

I nodded. "Too flamboyant even for Curry. But I'll bet it crossed his mind. Of course, Curry would have been on one of the tugs, headed out to the Japanese ship. He'd have had Leila's body"—I swallowed—"to dispose of at sea."

"And yours." Harry squeezed my hand. He slowed as a station wagon pulled out in front of him. On the bumper was a sign saying "Stop off-shore drilling! Save our coast!" "So," he said, "Curry would have established himself as a shrewd businessman. He could have waited out any public outcry while he was in Japan, and come back to work for Crestwood in Oregon or Idaho, in a much more important position."

I nodded. "He'd probably even have had *The Paper* sent to him so he could read about Edwina's reaction."

"But still, you said I was the cause of his killing Edwina. How could *I* be? He never even saw me."

Harry looked so distressed, I was sorry I had had to mention that. "Curry dropped Hooper off at Steelhead Lodge. Hooper had just seen you. He knew who you were. It was big-time for Edwina to have a noted expert call on her. Of course, he told Curry, a member of the historical society, that an important expert was here in Henderson conferring with Edwina. And Curry recognized your name, too. He knew you would see through the treaty right away. And he realized that Edwina would expose him, humiliate him, and block his great plan. So his choices were to let that happen or to kill her. For him, there must have been no choice at all. He dropped off Hooper at the lodge, then he had plenty of time to get to the fish ranch, pick up the nicotine and the Estrin bottle, and get back for the Slugfest. Since he was the area manager of Crestwood Industries, he'd been to the fish ranch often enough to know what was there. And the night guard was one person who wouldn't tell the sheriff he was there."

"But how did he go about it—I mean the actual killing? How did he know which pizza to put the poison on?"

I smiled. "Theoretically, that was the easy part. But it was the only area where there was a serious hitch in his plan. You see, part of the attraction of the Slugfest is its traditions. The audience likes to be able to anticipate what horrors await the judges; that's half the fun. So things are done the same way year after year. The trays with the entrees are lined up along the front edge of the food table. The judges march around it in the Grand Promenade. And for that, Curry made a point of getting the other judges up and going, so he could be last. So there was no one behind him to see him squeeze the nicotine onto the pizza. Then the cooks picked up their trays and served them, facing the judges. Think about the last time you were served like that."

He lifted an eyebrow. "It was at faculty meetings. For a while they had one person bring snacks, usually dry slices of cake on paper plates. The person who brought them passed the tray. I always assumed that was so the guilty party would be recognized."

"And when you took your slice of cake, you picked the one nearest you, right?"

"Well, I didn't want to make a big deal about choosing the least offensive piece."

"Exactly. When there are five dishes on a tray, the first two people take the ones in front, the third takes the middle dish, which leaves the ones in the rear corners. The two remaining people take the ones nearest them. It would be awkward not to."

He put a hand on my arm. "But I thought the guy in the first seat, your boss, got sick and ran out after the first dish."

"He did. It must have been a terrifying moment for Curry. By then the nicotine was already on the pizza. With only four judges, the pizza might have been moved, or even thrown out. But Curry salvaged things when he insisted Bert Lucci take Mr. Bobbs's place."

"Still," Harry said, tapping his forefinger on my arm, "suppose one of the other judges had taken that pizza."

"Then Curry would have to have aborted the whole plan. He could have knocked over the table, or made a spectacle snatching the pizzas and stalking out. There's a lot of leeway at an event like the Slugfest. People might have found his behavior odd, but they wouldn't have thought of poison. No one was considering poison then. Turn right here."

Harry pulled into Rosa's driveway. Cars and

trucks were crowded into every bare spot. It was, if anything, even more jammed than it had been last night. There was nothing to do but back out and leave the Volvo beside North Bank Road.

It didn't surprise me that the word of Chris's release had spread so rapidly, and that all his friends and Rosa's friends—which meant virtually everyone in town—had hurried here to share their relief. The fact that these same people had been here just last night to comfort Rosa would only make today's celebration more festive.

"But what about Angelina Rudd?" Harry asked as he pulled the car in by the hill at the side of the road.

"Well, she knew the fish were gone. But she wasn't privy to Curry's intentions. She might have overlooked a plan to embarrass Edwina; she certainly had no love for her. But she wouldn't have tolerated his kidnapping Leila. I think we'll find that her family's trip to Fort Ross was Curry's idea. He needed her out of the way for the weekend."

"Surely she must have suspected something."

"Not in the way you're thinking of it. Angelina and I both came upon the same empty room, but we didn't see the same thing. I saw a place that had been cleared out and I didn't know what for. Angelina just saw that her fish were gone. She knew that every fisherman in the Russian River area would assume that they died because ranched fish were inferior to begin with. People who considered the fish viable would blame their death on her incompetence— that's what *she* thought when fish died at other ranches. No one was going to believe her boss tossed them out for some reason she couldn't come up with. So, she wasn't thinking about Curry and his possible plans; she was caught up in what to do about this fish."

"She could have gone over Curry's head and called the home office."

"She couldn't take that chance. James Drayton, the head of Crestwood Industries, is known for his narrow, moralistic views. If she had angered Curry and he'd told Drayton that she had lived in sin before her marriage, she would have been fired—just about the time people were calling her incompetent. She could never have overcome that. There would have always been talk. And fish ranching in the Russian River would have been dead."

He nodded.

"Angelina had worked for years to get a position like this. Running the fish ranch wasn't just a job for her, it was a cause. With the fish ranch, she could save lives, she could triumph over the macho fishing culture that she blamed for her father's death and her childhood poverty. How often do you get an opportunity like that? But if the fish ranch failed, everyone along the river, where she had lived her entire life, would have laughed at her."

Harry sighed. "I guess that's the dark side, the price some people have to pay for living in the seclusion of this area."

Neither of us spoke as we got out of the car. I looked across North Bank Road. One of the two Warriors stood undisturbed, its top branches catching the last wisps of fog drifting in from the Pacific. Where the other Warrior had been for a thousand years, there was a sawed-off stump and the detritus of branches and cones around it. There were no laurels or eucalyptus trees near to mitigate the loss; the redwood branches had shaded the ground too completely for too many years to allow any seedling to survive. In time, Curry Cunningham would be forgotten. But the severed trunk of the downed Warrior would be a bitter loss to the people of the Russian

River area. Few of us would look at that naked stump without feeling an innocence departed.

We turned and made our way through the haphazardly parked vehicles to the house. As we climbed the kitchen steps, Chris Fortimiglio poked his head out and grinned. The welcoming aroma of tomato sauce filled the air. From the living room came a roar of conversation, intermingled with flurries of laughter. Chris smiled, shook his head, then shrugged. "How can I thank you?"

"Bring me some salmon when the *Rosa* docks."

"Some? You'll have a whole fish every time we come in. Vejay, you can plan on eating salmon three meals a day from now on."

"Contain yourself, I'm only one person."

Harry put a hand on my arm. I introduced him to Chris. Chris promised him salmon, too.

"Well, come on into the living room," he said, leading me through the doorway.

The room was even more crowded than it had been last night. Four and five people squeezed onto the sofas. Three women balanced on the edges of one ottoman and four children on another. And every foot of floor held Rosa and Chris's friends. Swallowing hard, I realized it was like it had been at the Fortimiglios' when I moved here, when all the winter people gathered to celebrate their friends' good fortune.

As I walked into the room, all the talk trailed off. I spotted Rosa by the door to the porch talking to Bert Lucci. With combed hair, a clean plaid shirt, and new jeans, Bert looked like the one who had been "quite a handsome man" in Rosa's youth. And as he gazed at Rosa he had an expression similar to Edwina Henderson's the day I'd come upon her sitting under her Warrior. Bert put a hand on Rosa's arm, then took her wine glass. She turned around smiling, and when she spotted me, her smile widened. Then she rushed over and hugged me, and everyone in the room cheered.

She clasped my hands. "Vejay, I'm so glad, so relieved. And Chris is . . ."

"I know," I said.

"And I'm so sorry I didn't trust you. I'm so embarrassed."

"It's okay. Really. I'm just glad to be your friend again."

"I should never have made you feel you weren't. You know Chris and I missed you, too. It was a bad time for us. But that's all over, and you're back."

Before she could say anything else, I wrapped my arms around her and gave her a squeeze. I felt a tear on my cheek. I wasn't sure if it was hers or mine.